SHELTERED

by

Debra Chapoton

This is a work of fiction. Names, characters, places, and incidents either are the product of the author's imagination or are used fictitiously.

Printed in the USA

ISBN-13: 978-1475249996

ISBN-10: 1475249993

Young Adult Books by Debra Chapoton:

EDGE OF ESCAPE

THE GUARDIAN'S DIARY (2013)

Preface

This novel touches on the following themes: homelessness, self-mutilation, schizophrenia, suicide, and the occult.

In America more than 1.3 million children are homeless at some time each year.[1] This is a sad statistic and one that needs a bit more publicity. 1 in 8 youth under the age of 18 will leave home and become homeless and in need of services.[2] 12-17 year olds are at more risk of homelessness than are adults.[3] Nearly 20,000 youth are emancipated from foster care each year.[4]

According to TeenHelp.com it is estimated that in the U.S. one out of every 200 girls between the ages of 13 and 19 cuts herself regularly. This number is rising.

Schizophrenia is a major psychiatric illness. It often first appears in males during their late teens and early twenties, a little later for females. Symptoms include distorted reality, hallucinations, suicidal thoughts, delusions, anxiety, and odd behaviors. Worldwide as many as 50 million people suffer from schizophrenia.

The Centers for Disease control report that suicide is the third leading cause of death for young people aged 15 to 24. There are several different factors that may cause a teenager to take his or her life, but the most common is depression. Hopelessness, anxiety, and feelings of being trapped in a life that one can't handle are also contributors to teen suicide. In many cases teenagers believe that suicide is their only option.

The occult, including witchcraft, mysticism, astrology, and even the current fad of vampires and werewolves, feeds a craze that has flourished for thousands of years. Demon possession and exorcism are Biblical and historical.

Take all five of these themes, stir well, add a few American teens, and the paranormal will seem normal.

[1] Ellen L. Bassuk, M.D. and Steven M. Friedman, Facts on Trauma and Homeless Children (Durham, NC and Los Angeles, CA: National Child Traumatic Stress Network, 2005): 1.

[2] C. Raleigh-DuRoff, "Factors that influence adolescents to leave or stay living on the street," Child and Adolescent Social Work Journal 21(6) (2004): 561-?572.

[3] J. Ensign and M. Bell, "Illness experiences of homeless youth," Qualitative Health Research 14(9) (2004): 1239-1254.

[4] U.S. Department of Health and Human Services, Administration for Children and Families, Children's Bureau. AFCARS Reports #6-10 (Washington DC: U.S. Department of Health and Human Services, 2005)

Prologue

Next Wednesday

Emily knew the precise moment that Ben returned, she felt him in her scars. She watched him carry some things to the house, heard the door close; she smiled when she heard him call out that Santa was here. He did that once before, in early December, insisting that she accept the gift he held out, not wanting her to wait until Christmas to use the mittens he knew she needed.

She went toward her door now, wondered what he had brought, and then heard Megan's voice below. Oh no, he probably brought something for *her*. She scuttled back to her nest by the window and stared outside, was still staring fifteen minutes later when she saw them walk down the street, Ben shouldering a shovel, his other hand knotted with Megan's.

She touched the skin on her arms, lightly at first, making it tingle. The image of Ben with Megan multiplied across her mind in broken mirrors, a repugnant picture that reflected her own self-loathing. She scratched at her scabs, felt the pricks of pain force away the ticklish sensations. She closed her eyes.

When she opened them she saw a figure standing at her door.

"Who– ?" she started, but the figment waned to less than a shadow. Still, though, there was something at her door. She rose slowly and held her hand out.

Its face was more womanly now, friendly, motherly. Yes, she knew this face. Its pearly white skin so shocking against the ruby lips, the stringy hair a match to her own. Her mother.

She stretched her fingers toward the face. The hallucination faded then sharpened. The eyes began to blaze. She drew her hands back to her own face. *What's wrong with me?* The delusion grieved Emily; all around her fluttered a longing.

And a deadly fear.

"Mom?" Emily sank to the floor and watched the face change to a silhouette, fogging away with a Cheshire grin, and then, at last, evaporating.

Leaving scattered crumbs of turmoil at Emily's feet.

SHELTERED

Friday

Chapter 1

Smoke curled past the woman's eyes; she squinted at Ben. He held out the money and repeated his offer. "It'll only take five minutes. Just say 'nice to meet you, you're welcome to stay as long as you need' and then ask me to drive you to the store or a meeting or something." He wiggled the money in the crone's face. "I'll bring you right back to this bar," he promised.

The woman kept her eye on the wad of bills, figuring out the extra number of drinks she could buy tonight. Ben could tell she was reaching the decision he hoped for. He raised the money to eye level and smiled his honest, dimpled grin, the grin that all the females in high school fell for, even the teachers.

Her hand shot out, but Ben was quicker. He held the money back, peeled off the top bill, and handed it to her. "I'll give you the rest after you convince her that you're Mrs. Kremer. Agreed?"

He half expected her to tuck the bill down her blouse, but she opened her purse, dropped it in and closed it. She took a final puff, crushed the cigarette butt under foot and grabbed the passenger door handle to yank it open. This wasn't the first time she had gone home with a stranger, but it was the first time she had entered a teenaged boy's littered sedan. And such a handsome boy, too, with that dark blond hair and clear blue eyes. She hadn't always been the best judge of character, but this kid was easy to read – he was innocent. She'd make sure to memorize the address to wherever he took her.

Megan walked three blocks from the main street café where she worked to the address on the letter. Bundled up against the January wind she clutched the borrowed duffel bag to her chest. Nearly half of her belongings were inside the bag. She used it like a shield against the sharp, dry crystals that attacked her bare face. She liked snow; she liked the Michigan winter, but she hated these burning whips of frozen rain. She pulled her scarf across her cheeks and nose with one hand and hurried on.

If this worked out she could get the rest of her things out of her friend's house and not have to go back to the Hall. It had been wonderful living with such a nice family. They had been there for her, gotten her a job, driven her to the court appointed visitations, and would have adopted her, she was certain, if such a thing were possible. But now they were moving away; they had to leave because of the economy. And Megan would never, ever leave. Not without Simon. And if she and Simon left the state they'd be chased, found, separated. She'd be locked away for sure in a place worse than the Hall.

Megan stopped at the corner and checked the address on an old city house. She was missing a secret visit now by coming here, but what choice did she have? If she could live in a rooming house, finish high school, get a second and maybe a third job, then eventually, sooner or later, she and Simon could be together.

She walked past one more house and found the right address. It was a narrow two-story brick home with a driveway that led to a ramshackle one-car garage tucked in a small yard behind the house. A blue sedan blocked another car in the partially shoveled drive. Every light was on inside and she could see the flickering glow of a TV in the living room. The left window revealed a dining room chandelier over a table piled with books. Two figures stood in the doorway to the kitchen beyond. A boy. A woman.

The sidewalk to the front door was un-shoveled. Megan debated her options. She didn't want to embarrass whoever forgot to shovel the sidewalk for her, but she didn't want to be too casual by showing up at the side door. Yet the porch light was on at the side. She made up her mind: instead of plodding to the front she walked up the trampled side path and knocked on the kitchen door.

It seemed to take longer than it should for one of the two people inside to answer her knock, but she waited without complaint, her head turned from the wind. She rested the duffel bag against her nervous knees. An old fashioned mailbox, bolted to the bricks next to the door, caught her attention. The metal lid was flapping in the same shivering rhythm as her legs.

"Hi! You must be Megan." Ben practically pulled her into the small vestibule as he grabbed for her bag. "Did you walk? I thought you'd get a ride." The fact that she had shown up on foot was unexpected and threw Ben into a flux of quick planning. He showed her where to hang her coat and leave her boots while his brain went into overdrive. He changed his plan, kept smiling, and carefully dropped her bag on the kitchen floor.

"I'm supposed to meet a Mrs. Kremer," her voice lilted up in a question.

"Right. I know. I'm Ben, by the way. I live here along with Chuck . . . and, uh, Adam." He saw her eyes get a little wide and he added, "But we're in the basement. You'll be on the second floor with Emily and Cori. Mrs. Kremer's room is on this floor. She's the buffer, in case you were bothered, uh . . ."

"No, that's okay." She followed him through the kitchen, puzzling where the woman had gone. "Is Mrs. Kremer here?" Megan's long brown hair sprang out with the static from her wool hat. She fingered through it and pulled it straight.

"Yup, she'll be out in a second, but I'm supposed to show you around first." He flashed her another of his famous smiles and waited for her to smile back. She did. She was cute. A tad shy. "Are those all your things? Were you planning on moving in tonight?"

"No, that's about half, but I only have the one bag to use, so I thought if I could, you know, I'd leave those things and bring the rest tomorrow."

Okay, Ben thought, maybe he could go back to his original plan.

"Sure, that'll work. Well, this is the dining room . . . where some of us study."

Megan merely nodded and took in the light green walls, the old blinds and the cheap pictures. They passed the tiny front entry.

"That door's always locked."Ben said. "We hardly ever use it."

The living room was small but bright; the pictures on the walls were dull. Ben flicked off the TV.

"Cori probably left that on." He lowered his voice to a conspirator's whisper, "She's kind of a bitch. You don't want to cross her."

Megan glanced down the hall. "Is she here?" she whispered back.

"No," Ben chuckled, "but the walls have ears. You never know who's listening." Another grin.

There were four doors off the short hallway in the center of the house. Ben pointed, "Bathroom, Mrs. Kremer's room . . . never go in there. The den. The door to the second floor."

He paused at Mrs. Kremer's door and cocked an ear. Megan stood still. There wasn't a sound in the house now that the TV was off. He knew the bar lady was in there, but she was awfully quiet.

The sound of a dresser drawer being pulled out broke the silence. Ben cleared his throat. "Uh, Mrs. Kremer?" The drawer slammed. Ben started to reach for the door knob and then stopped himself. "Ma'am?"

The woman from the bar coughed. "Yes?"

"I'm gonna show Megan her room now and then we'll come down to the living room." He waited a beat. "Okay?"

"Okay." There was a creaking sound, as if all her weight settled at once onto the bed.

Ben turned and opened the door to the second floor.

Ben was conscious of how steep and narrow the stairs were, the walls lined with peeling wallpaper. The landing at the top featured a small dirty window he wished he had cleaned. A single bare light bulb lit the hallway. There were several doors, all closed but one.

Ben ticked off the occupants' names, "Cori's in this one, Emily has the second one. That's the bathroom, linen closet, and . . . here ya go," he went to the only open door, "your room."

He flicked the light switch and stood at the entrance while Megan peered in. She was close enough for him to smell the fragrance in her hair. He stared at her profile while she inspected the space. He mentally measured her; she was an inch or two shorter than he. He liked everything about her, found her intriguing now that he could stand so close.

The room was small with one window that faced the neighbor's brick sidewall. Snow and ice accumulated along the outside edge and there was plenty of condensation on the inside sill. Megan's face fell when she saw the single twin mattress on the floor, no sheets, no blanket, no pillow.

"Oh," she said, "I guess I'll have to buy some sheets."

"Nope," Ben ushered her all the way in and closed the door. A small corner chest was visible now, stacked with all that she would need. "Everything's washed and ready. Compliments of yours truly. The machines are in the basement."

"You?"

"Yeah, and I'm sorry there's no bed frame. I keep checking the thrift stores, so . . . eventually . . ."

Megan's brow furrowed. Ben hoped he didn't give the impression he was odd; he didn't want to make it sound like this was his boarding house and he was running the show. He watched her move toward the closet and turn the old glass knob. The interior space was small. There might not be enough room for her things.

She looked back at Ben and smiled. "This is great. I hope Mrs. Kremer will accept me. Twenty-five dollars a week is incredibly cheap."

Ben's dimples stood out. "I know, she's really generous. But you have to do some chores. We all do. And then there's food." Ben rolled his eyes. "I hope you can cook. Emily does most of it, but we all chip in for groceries."

"Sure," Megan began, "but I usually eat at the restaurant where I work. One of the perks."

"Right." Ben leaned against the door and watched Megan pull her fingers through her hair again. She was better than cute, he thought, she was pretty. He liked the splatter of freckles across her nose. She looked . . . nice. He had learned the truth behind the rumors about her situation and that was why he sent her the phony note. He wondered if she'd tell him that truth if he asked. "So . . . uh, what's your story? I mean, Cori got herself emancipated at sixteen. Incorrigible, her parents said. She likes the label. She's all gothic and ornery. Emily was homeless; she has a mom and a brother living in a shelter somewhere. You'll like her, but she's pretty quiet and shy. Chuck and, uh, Adam, are nutcases. Well, Chuck is, anyway. So, why do *you* need a place to stay?"

Megan folded her arms across her chest and leaned against the closet door, mirroring Ben's stance. "Well, I guess you could say my parents divorced me. I've been fending for myself pretty much since the summer before tenth grade, so, about a year and a half now." Ben detected a sudden nervousness, didn't expect it, but out of the blue he saw that she was fighting to hold back the tears. Her eyes watered. She looked up at the ceiling and tried to blink them away. "Cool ceiling."

Ben looked up, too. The ceiling was plastered with little glow-in-the-dark stars that looked dimly green. He flicked the lights off. "Huh. I didn't noticed that before." The stars glowed faintly. "Must have been a kid's room before." He could have kicked himself for the stupid statement. The house had seen a century's worth of people; of course this had been a kid's room. He turned the lights back on and noticed that Megan was gripping the closet door knob.

Megan loosened her grip. She didn't know what to think of this Ben. He seemed charming, but she was startled when he darkened the room. She wasn't sure if this room was directly above Mrs. Kremer's room or not. Would the lady hear her if she screamed? Ben was flashing a dimple now. Megan relaxed and stepped forward; she felt silly for her brief anxiety. A loud noise from below made her stop and give Ben a questioning look.

"Wait here!" Ben said. He reinforced his order by closing the door behind him.

Megan listened to his feet pound down the staircase then looked around the room again. A mattress and a dresser. Not much, but all she needed for now. She had been contributing most of her earnings to her friend's family's expenses, but at only twenty-five dollars a week here she should be able to save enough. Enough to run. And run she would as soon as she graduated.

She sat down on the mattress and stretched out. From this angle she could see the dust on the floor. That would bother her; she'd find something tomorrow to clean the floorboards.

She strained to hear the voices below. Was there an argument? Had Mrs. Kremer changed her mind? It sounded like maybe Ben was pleading.

Or quarrelling.

Ben reached the bottom of the staircase and pushed the door open. The old barfly had come out of the master bedroom. He knocked on the bathroom door, waited. The toilet flushed and she immediately opened the door. He spied the counter behind her and wondered how many of the cosmetics were now in her bulging purse.

It didn't matter.

"Listen, Ken, I really gotta go. You know?"

"It's Ben and we have a deal. If you want your money . . . if you don't want to walk ten miles in a snowstorm, then you'll do like we agreed." He tried to look angry, pulled the money out of his pocket, and peeled off another bill. This time she was quick enough to grab it and it did disappear down her blouse.

"Fine. Just hurry up. What's her name? Melissa? Melanie?"

"It's Megan and you simply have to welcome her and tell her that I'll take care of all the details and you are too busy to sweat the small stuff. Got it?"

"Got it."

"And then you're gonna forget that you were ever here."

She made a zippered motion across her lips and winked at him. Ben gently pushed her toward the living room. "Sit. I'll bring her down."

He waited until she was seated. She crossed her legs and wiggled her foot. Ben picked up on her impatience. It was Friday night. She'd already missed happy hour. And it was at least a half an hour's drive in this snowstorm, or longer, back to the bar.

He cut through the dining room and went into the kitchen to grab Megan's bag. He took the stairs two at a time and knocked softly at her door before nudging it open.

"Hey, it's me, the bell boy."

Megan leaped up from the low bed as he entered. He dropped her bag next to the closet. "If you want, you can come down and meet Mrs. Kremer now. I have to drive her to a meeting in like five minutes. You can put your stuff away while I'm gone and then I can drive you home."

Ben moved toward the door. Megan unzipped the bag and dumped the contents onto the closet floor. "Done. You don't have to drive me. It's only a couple blocks back to where I work and my friend's dad is going to pick me up after my shift." She rolled the bag up and followed him out the door and down the stairs.

"Mrs. Kremer, this is Megan. Megan, Mrs. Kremer."

The woman acted more nervous. Ben eyed her sharply, raised a brow and gave the tiniest jerk of his head. She understood and rose from the chair, held out a hand, and spoke more slowly, "How do you do, Megan. Welcome to . . . to this home." She glanced at Ben, trying to remember her lines. "You are welcome to stay as long as you need to." She dropped Megan's hand and reached for her purse. "Ben will take care of the details. I'm very busy and I must leave now. Oh, I forgot something in the bedroom."

Ben was shocked. The woman wasn't sticking to the plan. What was she going to do? Steal some worthless object she had discovered in the bedroom? Time was running out; she was ruining things. He had to get her out of here before Chuck returned.

He looked at Megan. "Well, you heard her. I'm the detail guy. Just show up tomorrow with twenty-five bucks and you're in the club." He tried his most innocent laugh and she bought it.

"Thanks, do I get a key or anything?" She looked at him with clearer eyes than before. They drew him in and he found it hard to look away.

"Yup," he motioned for her to follow and they went to the kitchen where he pulled a key off a nail near the door. He waited until she finished putting on her boots and coat and then he handed her the key and her bag.

"Thanks."

"You're welcome. Are you sure you don't want a ride?"

"No, I'm fine with walking." She gave him a little wave and scooted out the door.

Ben watched for a long five seconds and then he rushed to the master bedroom.

Chapter 2

Chuck stomped the snow off his boots before opening the side door. He walked in and listened. Huh, no TV. Cori always left the TV on. She said it kept the burglars away.

He pulled off his boots and set them on top of an old pair, letting the snow melt into Adam's boots. Adam wouldn't mind.

"Honey, I'm home," he yelled just for fun. No one would be here yet. He was always the first one back since they had shortened his hours at the corner video store. People were renting DVD's through the mail or streaming them online; it was only a matter of time until the store closed. He already had his applications in at McDonald's and two other restaurants. People in this community still went out to eat. A lot.

Emily had made spaghetti again which they had all eaten right after school. Cori grumbled that there was too much garlic, which was a logical complaint for Cori since she looked like a vampire half the time. The garlic was probably killing her. Ben complimented Emily's cooking, as usual. Chuck ate his portion without complaint or compliment and then dished up another plateful for Adam. Adam rarely ate with the others. It was too much bother.

Chuck checked the fridge. Yes! Nobody had touched Adam's plate, especially not the never-present Mrs. Kremer. He had grown fonder and fonder of that woman; she was so rarely seen though he often heard regular sounds from her room. She was like clock-work listening to the news in her bedroom every night at eleven. Did she only come out to meet new tenants? She had impressed him when he came here last September. The word 'cougar' came to mind. He didn't see her again until Cori showed up at Halloween, such an appropriate time for a ghoul. Ben had said they were getting another new girl this weekend. Maybe Mrs. Kremer would take a meal with them then. He was scheduled to cook tomorrow. He always signed up for Saturdays because most Saturdays everyone else had other plans.

Chuck took the plastic off the plate and reheated the spaghetti in the microwave. He set the plate and a drink on a tray and headed to the basement. He was to the bottom of the steps when he heard Ben's car rumble to a stop outside.

Ben saw the fresh tracks in the snow. They were tracks from large boots, undoubtedly made by Chuck, or by his equally tall twin brother Adam. Identical twins. Ben smiled to himself. He wasn't fooled. The girls claimed they couldn't tell the difference. They said if it wasn't for Chuck slicking his hair back and Adam letting his hair fly loose beneath that stupid Fedora he always wore, even inside the house, that they would never be able to tell which was which. But Ben could tell and he suspected that they could, too.

Chuck was always slamming Cori. He denigrated her Gothic style, insulted her about her black-lined eyes, teased her about her clothes. But what he said never matched what he did. He followed her like a puppy, did her bidding, waited on her.

Adam, on the other hand, totally ignored her.

Ben closed the door quickly against the blowing snow. He set his boots next to two wet pairs. It looked like both Adam and Chuck had been outside. He could hear music coming from the basement. That would be Chuck; Adam always used an ipod.

He hung his coat up and then pulled a small bag out of one of the pockets. He had gone to the hardware for some locks. He wasn't sure what would work best, but he had a couple types of padlock, combination and key, as well as a slide and bolt lock for Megan's door. He had done the same for Emily when she arrived last fall. That little extra sense of security unquestionably soothed girls who were frightened. He didn't offer a lock to Cori, though, but then nobody would be stupid enough to open *her* door.

Ben set the locks down and decided to do a little special cleaning while he had the chance. He took several sheets of paper towels and the squirt bottle of cleaner and headed to the master bedroom. He wiped down the surfaces where he thought the lady from the bar might have left a fingerprint.

He checked the timer on the clock radio and the one on the lamp, then he left the room, pushing in the door lock on his way out. The bathroom got a quick once over; he didn't want to make it too clean or Emily might notice and be suspicious. After all, Mrs. Kremer never cleaned anything.

He pulled a small bottle of perfume out of his pocket and set it next to the hand lotion. That old woman, the dumbest Mrs. Kremer yet, thought she could steal from them. Well, she got what was coming to her, nothing more, nothing less.

He tossed out the paper towels and found that the garbage was almost overflowing. He grunted, more than a little pissed. It looked like he was the only one who would take the trash bags to the curb. He crushed the stuff down as much as he could. He acted as the father in this dysfunctional household and he was only seventeen. Sometimes he thought that this whole big plan was more trouble than it was worth. Then he remembered what was locked in the freezer chest downstairs. That was motivation enough to stick it out.

His real father had done two tours in Iraq. If he had inherited anything from him it was a sense of duty. Ben would get the job done.

He went into the living room and flicked the TV on. He was tired; this had been a harder day than most. He drove himself and Emily to school; he stayed awake for all of his classes – no nap in social studies or English – and then he took Emily to work. He made his usual stop-over at his mom and step-dad's house, messed up his room a little, threw some clothes in the laundry, took some food from the pantry and, of course, checked on his mom. She was usually drunk by 3:00 p.m. but she would remember his kiss, might even remember that he told her he aced his Chemistry test. Then he had driven over the county line and staked out a bar and waited for the right Mrs. Kremer. The next four hours had been very stressful. But he couldn't relax yet. If he fell asleep now how would Emily get home?

"Hey! Bennyboy!" Cori roughly shook Ben's shoulder. "Hey, wake up. Aren't you supposed to get Emily?"

Ben opened his lids to see Cori's raccoon-like eyes inches from his face. A new piercing on her brow looked swollen.

She gave him one more shake. "Not like I care or nothin', but the roads are pretty bad."

She straightened up and turned. He saw that she was wearing her army boots and tracking snow on the carpet. Her clothes reeked of smoke. She turned off the TV and headed for the second floor door. "'Night, Mrs. Kremer." When there was no answer she mumbled, "Bitch," and trooped up the stairs.

Ben felt dazed. He slapped his face a couple of times and pulled out his cell phone to check the time. "Holy sh- -." He sent Emily a text: he was on his way, the roads were bad.

Fully awake now, he marveled at Cori's uncharacteristic gesture.

"Sorry, Em," he said as she slid into the front seat.

Emily gave him a quick sweet look, swallowing her smile before it turned too wide. She buckled her seatbelt and looked down at her lap. "Thanks for picking me up."

Ben laughed. They had this conversation every day. She thanked him for the ride to school, to work, home again. Always shy, always patient. Her face was exactly the pale color Cori tried to get before she smeared on her vampire make-up.

Ben stole a glance. Emily's hair was a bit stringy and falling forward, hiding her straight nose and flat cheekbones. She would never be a beauty contestant. But Emily's strengths were math, cooking, and patience. She didn't need to be beautiful. She was fine the way she was. He could count on her. If he were the dad in their strange family then Emily was the mom, Cori the rebellious teen, and Chuck the crazy uncle. What would Megan be?

Ben slowed the car as he neared a busy intersection. There was too much traffic in this town, even this late at night. He had to make a left turn and the visibility with all of the blowing snow was diminishing rapidly.

“That car’s not stopping,” Emily warned. She was right. An SUV slid through, its driver on the phone. Ben waited through the yellow light, the red, and then cautiously advanced on a green arrow.

“Thanks, Em, you can back-seat drive anytime.”

He thought he heard a faint hum of agreement. She said so little, so rarely, that he was quite surprised that she had given him that warning. Perhaps she was finally warming up to him. They hadn’t had the best start; he made her cry on her first night staying at the house. He tried to make it up to her every day. She was his favorite project. Emily reminded him of his first pet, a puppy his father had let him pick out when he was six. Ben had chosen the runt of the litter, a scared pathetic little pup that had been his best friend for years . . . until his step-father ran it over.

“Did she come over?” Emily’s voice was so light it sounded far away.

“Who? Oh, the new girl? Yeah, her name is Megan and she left some of her stuff in her room. She’s gonna move in tomorrow.”

“Mrs. Kremer?”

“Yup, she was there for the meet and greet. You missed her again. She had to go . . . on a business trip or something.” Ben hated lying to Emily most of all. Her innocence was so raw; she had been hurt so much when her mom lost her house and the family turned to public assistance. And then when her mom and brother went missing, well . . . He wished there was a real Mrs. Kremer who could give her, give them all, the mothering they needed.

“Was she nice?”

“Mrs. Kremer? Oh, you mean Megan.” He put his blinker on for the last turn down their street. “Yeah, she seemed nice. More like you than like Cori, for sure.” Emily turned her face toward the window and let herself smile. Ben caught the reflection in the glass and realized that he had inadvertently complimented her. He’d have to try to sneak in other words of praise.

There was a time when praise was all he heard from his mom and his dad. Not like now. Dad dead; mom drunk; step-dad horrific.

Emily hurried from the car to the house and tried to slip out of her shoes and coat quickly, hoping to get out of the cramped entry before she was forced to share the small space with Ben. Being fourteen inches apart in the car several times a day was almost too much. She smelled him, breathed in the delicious scent of his cologne. She had bought it for him for their meager Christmas exchange and he had worn it every day since.

Ben came in as she hopped up a step to the kitchen.

"Em, your pants are soaked. We really need to find you some boots."

She only nodded and turned away. Her socks were wet, too, and she left a damp trail across the worn linoleum, the long frayed hems of her black pants mopping the dirty floor. She was saving up for boots . . . again. Perhaps, she thought, if she chose something more feminine than army boots this time, Cori wouldn't take them.

Emily paused at the door to the staircase and listened to the newscaster's voice as it filtered through Mrs. Kremer's door. For the seventy-third night in a row she wished it was her mom in there listening to the radio. She wished the door would open and loving arms would enfold her. She wished . . .

The radio broke off mid-sentence and out went the soft glow beneath the door taking away that strip of hope. *Good night, Mrs. Kremer.* Emily only thought the words. She closed the staircase door and fingered the hook and latch. The one time she dared to lock it Cori screamed a tirade. It was all right, though, for Cori to lock Emily out. Maybe the new girl would stand up to Cori's outbursts.

Maybe the new girl would be equally as bad.

With shoulders slumped and hair hanging forward, Emily crept past Cori's door and went into the bathroom. It was a mess. Obviously her housemate dyed her hair black again and left streaks of color on the sink and spots of water across the mirror. A pile of wet towels sat in the old tub. She softly closed the door and locked it.

A few minutes later, after she was sure the sound of the toilet flushing had not brought forth an angry sleeping bear, Emily eased open the door and sneaked into the new girl's room.

Cori had been here. Two heaps of clothes were mounded to the right and left as if Cori had emptied the closet by tossing things over one shoulder and then the other. What would she have taken? Probably nothing, Emily thought, based on the style and quality of what was here. The new girl, this Megan, wasn't into any particular fashion, at least not one that Cori would steal.

Emily started putting the clothes on the old wire hangers and folding the more personal items, which she placed in the top drawer of the dresser. Then she took the sheets and blankets and made up the bed.

A door slammed and she froze. She didn't relax until she heard Cori tramp down the stairs. Emily left Megan's room and went to her own where she could see down to the street. Cori's latest conquest had pulled up to the curb, anxious for a late-night date in a snowstorm. Nothing stopped Cori's love life. Emily could just imagine what this one looked like – spiked hair, piercings, tattoos, mean eyes, meaner hands and no doubt five or six years older.

She pulled back from the window when she saw Cori trudging down the driveway, coat open, wet hair swirling and freezing. Maybe she'd catch her death.

Ben heard the TV switch back on and then the whoosh of the kitchen door closing. Then there was a knock at his door.

"Ben. I need you to move your car so I can get out."

Ben opened his door to see Chuck standing there, all six foot two of him, head close to the low basement ceiling, hair combed back, looking eager and fresh.

"Chuck," Ben started, "man, you can't go following her in a snowstorm."

"She might need me. You know what kind of guys she goes out with. That dude could leave her stranded somewhere."

Ben huffed. "Do you have gas?" It was the question he always asked and Chuck's answer four times out of five was *no*.

It was no different this time. Chuck slumped and mumbled his response. Chuck would buy a couple of gallons of gas and then Adam would use the car, returning it to its spot with the needle on empty. Chuck walked to his job at the video store, walked to the alternative school, walked downtown, but Adam drove everywhere.

Ben felt sorry for him, knew what he was going to ask next, and spoke first, "Sorry, I can't help you. I have to be at the rink before midnight. But I'll keep an eye out for her along the way. Okay?"

Chuck gave a sullen nod and headed back to his room, leaden and dimmed.

Ben waited until Chuck closed his door and the music blared again before he went to the utility room. He threw his hockey bag on top of the chest-style freezer and put in all the equipment that he had laid out on the workbench. Gloves, mask, blades.

He made a quick stop in the basement bathroom. This room, like the basement bedrooms, was a previous homeowner's DIY project. The gray concrete floor was spattered with paint; colored lines snaked to the shower drain: blue and yellow, white and pink, with streaks of red and brown overlaying the older stains. It looked like dried blood.

Ben checked Chuck's pill bottle and counted out the number of meds left. There was one too many. Oh, great. Chuck probably wouldn't come out of his room tomorrow. Missing a dose always had consequences. Ben should say something.

But maybe Chuck would still take his pill tonight before bed. Ben decided to check at 3 a.m. when he came back from hockey, if he remembered.

Emily sat on the floor in her darkened room, door locked, blanket wrapped around her. She made a nest near the window so she could watch as Ben drove off. She prayed for his safety.

The storm let up and the city snow plow had gone down their street, leaving a mound of snow at the end of the driveway. Ben's car bumped over it in reverse and then headed off toward the arena.

She waved, unseen. How she wished she could watch him play hockey. She imagined him skating fast around the rink, slamming into other players, raising spurts of ice chips as he turned sharply or braked near the goal. Face offs, slap shots, backhands, saves, power plays . . . and in her fantasies he would wave at her where she sat in the stands, his focus more on showing off for her than on his opponents.

Emily sighed. Then it occurred to her that she could do something nice for Ben while he was gone. She could shovel the driveway and clear an adequate path to the side door.

A gust of wind swirled some snow off the roof. It eddied at her window, blurring the glow from the corner street lamp. She sensed a draft, smelled its freshness and shivered.

Ben always borrowed the neighbor's shovel. She rose up and unlocked the door. She padded down the hall to the new girl's room and went to the window. The neighbor would usually clear his drive and leave the shovel by his side door for Ben, but their lights were out, the driveway thickly blanketed, and there was no shovel to be seen.

There was nothing she could do for Ben tonight except pray. Emily had become quite regular in her praying. Every night she begged for her mother and brother's return. Every night she forgave her mother for abandoning her. Every night she asked for forgiveness for herself for all the lies. Every night she prayed for Ben. Emily knew what he had done. It made her grateful. And scared.

Cori was only half-drunk. The party in the tattoo parlor where she worked was small this Friday night, probably because of the snow storm. Jason picked her up and brought her back to the small building only because she promised him something she had so far managed to avoid. Jason was twenty-five and had opened the parlor a year ago. He had run away at fifteen, lived on the streets and made money doing tats with a second-hand tattoo gun. He morphed into an artist, a con man, and a sometimes druggie. He cleaned up his act after he spent a year at the alternative school and then six months in the juvenile hall. Cori knew all that from their daily chats. For some reason she could talk to him without getting bitchy or snarly or angry. They clicked.

She sat on the love seat in the front room, her boots off, her feet tucked up under her short black skirt. She played with the toe ends of her shredded black tights, twirling her fingers around and around the seamed tips. Her usual air of indifference melted with alcohol-produced mirth. Laughter was a reaction she forced herself to avoid at home and school. Her trademarks were moodiness, anger, and resentment. But after the second beer she began to giggle. Jason liked it.

The parlor was his home as long as he wasn't caught living there. A few months ago he took on Cori as an apprentice and was glad of it. Business picked up. Kids were coming in younger and younger. According to Michigan law Jason was prohibited from tattooing or piercing a minor without the parent watching and signing a consent form, but with more and more adults caving in to their kids' demands he was turning a considerable profit. He was able to shell out rent, pay Cori, and make daily trips to the bank. He gave a discount to the emancipated minors; they were the ones who brought him paying customers more often than not. And then there were the trendy twenty-somethings, the silly brides, and even the hip grandmas.

Jason, sitting half slumped in the client's chair, grinned at Cori and tapped his pierced tongue twice on his upper teeth. The other couple with them wandered to the back room where Jason had a sofa bed. One more beer each for himself and Cori and then he'd tell Jake and Sue that the party was over.

"So what did you do after you tied them up?" Jason asked.

Cori laughed too loud and took another slurp. "I watched *Dawn of the Dead* and told them that if they said anything to their folks their next babysitter wouldn't be as nice as me."

"But they told?"

"Yup. Everything I ever did . . . somebody narked on me . . . or a camera caught me." She laughed again and pulled at her toes. "What are they doing back there? I thought we were going to party?"

"Is that empty?" Jason reached across for her can, crushed it, and handed her a new one.

The city plow scraped along the street outside, its lights making the dark interior flash and glow with reflections that danced from mirror to glass framed samples to shiny displays of nipple rings and silver doodads. Cori popped the tab and rose up unsteadily; she settled back down on her other hip, leaving one foot on the floor.

Saturday

Chapter 3

Ben got in at 2:45 a.m., tired, aching, but wide awake. There were two sets of tracks going from the street to the front door, then the tracks doubled back to the driveway and continued to the side door. A third set of tracks went straight back to the street.

The door was unlocked, but that didn't alarm him. Cori was careless, believing their safety lay in the stupid theory that no burglar would enter a totally dark house . . . or a house with the TV on . . . or a house with all the lights on. He locked the door and threw his hockey bag down the steps. The TV was glowing but there was no sound. He tip-toed to the living room and found Cori sprawled on the couch, coat and boots still on. He bent low and sniffed.

He picked the remote control up off the floor where it had dropped from Cori's fingers. She had missed the off button and muted it instead. He flicked it off. It wasn't too big a waste of electricity, but he was trying to pay all the bills without dipping into his account. Maybe he should have Mrs. Kremer charge them for utilities. He dropped that thought as soon as it entered his head. The only one who would understand was Emily and he didn't want to punish her for the others' wastefulness. She was such a pitiable little kitten. Poor thing.

He looked down at Cori. Kind of like a stray feral cat. Also a poor thing.

Megan was both excited and sad to make the move. There was a tearful string of goodbyes with the family that had helped her through a most demanding time. But she was excited to take a huge step closer to being with Simon. She stuffed the rest of her things into two large black trash bags and threw them in the backseat. Her friend's dad, Mr. Felker, was going to drive her to the rooming house. He said he wanted to meet Mrs. Kremer.

"When is she arriving?" Emily's curiosity trumped her timidity; she spoke softly at Ben's back. He was dishing up some cereal for breakfast though it was nearly noon.

Ben shrugged his shoulders. "Sometime today." He stood at the counter, answering her in equally soft tones so as not to wake the black demon on the couch.

Emily wondered what they should do about Cori. She was sure to wake up loud and angry, hung-over and mean, especially if the new girl made any noise at all moving in. Even big old Adam had crept carefully past her to plant himself in the den first thing this morning.

"Oh, she's here." Emily breathed out the announcement in one excited breath.

She watched from the dining room archway as a man lugged two garbage bags behind a girl with long brown hair. *She's pretty,* Emily thought, *and tall.* She stared as Megan walked with purpose and confidence toward the house. *She won't be shy. Ben will like her more.* Emily swallowed a lump of jealous fear.

"What the f---!" Cori was awake.

Ben and Emily exchanged glances then rushed to the living room at once.

"Are you okay?" Ben asked. "You need anything?"

Emily stood still, staring at the raccoon-like mask that was Cori's smeared face. Black eye-liner ran in streaks down her cheeks; there were dark smudges on the backs of her hands where her face had rested for lack of a pillow.

Cori clunked her booted feet to the floor and swore again. She put her head in her hands and groaned. "I think I'm gonna be sick."

"Take her to the bathroom," Ben ordered. "I'll get the door."

Cori swatted away Emily's hand and stood up, then clutched at Emily for support as she teetered forward. Emily helped her to the bathroom, closing the door behind them. Ben grabbed the remote, turned the TV on, and raised the volume just as there was a knock at the side door. He could only hope that the silly rerun would mask the gross sounds Cori was making.

Megan smiled at Ben with hidden emotion as he opened the door. He stood back so they could enter. Megan made a hasty introduction of her friend's father as he dropped her bags onto the kitchen floor.

"I'd like to meet this Mrs. Kremer," Mr. Felker said as he reached back to close the door. "It's wonderful what she's doing for all you kids." He glanced down the basement stairs and then into the kitchen. "A rooming house, huh? Kind of like a fraternity or sorority, isn't it?"

"I guess so. Uh, Mrs. Kremer isn't available right now." Ben took a big chance and added, "She's got the flu or something. She's in the bathroom." He nodded in that direction and Megan took another step through the kitchen. Mr. Felker followed. The toilet flushed and a string of expletives were only partly muffled by the sound. They all could hear Emily repeating *sorry, sorry* as there was more banging, coughing, wretching and cussing.

"Sorry 'bout that," Ben said. "I've never heard Mrs. Kremer swear before." A true statement.

Megan shifted her gaze from the hallway back to Ben and then to Mr. Felker. "I'll be okay, really. Don't worry."

The man's frown didn't fade, but he gave Megan a quick hug, promised to check back with her before they left town, and shook hands with Ben.

"Nice to meet you, sir," Ben said.

Meg smiled at his politeness and hid her relief that Mr. Felker was as accepting of Ben's genuine maturity as she was. She wanted to judge his character correctly; he acted older than the boys she was used to.

She was sorry to hear that Mrs. Kremer was ill, but glad to avoid all that adult-talk with Mr. Felker asking probing questions. He could spot a lie still between your teeth. Although Mrs. Kremer treated her nicely enough when she met her last night, she didn't fit the stereotype of a sweet and charming housemother. It didn't actually matter if Mr. Felker approved of this whole rooming house thing, though. He wasn't family and even if he was, her own parents had pushed her out, signed the papers, and made it legal for her to make her own decisions.

"Well . . . call if you need anything." Megan nodded at the offer and said another goodbye as he ducked out the door and tramped through the snow.

She turned back to Ben. "So . . . uh, Mrs. Kremer is sick?"

She knew he was staring at the freckles on her face and she self-consciously rubbed at her nose. Boy, his eyes were blue, so blue. A really, really clear baby blue. Like Simon's, she thought, only . . . sexy.

"Uh," Ben held back for a second, deciding, "uh, no, not really. She's not here actually." A questionable but true statement. "I wasn't sure if Mr. Felker was gonna let you move in to a house of teens, so . . ."

"That's all right. I understand. So who's sick?"

The bathroom door burst open at that moment along with the door to the den. Suddenly there were five teens assessing one another.

"Who is *she*?" Cori demanded.

"The new girl," Emily murmured.

"Shut up! I didn't ask *you*! Who is she Ben? What's her name?" Cori leaned against the bathroom doorframe effectively screening Emily from view.

"I'm Megan, Megan Blakeney. I'm moving into the third bedroom upstairs. You must be Cori," she said taking a couple steps toward her. Ben reached for her arm and held her back.

"And why must I be Cori? Did somebody tell you the black sheep was Cori?" She ignored Adam and passed him to first knock and then pound on Mrs. Kremer's door. "Hey, bitch!" She pounded again. "We don't want another messed up kid here. Tell her she can't stay!"

Ben went straight for Cori who was starting to weaken the old door with her incessant battering. "She's not in there."

Cori swatted at him. "She's never in there! She hasn't been in there in three months!"

Ben glanced back at Megan whose face was two shades paler. Emily slinked back into the bathroom and Adam tilted his Fedora forward over his eyes.

"Cori!" Low yet forceful, Ben's voice found purchase in Cori's hazy brain. She took a step toward Megan then turned and made for the bathroom again, whisking past Emily and shoving her out. Emily pulled the door closed and stared at her feet.

"Guys," Ben motioned Adam and Emily toward the kitchen, "Adam, Emily, this is Megan. Megan, meet Adam and Emily, the two quietest people on the earth."

Adam stepped toward her and swooped his hat off, making a low bow like an English actor. Emily lifted her eyes and raised her hand.

Megan couldn't help but smile as she nodded to Adam and returned little finger waves with Emily. "Nice to meet you."

Ben tried for more damage control. "Don't pay any attention to anything Cori says. Em, why don't you help Megan with her bags?" He looked at Megan. "Guys aren't allowed upstairs. Especially when Cori is in one of her moods." He opened a kitchen drawer and pulled out a brown paper bag. "Some locks. You can guess what for." The deep dimples appeared. "I'll help you later."

Megan took the bag and followed Emily.

Emily led the way, dragging one of the bags sideways up the narrow staircase. She stepped aside at Megan's bedroom door and let her enter first. Quickly she explained, "I hope you don't mind." Her voice was soft and Megan gave her a questioning look. "I hung your things up."

"Thank you." Megan tried to remember what Ben told her about Emily. Quiet and shy? Yes, definitely. "Did you make the bed, too?"

Emily nodded and looked like she had something else to say. Instead she dragged the bag toward the closet and worked on untying the yellow plastic knot.

"It's nice of you to help." Megan hoped she'd be able to get more words out of Emily, but maybe she had reached her limit. She thought of a number of questions to ask, starting with what was going on with Cori. Cori was the one Ben said was incorrigible, a word she hadn't heard before he used it. She thought she knew the meaning now. Ornery wasn't strong enough.

"So . . ." Megan chose a safe question first, "do you like living here?"

Emily only shrugged her shoulders and worked harder to loosen the knot. She stretched the mouth of the bag and pulled out an armload of carefully folded clothes.

"Do you like Ben? He seems nice." Megan worked on opening the second bag but watched Emily for a reaction. She wasn't going to give much away with words but her body language was easily readable.

"He's okay." Emily crossed her arms over her chest. Megan thought she might be hiding her feelings with a lie. She watched her closely. Emily said, "The guys here are okay, but-"

"But what?"

"Cori . . . she went through your things."

"What?"

"If anything is missing . . . *she* took it. It wasn't me."

Megan was afraid to get angry; she didn't want to upset Emily who suggested such fragility. Now she understood why Ben had given her the bag of locks.

"It's all right. I don't think we're the same size any way. She's looks as big as a horse."

That made Emily snort and then she giggled. It broke the ice and both girls laughed and relaxed. Megan talked and drew Emily more and more out of her shell as they hung clothes and arranged items in the room. Megan tucked a small yellow photo album and a packet of papers in her top drawer and wondered if any of the locks Ben provided would allow her to bolt the drawer closed.

"What did Cori mean," Megan finally asked, "about Mrs. Kremer not being here for three months?"

Ben stood back as Cori took over the kitchen, pulling several things out of the fridge to make herself a sandwich.

She took it into the dining room and shoved aside the books on the table and used a paper towel as a plate.

"What're you staring at?" She took a bite of her sandwich, not bothering to lift her head to Ben.

Ben sat down at the table with her. "Cori, what are you trying to do? Don't you want to keep things like they are?" He watched her pull a piece of crust off, her black fingernails contrasting with the soft white bread. He didn't expect an apology, but he had to make her regret her outburst. "Do you have anywhere else to live?"

Cori's eyes went dark, as bitter and malicious as ever though she had washed off the streaks and shadows. "You think *you're* kicking me out? Who put *you* in charge?"

"I'm not . . . I didn't mean . . . listen, Mrs. Kremer was here yesterday. You can ask the new girl, she met her. But . . . if it ever got out how much she leaves us alone then this sweet deal, and our independence, will disappear." He watched her eyes roll when he mentioned the new girl; he wasn't getting through to Cori. If she ruined his plan, she'd be the one to disappear; he'd make sure of it. But he didn't want to start from scratch again; it would be best if he could convince her to shut up until Megan was happily established and there was no chance of Mr. Felker or a school counselor or a social worker getting wind of the arrangements here.

The silence stretched as Cori chewed. "Fine."

Ben got up and went back into the kitchen for some tools. He looked into the living room where Adam sat, arms folded, hat tipped forward, hair sticking straight out the sides. "Hey, Adam."

"Hey, Ben."

"Chuck staying in your room all day?"

Adam used an index finger to tap back the front end of his Fedora. He winked at Ben. "That he is."

"Tell him Cori got back safe."

"He knows." He leaned back, re-crossed his arms and, from where he was sitting, stared from underneath the hat brim into the dining room at Cori.

Ben cracked his knuckles and stifled a sigh. He took the stairs two and three at a time, but quietly. He reached

Megan's room right as he heard her ask Emily, "What did Cori mean about Mrs. Kremer not being here for three months?"

"Knock, knock. It's the bell boy slash locksmith." Ben entered armed with dimples, hammer, and screw driver.

"Oh," Megan dug through her pockets. "I'm supposed to give this to you, right? Since Mrs. Kremer isn't here?" She held out two tens and a five.

"Uh, no. You have to stick it in an envelope with your name on it and shove it under her door. There are envelopes in the kitchen."

Megan stuffed the money back in her pocket. "I was just asking Emily about what Cori said–."

"Forget it. She's nuts. Mrs. Kremer's here a lot, though she does travel. She's weird, kind of reclusive . . . but she's kind-hearted or else why would she let a bunch of misfits live in her *lovely* house?" He paused. "Especially the ever-sweet Cori." He glanced toward Emily. She wouldn't raise her eyes. "So . . . door lock?"

Chapter 4

Megan locked her special things in her closet before she left her room. The latch on the bedroom door only worked if she was in the room, keeping people out. While she was at work or school her belongings would be vulnerable to Cori. Ben offered to drive her to Home Depot to pick out a new doorknob with a locking mechanism, but he confessed that he didn't think he had the skills or proper tools to install it. She told him she'd be fine with what he brought. The closet already had a metal clasp that the padlock easily secured and the hammer was all they needed to nail in the hook and ring on the bedroom door. She wasn't about to start off in this new situation acting all paranoid.

Paranoid? She laughed to herself. Ben was the only normal one so far. Cori was a maniac, Emily super shy, and Adam acted like an observer, as if he were solely here to take mental notes on everything. She wondered what Chuck was like. Ben told her yesterday that he was a nutcase. What exactly did that mean?

She had at least a half an hour before she needed to walk to work. She looked out the window to check the weather. The sun was out and the snow gleamed.

There was a timid knock at the door.

"Come on in, Emily."

The door creaked open and Emily stood there pulling at her sleeves. She looked down the hall and then back at Megan. "He lied," she whispered.

"What?" Megan took a step forward, watched Emily back up a half-step. "Come in. Shut the door." The hair on her arms prickled. "What do you mean?"

Emily took another step back and shook her head. "This house isn't lovely . . . what he said. It's . . . it's haunted."

Megan would have burst out laughing if Emily didn't look so pathetic and dismal. Maybe her problem wasn't shyness; maybe she too was psycho.

Emily glanced down the hallway again and started moving her lips. There were no words that Megan could hear.

"Come on, sit on the mattress." She reached out to pull Emily in and noticed stains of blood around her sleeves, a smear of red on one thumb. She touched Emily's shoulder instead and steered her toward the bed. "I've got a few minutes before I leave for work. Are you afraid to be here alone?"

Emily allowed herself to be directed to the edge of the mattress and plopped herself down at the foot end. She shook her head, "No, I'm used to it."

"I don't believe in ghosts," Megan stated. "But I can see how this house could be creepy." She tried to laugh. It sounded fake to her own ears. "Ask me what I think tomorrow."

"Demons, too." Emily gave her warning in the tiniest of voices. Megan wasn't sure she even heard correctly.

"How about vampires?" She was growing uncomfortable, afraid she'd have to run down the snowy streets to be on time.

"Not real."

Well, that was encouraging, only two out of three impossible threats to her newfound independence.

"Emily, I need to leave for work. Can we talk about this when I get back? Around nine-thirty?"

Emily stayed out of Cori's way while she cleaned up and then left for work. When Ben came down from Megan's room Emily heard Adam ask him to move his car so he could leave. It wasn't much later that Ben took off; Emily suspected he was going to that other address she had seen on his license. She didn't mean to snoop, but he had left his wallet on the kitchen counter once.

After Megan left for work Emily sat in the living room, listening to the sounds in the old home.

It was Chuck's turn to make supper, but it didn't look like he was coming out of his cave. As long as he wasn't going to cook Emily wished he would leave like everyone else. She was aching for a chance to explore the basement again. Of course she went down there once a week to do her laundry, but there had only been one time when she was sure she was home alone. That was over a month ago. She had peeked in their rooms, but not gone in. Something niggled at her memory. Was that when the nightmares started? Did she see something that bothered her?

Maybe she should look again.

Emily gathered up an armload of dirty clothes and went downstairs, switching on more lights along the way. At the top of the basement stairs she noticed that both sets of the twins' boots were gone. Maybe Chuck had left with Adam. She stared at the floor a moment and replayed the few words Adam had said to Ben: *move your car, got someplace to be.* Well, he could have meant *we* not *I*. She started down the stairs.

"Chuck? . . . Chuck, I'm coming down to do laundry."

At the bottom of the steps she stared toward the first bedroom. "Chuck?" and a little louder: "You in there?" There was no music, no snoring, nothing.

She went to the utility room and stuffed her things in the washer, added soap, and adjusted the dials, but she didn't start it. It was her chance to know Ben better: to be in his room. She disregarded the little battle in her conscience debating right and wrong, privacy and trust. She could punish herself later. Her heart began to pump faster. Maybe she should work up the nerve to enter Ben's room by investigating Chuck's first.

She knocked and jiggled the doorknob before pushing it open. She stared into the room. They had bunk beds that were too short for such tall guys. No wonder they were often unpleasant. There was a third mattress on the floor. Perhaps they took turns stretching out there. Music posters hung on the walls and across from the beds was a bookcase filled with everything except books. Two piles of clothes filled the corner near the small basement window; one pile was stacked neatly with the plain, logo-free shirts that Adam favored and the other pile looked like Chuck's grab-and-go stash. Maybe they were clean, maybe not. The place smelled like a locker room.

Before she left the room she picked up a certificate and read the inscription: Charles Burdick, 1st place, boy's 100 yard dash. It was dated five years ago. Chuck had won first place in his sixth grade field day. Why would he still have this out? She set it back down exactly where it had been and left the room.

Her heart settled down a bit, but she had two more rooms to explore. She told herself that looking at the twins' room was innocent because she actually didn't care about them; she wouldn't need to cut herself for that trespass.

The basement bathroom was gross. She didn't step all the way in. Funny, there were only two toothbrushes at the sink. Emily decided that Ben was smart enough to keep his stuff in his room.

Now the adrenaline surged. She touched Ben's bedroom door knob and held her breath.

She blew out slowly as she entered, then noticed a much better smell than in Chuck's room. Ben's room contained two windows. The room was fairly neat, sparse even. It looked like he didn't live here. The bed was neatly made though there was no bedspread. Emily touched her heart unconsciously and gaped at Ben's decorating: hockey posters.

She ran her fingers along the edge of the bed and traced an outline of his head on the pillow. She buried her nose in the pillowcase and took more pleasure in the faint scent of his cologne than she should have allowed herself. The pounding in her ears was muting her hearing. What if she was caught in here?

She raised her head too fast, light headed. She panicked at the thought of fainting here and having Ben discover what a trespasser she was. Emily dropped to her knees and started crawling out of the forbidden space.

And that's when she saw them. The exposed parts of the basement floor, where the throw rugs didn't cover, showed dark red and brown stains exactly like in the laundry room.

Megan got a ride back from one of the busboys who, she was sure, had a crush on her. When they pulled into the driveway there were no cars there. She got her key ready, expecting that although there were plenty of lights on, the house might be locked.

She was right. And after pulling off her winter things she relocked the door. She paused a moment to listen. There was a frantic tumble of feet on the staircase above her head. She didn't want to scare Emily so she called out right away, "It's me. It's Megan. I'm home."

Emily rounded the corner of the kitchen and slid to a stop. She was paler than before.

"Are you all right? You look like you've seen a-" Megan stopped herself. "Are you all alone here? Did something happen?"

Emily pulled at her sleeves and shook her head, her hair flapping in little tremors. Both girls jumped at the sound of the dryer buzzer. Emily crooked her finger at Megan to follow her downstairs; she still didn't say a word.

She broke the silence at the bottom step when she pointed to the left and said, "Twins." Then she identified Ben's room and the bathroom as she led Megan into the utility room. She pulled her things out of the dryer as Megan surveyed the room.

Ben's open hockey bag was sitting on the freezer chest, a flap hanging down covering the padlock on the freezer.

Megan gasped as she looked at the floor. "Are those mouse turds?"

Emily followed her gaze. Mice were the least of their problems. Didn't Megan find the stains disturbing? She clutched her clean laundry to her chest and said, "Maybe, I don't know." She started out the door and Megan reached for the pull string on the single light bulb. Emily stopped her, "No, we always leave that on."

Megan trailed after her up two flights and stopped at Emily's door. She could see into her room and spotted the twist of blankets on the floor by the window. It looked like a nest.

"Can I see your room?"

Emily nodded and stepped in. Megan followed.

The walls were plastered with pages from magazines: everything concerning the *Twilight* saga.

"Nice," Megan said, not meaning it. "Oh, this is cool." She meant that. She picked up Emily's knitted satchel. It was light, stylish and pretty.

Emily opened her closet and started putting her things away. She spoke then, finally sounding normal. "Are you hungry? I made some mac and cheese."

"No, thanks, I ate at the restaurant where I work." A pause, she set the satchel down. "Where do you work?"

Emily named a clothing store in the strip mall a couple of miles away. Her reluctance to give a longer answer made Megan think they were back to square one again. Was she going to have to start over with this girl every five minutes? She started to open up earlier today. Now she was like a vault.

"Well," Megan turned toward the door. "I guess I'll see you tomorrow. I don't go to work until four."

"Sundays," Emily shook her head, "I work eight to five." And then Ben drives me to all the shelters looking for my mother, she wanted to say aloud, but that was too much to share yet.

It was after midnight when Emily thought she was waking up because of a car door slamming. She heard that muted yet crisp thump that certain sounds echoed when the temperatures dropped below freezing.

But she wasn't awake.

And she wasn't dreaming.

Something was pressing against her chest. Her arms were pinned down and her feet felt bound at the ankles. Her eyes wouldn't, or couldn't, open.

The scraping started at her neck. Claws or nails or needles were making at least a dozen scratches down her throat, over her shoulders, toward her elbows, stopping abruptly where the razor cuts began.

She couldn't breathe.

The scraping started at her neck again and this time the claws gouged over her breasts and down her middle and down farther.

And stopped.

Emily struggled to open her eyes and when she thought she had, all she saw was pitch blackness. No street light glow, no flicker from the candle she left burning on the dresser.

Her whole body tingled with bubbles of adrenaline, rushing to all parts at once. If only she could move. What, or who, was holding her down?

Fear heaved through her small frame, rushing up from her feet, meeting the claws at her middle, and flooding up to her brain.

Fear made her gasp for air. She tried to break free of the demons that held her down.

A soft undertone of air or breath spoke words to her anxious soul. Be calm. Go back to sleep.

But instead she groaned.

Megan didn't fall asleep. She had too much on her mind and the creepiness of the old house, and the loneliness, got to her. She explored the first floor again, trying not to be too snoopy, hoping the others wouldn't arrive to find her boldly going through the cupboards and drawers. She even jiggled Mrs. Kremer's door knob when the radio in her room started up at eleven p.m.

On her knees at the door she could see underneath and into the room several feet. She shoved her rent under the door hours ago, as instructed, but now she couldn't see any sign of her envelope.

She stood up and felt the upper ledge of the frame above the door. Dust.

She went to the bathroom door and did the same. Nothing. She hoped to find one of those little metal things you stick in the knob to release the mechanism. A bobby pin or paper clip might work, too.

She looked toward the den and had a thought.

Yes! Above the door frame rested a metal pin, hooked at one end.

Chapter 5

Ben loved Saturdays. He could always count on his mother staying sober until evening when his step-father would take her out and he'd have the house to himself. The office was off-limits to him and he had been harshly disciplined the first time he used the desk top computer in there. But it was routine now for Ben to hack into Rose Properties, Inc.'s accounts and make certain adjustments.

His step-father's company bought, sold, renovated, and rented foreclosed homes and condos, and lucratively exploited the economic downturn. A luxury suburban home that some laid off car executive borrowed half a million dollars against was snapped up by Rose for as little as $200,000. Renting it back to the same family put money in both their pockets. Ben knew that Ed Rose wasn't philanthropic, so he liked to check through the accounts receivable and give a little electronic help to those whose payments were late or short.

A year ago Ben conceived his plan when Rose Properties bought six city houses in a dilapidated but safe area. All six were bank owned and languishing in neglect. Rose bought them all and offered them for rent at break-even prices with three year leases. His step-father alternately carped and crowed about the deal and Ben got his idea. He jumped on the one that came with furniture, negotiating through the mail. Then he told Ed that a lady came by and he'd given her the keys to the house. At first his step-dad was furious, but then Ed patted Ben on the back, the only friendly contact they'd had, when Ben handed him the imaginary Mrs. Kremer's money order for the first three months' rent. From then on Ben split his life between hockey-playing-honor-student and invisible-landlord-to-emancipated-and-needy-teens.

"Holy cow," Ben mumbled as he opened the last program and looked up his step-father's finances. Something wasn't right. A jolt went through his body along with a hunch. He clinked on the history button and scrolled down. "No way . . . no way!" Ben's agitation grew as the realization dawned on him that his mother must have given Ed the passwords to his own accounts. His inheritance, the government's death gratuity and a small life insurance payout, were under his mother's control. He found the passwords two years ago and became his own secret executor, funneling small amounts to a teen savings account he held jointly with her, but which she ignored.

He unclenched his fists and cracked his knuckles. If he changed the passwords now would his step-father be suspicious? He needed to think this through. He didn't want to rock the boat.

He cleared the history cache for the last hour and logged off. He leaned back in the desk chair and stared at the blank screen. Several illegal ideas sprang to mind, but he'd watched enough TV to eliminate them all as foolish. As much as it burned him Ben decided he'd have to pretend to be ignorant of the situation.

And then he spotted the envelope. Old fashioned mail. But the return address was the house next door to his rooming house. The Petersons. The people who lent him the snow shovel. The people whose mail he picked up when they went away at Christmas.

He pulled the letter out. *Dear Mr. Rose, We rent from you at 324 Elm, next to another of your properties, 328. We are bringing to your attention that several teenagers seem to be living there alone without adult supervision. We would like you to check into the matter. We are planning on reporting the situation to the authorities but thought it best to alert you first. Please do something by the end of the month. Sincerely, Mike and Charlene Peterson*

Ben reread the letter, checked the date, and searched the desk for any other correspondence. Had his step-father already replied? Would the Petersons really contact the authorities? Which authorities?

He panicked when he thought of how quickly teens were hauled off to foster care on TV shows. Would he have a chance to take care of what was in the freezer? Maybe the trunk of his car would be a safer place for that 'treasure'.

Megan fingered the thin door key and pressed it into the hole in the knob. A couple of fumbling twists and pokes and the mechanism sprang. The sounds of the house amplified in her pounding ears: the hum of the furnace, the drone of the fridge, the radio behind the door that earlier bore Cori's beating.

She pushed it open and slipped into the bedroom, closed and locked the door behind her. The shades were drawn; the bedside lamp was on, providing plenty of light to snoop around. The closet door was closed. She started there. Four blouses, two pairs of slacks, three dresses, a night gown, a jacket. Not much of a wardrobe. She conjured up an image of Mrs. Kremer in the first dress. Not likely. It was a petite, size 4, and the next one was a woman's 22. The pants were size 10 and size 16, all the blouses medium. And nothing smelled of the cigarette smoke that Mrs. Kremer's clothes had.

Megan frowned at the floor of the closet – no shoes.

She checked the dresser. Pillowcases and scarves in the top drawer. Nothing in the second and third. No personal objects anywhere.

The radio shut off. Megan froze.

She could hear groans. The table lamp went out on its own; she stayed still.

Emily's groans rose to her own ears. Her body began to convulse and she jerked free of the weight that held her down, yet was unable to control the violent shaking that sent her arms and legs and torso into a demonic dance of trouble. Her head began to whip back and forth and she tried to form a prayer, fear and wishing mingling as one.

Ben drove back to the rooming house. His headlights flashed across the front of the house, momentarily illuminating the dark living room. There was no blue flicker from the TV, most of the lights were off in the house; already Megan's presence changed the rhythm of the place. He knew she didn't have a boyfriend. Not anymore. As pretty as she was, it was surprising that she didn't. He had scoped her out thoroughly for two weeks before he decided to help her out. He never saw her with any guys.

He parked and went up the steps. A piercing shriek from above made him hurry through the door. If Emily was all alone . . .

Megan had her hand on the door knob ready to sneak out when she heard first the scream and then the back door bursting open. Footsteps ran past her door and up the staircase. Cori?

She locked the door and pulled it closed, stuffed the key in her pocket and ran up the stairs.

Emily cried out as soon as Ben entered the room. He flicked on the light and repeated something over and over. She felt the warmth of Ben's hands gripping the sides of her face and calmed down.

Another nightmare. It wasn't real.

Emily sat up, pulled the blanket to her chin and sniffled.

"Are you gonna be okay?" Ben dropped his hands and moved back a few inches. He saw Megan standing at the door and explained, "Nightmare . . . again. Didn't you hear her? Where were you?"

Emily glanced at Megan and then lay back down, turned toward the wall, and covered her head with the blanket. "Get out," she said, half-muffled by the pillow. She was horrified that Megan had seen her like this. Such humiliation would need a penalty.

She heard Ben move away, saying a few more calming words, like everything would be all right, he'd leave the light on, Megan was here for her. And then there was the click of the door closing tightly.

Ben repeated his question in a whisper, "Where were you?"

Megan lied, "Laundry room."

"Well, get used to the nightmares. Always when she first goes to bed."

"Does Cori usually wake her up?"

Ben walked with her to the steps. Megan made like she was going to go down, too, so he talked over his shoulder as they descended. "Never. Come to think of it, I don't remember Cori ever being in the house when it happens."

"That's strange."

They reached the first floor. "We should probably stay up a while. Make sure she gets back to sleep." Ben wanted to get to know Megan without the others around. Now was as good a time as any. They had the place virtually to themselves.

He plopped himself onto the easy chair and turned on a lamp. Megan took the couch and sat on one leg.

"Well, think this is gonna work out for ya? In a house full of crazy teens?"

"Hmm," Megan started twisting her hair for something to do with her hands, "seems okay so far, but . . ."

Ben's dimples faded and he sat forward. "What?"

"Well, first of all, I don't even know your last name."

"Kinlaw, Ben Kinlaw . . . and Emily is Emily Courtland. You can ride with us to school in the mornings. Or wait for the bus."

"Thanks, a ride sounds good, but won't it be too crowded?"

"Nope, Chuck and Cori go to the alternative high school a few blocks from here."

"What's alternative about it? Art? Music?"

"Hardly. They get the basics plus anger management, therapy, and a smoking patio."

Megan swallowed, "So . . . they're like the losers who can't make it in school but get another chance." She thought about it as Ben gave the tiniest of head nods and cracked his knuckles. "Adam seemed normal. What's his problem?"

"Well, uh, the better question is – what is Chuck's problem? And the answer is – he's schizophrenic."

Megan gave a little gasp. "Is he dangerous? Is that the real reason you gave me a lock for the door?" She sat up a little straighter and thought of what she'd found out in the master bedroom. Who was that woman she met yesterday?

Who took her rent money? Had she made a huge mistake in moving here?

"No, no, don't worry about Chuck. And Adam is harmless."

The dimples spread across his face again and Megan couldn't help but melt a little. This whole situation had to work out for her; she was already in deep with court appearances and paper work and social workers. Would living in a home with psychos totally ruin her chances to get back with Simon? The little tingling in her belly was either fear or attraction. "What about Cori? Why is she there?"

"Because she's Cori. She's anti-everything. Rotten to the core. Bad home life, low self-esteem, bullying, drugs, shop-lifting, you name it. But she's lightened up a lot since she moved in here. There's hope for her."

Megan knew what her own problem was and now knew about Cori and Chuck and poor, shy Emily, but what about Ben? He was adorable. It was like he was the shepherd. It crossed her mind that maybe he was years older than he looked; maybe this was some grad school research project.

"Why are you here?" Megan got the words out slowly, watching his face for signs of lies.

"My dad was killed in action, my mom's in rehab, I have to live somewhere. Don't worry, I'm not crazy. In fact, you can check the list in the main office – I'm always on the honor roll."

Megan twirled her hair and tried to form her next question about Mrs. Kremer when headlights swung across the front window and a car pulled up and out of sight. A moment later they heard a car door slam and then the side door exploded open.

"You first."

"No, you first. Out of my way."

Ben chuckled. "Hey, Chuck," he called, "come and meet Megan, our new roomie."

Something was thrown down the basement stairs, there were hushed whispers, and then a tall, thin boy walked into the living room. He was finger-combing his hair behind his ears. He stopped and looked from Ben to Megan.

"Hello," was all he said.

Megan greeted him back, watching for signs of something. Weirdness, danger, something. But he only showed the signs of shyness; he hunched a little, was much less sure of himself than Adam who had bowed with a certain elegance. Chuck had no style.

"You okay?" Ben asked him.

Chuck stared for a beat or two before replying, "Sure."

"Take your . . . vitamins, buddy."

Chuck's eyes flew to Megan to see if she discerned the hidden meaning. "Right," he said.

Ben lay in his bed thinking of his problem with his step-father, but he couldn't focus. All he thought about was Megan. After Chuck went downstairs, hopefully to take a pill, they talked until nearly one a.m. He liked her and he wanted to tell her the truth, but he sensed there was something she was holding back, not only the secret he already knew about. She did tell him about her old school, how she was a cheerleader in junior high, but had to give it up for some health issues. When he had asked more about her family she said it was complicated and left it at that.

Megan asked him about his father and if he wanted to go in the army some day. The thought had been buried, but he blurted out to her half of his secret plan: that he would apply to the best colleges, get a degree in political science, and then do something to help the world – he wanted to honor his father.

He blinked in the darkness. Megan was going to side-track him, make him lose focus, if he wasn't careful.

But he was so lonely.

He watched the red numbers on the clock until they read one forty. Everyone should be in their deepest stage of sleep by now, he reasoned. He threw off the covers and hunted for the key to the padlock on the freezer. This would be a good time to make the transfer from freezer to car trunk. He'd have to make two trips to carry the heavy plastic bins up.

Megan couldn't fall asleep though she was exhausted physically, mentally, and emotionally. She tried to think only of Simon, but her thoughts kept returning to Ben's dimples, his smile, and the way he talked with his hands and then punctuated with knuckle cracks.

She nearly told him about her snooping. She wanted to be honest with him, especially since it was apparent he was the only normal person in the house.

The nightmare thing with Emily seemed weird. Ben was so mature in his handling of the situation. Poor Emily looked ashamed of having a bad dream. Maybe this week Megan could talk to her about it. Maybe she would tell Emily about Simon.

The moment she drifted off to sleep she thought she heard her door latch rattle.

She dreamed she could see it lifting up, the door open yet closed, strange shapes sifting through the slats, hovering and taking new forms above her low bed.

She tried to shake herself awake, but found she couldn't move a muscle. There was pressure on her chest, her head, her legs. Was she having Emily's night terror?

Her heart began to pound too fast, but the pressure, though it weighted her down, did not prohibit her from rising up. Her planked body levitated, eyes closed, ears unhearing, voice mute. She tried to scream, but could barely manage a groan.

Paralyzed. Mid-air.

And then . . .

Sunday

Chapter 6

Very early Sunday morning Cori returned. Jason dropped her at the street and started driving away the moment she closed the door. She swore at his taillights.

The house was dark except for a candle in Emily's window. Stupid girl was going to burn the place down.

Cori stomped through the main floor extra hard. Take that, Benny boy. And screw you, psycho twins. She ascended the stairs a little less angry, but no less high, then made all kinds of noise in the bathroom. When she came out she flicked off the hall light and stood in the dark. She looked intently at Emily's door and debated whether or not to go in and blow the candle out. She touched the door knob and pushed. The stupid little wallflower hadn't locked her door. Cori crossed the room and rather than blow out the candle she simply took it with her, glancing at the quivering lump under the covers as she passed. Pathetic.

She didn't bother to close the door behind her.

The candle cast flickering shapes down the hall. Cool. She tried to remember which drug Jason gave her last. She paused at the new girl's room. A quick check of the door and she knew that Benny boy had helped new girl with a lock. Cori cursed aloud. She set the candle on the floor and dug through her pockets. She had nothing that would work. She went to her own room and looked around. Her head began to nod in mock anticipation as she picked up a wire clothes hanger from the floor and bent the rounded end into a sharper angle.

Slowly, quietly she opened Megan's door the eighth of an inch that the latch allowed. She slipped the wire through and lifted up. The hanger caught the latch and she unhooked it in seconds. Her short black-polished nail tapped the door the rest of the way.

The candle still flickered from its spot on the floor. The tiny light made Megan's shape loom larger and higher on the wall.

Cori fell against the door frame, grabbed it for balance. She couldn't believe what she thought she saw. The new girl was floating at least half-way between the floor and the ceiling.

Cori strained her eyes, grabbed for the candle. She burned her palm and thumb and swore again, stumbling backward. The candle went out, the hanger struck the floor and Cori backed away. She damned Jason for giving her something weird; she damned the new girl; she damned the candle.

Emily thought she could smell the bacon, hear it sizzling. Sundays were the best and worst day for her. Ben would make eggs and then drive her to her job where she'd stand at the clerk's counter for nine hours, minus a half hour lunch and two breaks. It was boring, tedious, and uninteresting. But it was an escape from the rooming house and Cori's domination. Cori demanded that Sundays were her day to rule the house since it was her day off from the tattoo parlor. And since Ben didn't stick around on Sundays Cori made slaves of her and Chuck unless they stayed out of her way.

"It's seven fifteen, Em, time to get up," Ben called from the bottom of the stairs.

She could hear him more clearly than usual. She turned over and was surprised to see the door open. Now she remembered; she freaked out over a nightmare and Ben and Megan came to her room. But she remembered him closing the door.

She sat up in bed and looked around the room. Her big pine scented candle was gone. If Cori took it then it was gone forever. But if Ben blew it out and moved it . . . maybe . . .

She went barefoot to the door and looked down the hall. The candle sat on the floor in front of Megan's room, the door open. She heard a thump and a startled cry from Megan.

Emily took a quick look at Cori's door before moving, then hurried toward the candle. She scooped it up and turned back to her room without looking into Megan's. But Megan saw her.

Megan's eyelids jerked open the instant she slammed onto the floor. Her head hit the mattress, but her body was on the old hardwood oak strips. She caught a glimpse of Emily as she snatched a green cylinder from the floor in front of Megan's door. A door that should have been closed. And locked.

Like thumbing through a series of snapshots her mind flitted through the events of the previous evening: Emily's nightmare, talking with Ben, meeting Chuck, locking her door.

The nightmare.

Was it scarcely a second ago? Did she only dream she hit the floor hard?

She scrambled to her feet and ran after Emily.

They talked as Emily got dressed behind the closet door. Then Megan pulled a sweatshirt on over her pajamas before they both went down for breakfast.

"Tell him," Emily whispered as she and Megan entered the kitchen.

"Tell me what?" Ben asked. He grabbed a plate from the cupboard and handed it to Megan. Emily shrank back as she watched him smile at Megan; he never looked her way, not even when he handed her the second plate.

"I don't believe in ghosts," Megan began with a little snort, "at least I didn't think I did. But there might be something haunted about this house. I had a nightmare, too. Woke up half off my bed, as if I'd fallen out."

"But it's on the floor."

"Right." Megan dished up her eggs and waited for Emily and Ben to do the same. "But it still felt like I hit the floor hard." She followed them to the table and sat across from Emily.

Emily tried not to stare at Megan. *Why does her hair look so good?* Jealousy flushed her cheeks and she sat smaller in her chair. Ben and Megan continued the conversation without including her. She took two bites of eggs and lowered her fork to her lap. She scratched the tines along her wrist and chewed harder.

"Is there an attic?" Megan asked.

"Yeah, but the access is in Cori's closet."

"I wonder . . ."

"What?"

"Well, I just wonder about the history of this place. Like maybe there was a murder here or something. Maybe there's a trunk in the attic with, you know, newspaper clippings and junk that somebody from a hundred years ago left." Megan finished her eggs and looked across at Emily. She realized her mistake and changed directions. "Maybe if we found out that nothing ever happened here, no ghosts or anything, then maybe your nightmares would stop."

Emily bobbed her head. "But you had one." she said it so softly that she thought perhaps she'd have to repeat it to be heard.

But Ben answered, "Nightmares are like yawns, very contagious." He tried for a real laugh and Megan was quick to join in. "Anyway, I seriously doubt Cori would let us through her room to get to the attic."

Emily took her plate to the sink. She heard Ben tell Megan that he'd be back after he did some errands if she wanted to continue their conversation from last night. Emily frowned. Ben never stuck around here on Sundays. At least that was what he always told her. She turned the water on its hottest temperature and let it scald her left wrist. She felt a little better.

She needed to comb her hair, wash her face, and brush her teeth, but that would mean ten more minutes for those two to talk alone. "Ben," she raised her voice a couple decibels, "Ben. I'm ready to go."

Megan figured she had some time to shower and dress before Ben got back. She started up the stairs quickly then slowed to a quieter stealth when she remembered who was still sleeping up there.

Haunted house, right, she thought. She liked a good zombie story or vampire movie same as the next person, but a nightmare couldn't hurt you, bite you, kill you. She wasn't as sure about Cori.

The pounding on the front door was another matter. Who would be knocking this early on a Sunday morning? Her heart froze with the possibilities. If it was the police . . . something about Simon? No, they couldn't know yet that she lived here unless . . .

She went to Emily's room and hesitated a second before pushing the door open. She went to the window, stepped on Emily's nest of blankets, and looked out. Relief. The car out front was not a police cruiser. She could see tracks in the snow, but even with her face right up to the top of the window she couldn't quite see who was down there on the porch.

Another pounding on the door. Would Cori be roused by the noise? And what about the twins in the basement? It shouldn't be her responsibility yet to answer the door. Whoever was down there was probably one of their friends.

Two more knocks and the person stepped back and into Megan's view. She jerked back and to the side, out of sight, as the man raised his face toward the window.

"I'll be back!" he yelled, his voice hardly muted through the old panes of glass. "Marty *Kremer* will be back!"

Megan gambled on another look and watched the hugely obese man waddle back to the car. Marty Kremer? A relative of the woman she met? She should have gone down and let him in, but . . .

"What are you doing in Emily's room?" Cori demanded.

Megan's hand flew to her mouth to stifle a gasp. "You scared me!"

"I scare everybody." Cori crossed the room, shouldered Megan aside, and looked out the window. "Who's he?"

"I don't know, I mean, he hollered that he'd be back. Said he's Marty Kremer."

"Shit. He's huge." She watched him struggle to fit into the seat, start the car, and pull away. "Didn't look like the bitch's type. She could do better."

Megan was ready to disagree, to say that the woman she met seemed like she'd hook up with any guy, but instead she stared at Cori.

"What happened to your face?"

Cori turned abruptly and spat out the words, "None of your business."

"Cori, please, can't we be friends? After all, we're living together."

"What's your name again?"

"Megan."

"Well, Megan, my kind and your kind can't be friends." Cori turned.

"Wait. I know you went in my room. Did you take anything?" Megan stepped closer, not threatening, not even confrontational, but sure of herself.

Cori sneered. "You don't have anything I want. What are you, some stupid rich bitch that got grounded once? Why do you need to be here?"

Megan cleared her throat. She never imagined that she'd tell this to Cori before Ben or Emily. "My parents disowned me. I had a baby." The tears started to come, unwanted. "His name is Simon and I hardly ever get to be with him." The sobs began and she lowered her head. Her whole body shook. She covered her face with her hands and cried in earnest. When she finally got hold of herself she lifted her head, ready to explain the rest.

But Cori was gone.

Chapter 7

Chuck listened from the kitchen. New girl was crying. He scraped out a few chunks of dried eggs from the pan on the stove then took a box of cheerios into the living room. He took his pill and now felt kind of mellow. Hoped Cori would come down. Maybe she'd give him a hard time. As usual.

She wanted him. She was clearly playing hard to get. I need a cigarette.

No you don't.

Adam, just leave me alone.

New girl is kind of cute. Maybe I could make Cori jealous by paying more attention to her. To Megan.

That might make Ben mad. He was kind of into her last night.

Chuck's mind went blank and he stared out the window.

Megan showered and dressed and went down to the living room to wait for Ben. One of the twins was sitting in the chair watching the road; a box of cereal was tipped at his feet.

"Good morning . . . Chuck?" He was wearing the same Kid Rock shirt from the night before and since he wasn't wearing a hat, she was certain she'd guessed right.

Slowly he turned his face her way. His gaze was vacant, empty, and a tad frightening. For a split second Megan imagined that a demon was arched to pop out of his skull and attack her. The thought vanished when she heard a gurgle from his throat.

"Morning," he struggled to say. He twisted back toward the window and went rigid.

"Um, last night Ben told me I could use the computer in the den. That okay with you?"

His head nodded slightly. Megan left him to his stupor and entered the den.

The small room was drafty, but she was too intent on her mission to be bothered running upstairs for a sweatshirt.

She started a Google search with the address of the house and got 509,000 results in 0.46 seconds. The first thing was a map with a green arrow indicating the old house's location. Real estate news, data, and statistics followed along with totally irrelevant stuff about Pottery Barn, a pizza place, and several libraries. She jumped ahead ten and twenty pages deeper into the search results and found nothing. The side bar caught her attention and she hit "news" under the search options and was disappointed again when no results appeared.

Next she tried a search of newspaper archives. Pay dirt. She found an article from 1933 that detailed a horrific murder that took place two blocks from the new high school: *Small towns are not immune to tragedies of this magnitude,* the article began, *but it is a shock just the same to have a calamity such as this occur here. In an extraordinary religious cult ceremony and orgy Bobby Joe Kinton killed his own mother and sister. Police officials have confirmed that a group of twelve Kentucky mountaineers relocated to this community in 1932 and continued to practice devil-worship, voodooism, and animal sacrifice. The bodies of the two women were found partially burned, stabbed, and dismembered. Neighbors on Elm Street had reported screams coming from the house next door on two previous occasions.*

Megan scanned the rest of the article. She wondered if she was now living in a house that once was the site of a human sacrifice. She chilled at the thought. What, besides the devil, would drive a son to kill his mother and sister?

The reference to Elm Street and the "new" school sidetracked her onto another direction. She found the address of the school, built in 1928. Further sleuthing and she learned that the school was used as administrative offices in the 70's and 80's and then reopened in 2001 as the alternative school that Cori and the twins attended. Interesting, but she wanted to know more about the murder. She tried Bobby Joe Kinton's name, but Google had no results, not even Facebook.

Megan wondered if she could check the county records. The Freedom of Information Act must apply. Maybe there was a deed or something in the mother's name, but, considering the type of people they were, her last name was likely to be different from her son's. She might as well drop the whole thing. Nightmares, ghosts, murders. She knew why she was distracting herself with this: she was avoiding thinking about how she blurted out her big secret to Cori.

She'd have to say something to Ben now. So much for trying to impress a guy.

Ben dropped the uber-silent Emily off at her work and then circled around to his mother and step-dad's house. If he parked on the next street and came in through the walk-out basement they wouldn't know the car hadn't been in the garage all night. He had set the house alarm, but chances were good that they had been too drunk to think of re-setting it. But if they did, he'd have 30 seconds to run up to the foyer and disarm it. He could do it in 10.

"Ben!" Ed Rose was on the weight lifting bench. "What are you doing?"

Ben closed the door quickly and stomped his feet on the mat. "Uh, I went outside right before you came down here. Didn't you see me?" He looked out the door window at the solitary tracks he'd made in the snow. That would be hard to explain if Ed looked.

"No. Hey, come here. Spot me."

Ben threw his coat on the chair and slipped off his boots. Already his mind was inventing plausible explanations – lies – to cover himself. As he stood at the head of the bench he thought of something else: the Petersons. How could he bring up the subject of his step-father's rental houses without arousing suspicion?

Easy. Ed Rose thought his step-son was a bookworm, a geek, and a loser. A little flattery should play to the old man's ego.

"Um, Ed, we're studying financial stuff in economics class. My teacher said nobody can make money in real estate now and I said Rose Properties does."

"Damn right." Ed grunted with the weight, pushed it straight up.

"Well, how come you do?"

"Volume, low interest, steady renters," he grunted again, "a number of things."

"Aren't renters a hassle?" Ben hoped this was a good segue.

"Only if they don't pay on time."

"What if," he hesitated, trying to frame the question, "what if your renters are, you know, unreliable or something. Like they wreck the house or have parties all the time or don't mow the grass and the city gets after you."

"I kick 'em out in a heartbeat." He finished and sat up, wiped his brow.

"You can do that? Even if they've paid their rent in advance?"

Ed's laugh was not only evil, it was sardonic. "I've got people who can handle . . . evictions . . ."

Cori stretched and yawned. It was almost noon on a Sunday. Perfect. The only thing wrong with this weekend was that it was close to being over.

And her jaw hurt. Then she remembered. She came home at four or five a.m., saw something incredible, hit her head stumbling through her room, and passed out. A noise awakened her a couple of hours later and she confronted the new girl in Emily's room. There was a fat guy outside and . . . the new girl was a mother. Holy sh--!

She rubbed at her jaw and felt some dried blood. Her stomach growled. She'd had dreams in her life that had stayed with her long after and changed her perceptions; she'd had nightmares that blackened her head like the dye in her hair, coloring the thoughts of her mind but then fading to a haze. Cori took no moment to think – she was better at reacting. She fled the room.

When she reached the bottom step she listened before touching the door. The place was dead silent. She opened the door and took an elastic step out.

She was surprised to see the new girl in the den and Chuck in the living room. She kept her facial expression terse in that every-day scowl of hers and purposely crossed the living room and took the long way to the kitchen.

"Hey, pizza-face," Cori mocked as she passed Chuck.

He turned as she spoke and flung a peculiar look in her direction: a look of hatred. His facial muscles hardened then relaxed. He did not speak until she reached the kitchen.

"Hey, Cori," Chuck replied, softly. He stood and stretched, rubbed his eyes, and followed her. "Can I help you with anything?"

"Get outta my sight. Go screw a light bulb or somethin'."

"You need that pan? Lemme wash it for ya." He grabbed the egg-encrusted pan and made for the sink.

Cori smirked. "Did *you* make eggs? I don't believe it."

Chuck's shoulders slumped. He began to scrub the pan.

"Hey, new girl!" Cori leaned into the hallway. "Come wash your dirty pan out. We're not your slaves."

Megan appeared in the doorway and watched her housemates' backs as Chuck cleaned and Cori hunted for cereal.

"Shit, we're outta Cheerios."

"I'll get 'em." Chuck's long legs meant it only took him a couple of strides to and from the living room to retrieve the box. "Here, Cori." He said her name like a kid with a crush.

Megan took Chuck's spot at the sink and finished washing the pan. The small room guarded their careful movements as they braided their way around one another. Despite Cori's ill-temper Megan's revelation put a chink in her scaly armor; Chuck's devotion and her own insecurities broke her scowl, but neither Megan nor Chuck saw the change in her demeanor. Cori took her cereal bowl to the dining room and stood at the window to eat.

"So, Chuck," Megan began, "I was just looking up some stuff on the internet. Did you know there might have been a double murder in this house?"

His reaction was not what she expected. Chuck's lips parted, as if to speak, but he merely drew a breath in then let it escape with a sigh. "I love murder," he whispered.

Megan chilled. She stepped away from him and into the dining room. "Cori, Ben said there's a way into the attic from your room. Can we look up there?"

Megan felt colder yet as Cori's eyes boiled at her with some dark and unnamed emotion. Then she spoke, "Listen, new girl . . ." Her jaw tightened, "Maybe we need some kind of initiation or orientation or . . ."

"Hazing," Chuck breathed.

Cori ignored him. "Or whatever. You gotta learn the rules. Nobody goes in my room. Not even Mr. All-important-Ben."

Megan backed away then had a thought. "Hey, do you think Mrs. Kremer could be a descendant of the victims?"

Cori rolled her eyes.

"They could have left kids. Or the murderer could have had a kid."

Cori clenched her spoon. New girl was getting to her. She set her bowl down on the table and took a step toward Megan. "Tell me your impression of Mrs. Kremer. Describe her."

"Um, old, older. Brownish hair."

"Not blonde? How long?"

"Not long, hardly over her ears. Short dirty nails. Trailer trash," Megan said remembering with a jolt how that term had been used to belittle her once.

"Would you say she was a thirty-something business executive type?" Cori crossed her arms and moved further into Megan's space.

"No," she answered, holding her ground. She sent a flickering glance toward Chuck who framed the doorway. His brow corrugated into lines of wonder, but he said nothing.

Megan dug one hand into her jeans pocket and pulled out the piece of metal she found above the door frame yesterday. She waved it at Cori. "I dare you to go in her room."

Ben finally got away in the afternoon when he told his mom he had a project to work on at the city library. She was on her second glass of wine from a bottle that Ben had watered down. He left her to rattle around the big house alone.

Ed had escaped earlier, after his workout, claiming that Sunday was the only day he could scout real estate, walk through open houses, and make deals. Funny how so many deals brought him home late smelling of smoke and booze.

Ben drove fast, anxious to spend some time with Megan before she went to work. Some concern about leaving her alone with the others also affected his speed. He couldn't trust Cori to hold her tongue. The comment with reference to Mrs. Kremer was worrisome.

He pulled into the driveway behind Chuck's car. As soon as he opened the side door he heard the arguing.

Three voices came from the back of the house.

"What are you guys doing in here?" he asked as he entered the den.

Megan was at the computer. Cori and Chuck hunched over either side of her.

The look in Cori's eyes stopped him before her words did. "We're googling Mrs. Kremer. What's her first name anyway?"

"I . . . I don't know. Why are you . . . what are you looking for?" Ben cracked every knuckle, moved closer to the monitor.

"Try Marty Kremer. Martin, I mean," Cori offered. Her scowl was gone and her face held more color than usual.

"What are you guys doing?" Ben demanded again.

"Some man . . ."

"A fat man."

"Yeah, some fat man showed up this morning pounding on the door. Said his name was Marty Kremer."

Ben stepped back. *How could this be?*

Megan stood up. "Ben, we're pretty sure there isn't a Mrs. Kremer. There isn't, is there?"

"What, what do you mean? You've all met her."

"We've all met somebody different," Cori said. "Tell us, Ben, what *does* she look like?"

"Well," he looked from face to face then held his hand out as high as his ears, "she's about this tall or this tall depending on if she's wearing heels or not." He lowered his hand a few inches.

"What color is her hair?" Cori asked.

"Like you, she changes it. So, I guess I don't really know." He pulled his thumb till the knuckle popped.

Megan was looking at him more intently than the others, reading him.

Ben popped his other thumb. "Listen, why are you guys so interested all of a sudden? Because of this Marty guy?" He unexpectedly struck on an answer and tried to look surprised. "Maybe it's her husband. Maybe she's not here much because she lives with him and this place is a secret."

The other three were relaxing their frowns gradually. Ben knew he could save this by weaving a tale close to his own. "Yeah, that makes sense, now that I think about it. She must be keeping this place behind his back. Maybe she's going to leave him someday and needed somewhere already set up. She couldn't afford it without our rent, so . . ." The fiction was pulling them in; he had at least one of them convinced.

"But what about her clothes?" Megan walked around Ben and into the hallway where she pushed open the door to the master bedroom.

"You've been in her room?" Astonishment strangled some of his words. He followed Megan in and looked around as if he were viewing it for the first time. "What did you find?"

Megan opened the closet door. "The clothes are different sizes. No shoes."

Ben thought hard. He had grabbed the first things he found at the Salvation Army store, never checking the sizes. "Huh. Maybe my theory is right. She doesn't actually live here."

Chuck and Cori grouped up alongside him. "No duh, genius," Cori scoffed. "We're being used."

"What did you find out on the internet?" Ben asked.

Megan brushed past him, squeezed his elbow as she did, and gave him a look. She led the little group back into the den and punched a key on the computer. "See?" she said, standing back.

Ben slipped into the chair and looked at the page then used the back button to scroll through all of their searches. "So . . . nothing?" he guessed.

"Nothing about this house or the Kremers or anything," Megan said. "But I did find out that there was a murder in this neighborhood, probably in this very house, a long, long time ago. Well, two murders actually."

Ben glanced at Megan and caught a glimmer of something in her eyes. Was she trying to change the subject on purpose? "Show me," he said.

Emily finished her shift and waited while the owner counted the money and then, satisfied that neither Emily nor the other employee had cheated her, the owner dismissed them and locked the store. The other girl hurried off to her car and Emily stood close to the building and waited for Ben.

What if he didn't show up? What if he got so involved with Megan that he forgot all about her?

A gentle snow began to fall, the flakes fat and wet. Emily lifted her face to the sky and questioned God. Why did everyone abandon her?

A blue sedan pulled up to the curb and Ben honked.

Emily got in and said nothing.

"Sorry I'm late. I dropped Meg at work first," Ben said. "Wanna get a burger and fries? We need to talk."

Emily tightened her seat belt and kept her eyes averted. "Sure." She didn't fail to notice how he shortened the new girl's name. What was next . . . intimate pet names?

"Good. You're not gonna believe what's gone on today."

Emily felt her face reddening and loosened her scarf. What kind of news was he going to soften with a burger and fries?

Ben opened the door for Emily and asked her to snag a corner booth while he ordered the food. When he brought it to her he waited a second for her to lift her arms and head from the table. He noticed how slowly she was moving. Sundays were hard for her, he knew. Despite his efforts to help her find her mother and brother each week, it was turning out to be a lost cause.

"Here, Em, I got you a milk shake, too." His dimples weren't quite as deep as he tried to lift her spirits with a smile.

Emily yielded a short response and unwrapped her burger.

Ben started on his fries and waved a few as he spoke. "So, I got back to the house this afternoon to find all the others in the den camped out around the computer. *Talking*." He emphasized it by jabbing a fry into his mouth. "And guess what?" He waited for Emily to make eye contact. "They went in Mrs. Kremer's room." She gave him the surprised look he expected and he went on, "And we all think that she's never around because she's leading a double life."

Emily held his gaze with a sorrow that disrupted his train of thought. He understood then that she knew.

"Oh, Em, I'm sorry. What?"

"You're so nice to me. I don't want, you know, I don't want to let you down or anything. But I know there isn't a Mrs. Kremer. You own the house, right?"

Ben decided he needed to be straight with her. Honesty was the best policy, his real father always told him. How had he gotten so far away from that standard? Reluctantly he confessed a tiny part of his plan to her and swore her to secrecy.

By 6 p.m. the winter night darkened the streets. Cory made herself and Chuck some soup and yelled downstairs to Adam to see if he wanted any. There was no answer above the loud music. She tried some curses. Still no answer. She and Chuck ate in silence though he stared or wiggled or spoon-tapped trying to get her attention. Her agitation with him grew as she sorted through a buffet of emotions, settling on indifference.

She cleaned up the kitchen without comment or complaint and then went into the living room and turned on the TV.

Chuck went downstairs. A few moments later Adam came up and politely asked Cory what she had left him for dinner.

She flipped him off and raised the volume on the TV. Adam touched his hat in mock salute, grabbed his coat, and left. A morsel of regret mushroomed in her gut. It wasn't Adam's fault that she was tired of Chuck trailing after her, trying to catch her interest in unfortunate ways.

As soon as his taillights diminished in the window reflection she got up and carried a kitchen chair up to her bedroom. She was more than vaguely interested in checking out the attic. With only Chuck in the house she assumed that she could do some sleuthing undetected.

She stood on the chair and pushed up on the ceiling panel. A waft of gray dust and insulation feathered down on her head and shoulders. She took care to slide the panel over without dislodging too much more of the filth.

The light from her room did not reach up into the black space, nor could she climb up from the chair; she would need a ladder and a flashlight. She thought she'd seen both in the utility room.

Two honks of a car horn outside distracted her. Was it Jason? She had told him she'd see him tomorrow. Maybe it was a neighbor. She carried the chair back down to the first floor and set it in the kitchen right as someone pounded on the front door. Stupid ass. She peeked around the wall and saw the large head of this morning's persistent "Marty Kremer".

And he saw her.

Shit. She didn't want to deal with this. "Chuck!" she yelled and headed for the stairs. "Chuck, it's that guy!" She reached the bottom step and pushed his door open. "Chuck?" The room was empty; clothing was strewn around;

a spaghetti smeared plate stared at her from the nearest corner.

The pounding upstairs now came from the side entry 13 unlucky steps above her. She looked toward the open doors of Ben's room, the bathroom, and the utility room. No Chuck. She was alone. The door above swung open and the fat man broke in.

Chapter 8

First Ben and Emily checked the Women's Shelter, then the Mission, then the Crisis Center, followed by a long drive to a suburban Oasis and finally the YWCA. They always started with the Women's Shelter because that was the last place Emily had seen her mother and brother. At some of the places they had to be more like stalkers than visitors and wait as patiently as possible to talk with women who didn't view the teens as a threat. So many of the women were victims of domestic violence that they suspected their abusers of trapping them even with teens as innocent looking as Emily.

At most of the places, though, they were greeted by a gate-keeper who listened to Emily's description of her mother and brother and then sadly shook his or her head.

Six weeks ago they came close to an answer when a woman leaving the Crisis Center remembered Emily's mother from the week before. But, she said, that particular woman and boy left in a van with three others to go to a farm in the south. The idea that any mother could leave so swiftly and completely re-opened a wound that had failed to scab over. It was true enough that her mother encouraged her to go out on her own. That happened when Emily came back to the shelter from school with a letter – the letter from Mrs. Kremer offering her a place to live while her mother got back on her feet. At first her mother told her when she was changing abodes, moving to a church basement or a friend's house. Then Emily had to hunt for her. Thankfully she had that option because of Ben. They found her twice and then . . . Homelessness tore apart her family.

"I can't think of anywhere else to try, Em," Ben said. He signaled a left turn out of the Y's parking lot and headed north.

This was the part of their Sunday night ritual when Ben tried to be cheerful and Emily tried to hide her silent sobs by pretending to be coughing. One never fooled the other.

But tonight was different. There was no joking and no crying. Emily had questions.

"So . . . are you going to tell the others . . . what you told me?"

Ben huffed. "No, I don't see the point."

"Megan seems smart."

Ben smiled; Emily noticed. "Yeah, I think she is. She knows her way around the internet for sure. But I don't know about that murder stuff." He glanced at Emily when he checked traffic to the right. Then he asked, "You don't believe in ghosts, do you?"

Emily kept her head from moving in any direction and turned the question back on him, "Do you?"

"Course not. But I think maybe your nightmares are related to the stains on the laundry room floor. Have you noticed that you have bad dreams on the nights after you've done your wash?"

Her face puckered in thought. She didn't say anything right away. "Are the stains blood from the murders?"

"Uh, we don't know if there were murders in the house. That's probably just old paint on the floor. It looks like blood, but it's not. Okay?"

He checked to see if she was nodding. His eyes scanned the dashboard.

"Whoa," he said. "We've got like ten minutes to make it to the Steak House Grill. I told Meg we'd pick her up after her shift."

Emily stuck her hands up opposing coat sleeves, rubbed her fingernails along the thin scabs, and wondered if she'd be asked to move to the back seat.

Megan climbed into the back seat and chattered the short three blocks from the restaurant to the house. She leaned forward and touched Ben's coat collar as they turned the last corner and tapped instead of pointing.

"That's the fat man's car. The guy who said he was Marty Kremer."

Ben turned his head slightly to ask her, "Are you sure?"

"I think so. And look, there aren't any lights on. Where's Cori?"

Emily lifted her hand to point to the driveway, and Ben anticipated her thought. "Chuck's car is gone. Still, it's not likely that she'd go anywhere with Chuck. She won't even let him drive her to school when it's pouring."

He parked in the drive and they all got out. Emily stared up at the darkened bedroom window.

"Do you hear that . . . chanting?" Megan asked. She was right behind Ben as he went to the door. Emily hung back.

"The door's not closed all the way." The alarm in Ben's voice spooked both girls. Emily pulled her coat sleeves tight across her chest, but followed.

The little group poured through the entry and overflowed into the kitchen. Megan flicked on the kitchen light.

"Who's here?" Ben shouted. The girls froze, waited, stared at Ben. The humming was louder, coming from the basement. One note. One droning, breathless "Aaahhhmmm". Five seconds long. A short break, like a gasp for air. Another whining note, the same syllable.

Ben charged down the stairs.

Emily shook her head at Megan and opened the silverware drawer. They both grabbed paring knives and started after Ben.

Cori thought she was bad. Bad like tough, cool, wicked. A hard ass. A tough bitch. She loved a good cat fight. That was what had gotten her kicked out of regular school to begin with. Cori was irredeemable. Or so she liked to think.

She didn't feel so tough, though, when a bald man, more than twice her weight and size, busted into the house and stared at her from the top landing. Drunk, she thought, as she watched him grasp the handrail and weave to the left, stumbling down three steps before catching himself.

The urge to scream was stilled by the same fear that created the terror. She was alone. She was trapped. Even if the boys had locks on their doors, even if she could barricade herself in one of their rooms, there was little chance that such a big man wouldn't or couldn't break down the door.

She held her ground. It wasn't bravery that glued her to the spot. It wasn't fear or terror or panic. Something else came over her and as this stranger reached the bottom step she held out both hands, palms facing ahead, and she began to chant.

"What?" this Marty Kremer laughed. "What are you doing? You stupid kid." He lurched to the right and fell onto the cold concrete.

Ben reached the bottom step and saw first the folded form of Cori, crouched in the corner. Her eyes were bloodshot and teary, but the black make-up, still in place, accented the force and control that dominated her expression. She didn't look afraid or troubled; her eyes did not yield their focus, her chants did not pause, and her body did not relax.

Another step forward and into the basement and Ben saw the miraculous thing that Cori was centering on: a heavy set man floated waist-high in the air as if strung from invisible marionette wires. His head hung a few inches lower, eyes closed, a string of drool reaching to the floor. His jacket was open; the zipper tip fluttered. Ben's mind could hardly wrap itself around the reality. Each little detail burned itself into his mind – the smell of beer, the ashy scent of smoke-permeated clothes, a sour whiff of sweat.

Behind him Megan and Emily's soft steps hammered like thunder; he heard their hearts pound to match his own.

He looked again at Cori and then back at the hovering lump. He felt tourniquet squeezes on both of his arms as each girl in sequence gasped, swore, and grabbed him tighter. No words would form in his mouth; he felt compelled to join Cori's chant, but he resisted. The pressure on his right arm lessened and Megan's voice was soft by his ear.

"Cori, Cori," Megan gently repeated, "Cori, you've got to let him go. It'll be all right. Cori?"

The sound from Cori's lips sharpened and then stopped. The man drifted to the floor, puddled, and didn't move.

"Tell us what happened," Megan whispered. She remained clutching Ben's elbow with her left hand, holding the knife ready in her right.

"I don't know . . . exactly." Cori cursed repeatedly, shook her head from side to side, and rose up. "Check his pockets." She pointed. "See who he is. I got him . . . to tell me that he found out about us . . . about a group of teens living here without adults . . . he heard it from some woman . . . some woman at a bar on Friday." She swore again and leaned back against the wall, held her hands up in front of her face, and stared at her palms.

Ben wet his lips. "Mrs. Kremer, you mean?"

Cori ignored him. "He thought he could come here and threaten us . . . use us . . . live here even." She turned her palms outward, stretched her arms out, and levitated the body again.

Ben took a step forward. Megan and Emily released him and he continued on toward the body. Two more steps and he stopped.

"Check his back pocket for ID." Cori moved her hands and the body tilted toward Ben.

"Is he dead?" Ben asked. He could see no sign of life; he heard no breath.

Cori lifted her hands and the body bounced up to the ceiling, hit it hard, and fell back to its last suspended spot. The man groaned.

"Check him!"

Ben did as ordered and pulled a wallet from the back jean pocket.

"Says he's Marty Muscott," Ben read from the license. He snooped through the rest of the wallet and found nothing but a five and six singles, a car registration, a couple of gas receipts, and a post-it note with a phone number. "Nothing else." He looked at Cori for direction.

"We have to get rid of him."

Ben chilled at the thought. "We could check him out on the internet first." He stepped back and handed the wallet to Megan. "Hurry," he said. Both girls fled up the stairs.

"How are you doing this?" Ben kept his eyes on the man, but spoke to Cori, moving like a cat closer to her.

Cori didn't answer. She began to chant again.

Megan couldn't get the computer to obey her commands. A white fog covered the screen and she had to bring up the task manager to quit the Google search. She started over, searched through the Norton toolbar, and began with his name.

Emily sat in the corner chair and watched the door. She held her knife and Megan's in her lap, ready, deadly, hushed.

"Look at this," Megan broke the silence. "He's on parole." She turned to Emily, saw her white knuckles, and rose up to give her a hug.

"It'll be all right," she said as she sat back down. "I have an idea. And if it doesn't work we'll call my friend's dad." She went back to the keyboard and did a search of the phone number that was on the note. She wrote down a name and address and then checked out that person. Apparently it was Marty Muscott's parole officer. She did a search to see what constituted a parole violation that would get Marty sent immediately to jail, do not pass go.

"Okay, Emily, this says he's in big trouble if he crosses the state line or leaves the country. Or if he has a gun. Or if he commits another crime." She stood up and held her hand out for the second knife. She kept the wallet and her notes in her left hand and led the way back down to the basement. But Emily didn't follow.

Cori curled her lip into a smirk. She liked this control. There was a measure of nausea that surged through her gut every few seconds, but it was outweighed by the power, authority, and supremacy that she felt.

She stopped chanting and sank down along the wall until she sat on her butt, legs crossed. Ben inched closer and she allowed it. An inner voice told her that she could levitate him, too, if she wanted, but Ben was too docile to be a threat and what if she lost control of the fat man?

She shifted her gaze to Ben as he lowered himself beside her. His voice was steady as he asked her, “What are we gonna do, Cori?”

“We?”

“I’ll tell you the truth. There is no Mrs. Kremer. I’ve hired people to pretend to be her.”

“Mr. All-important-Ben, after all. Why am I not surprised?”

Ben cracked his knuckles, stopped himself when the sound resonated. “If this guy exposes us because that old crone flashed the bunch of twenties I paid her and gave him our address, well . . .”

“I can keep a secret if you can.” Cori whispered, then moved her hands in a way that made the fat man somersault like a football.

Megan appeared at the bottom step. She rushed the last little distance and went down on her knees next to Ben; she faced Cori.

Before she could speak Cori glared at her. “You’re next, new girl.” She wouldn’t succumb to any more gentle entreaties from this little goody-two-shoes.

Megan clenched her fist to quell the urge to slap Cori; the paper crumpled. “This guy is an ex-con on parole for breaking and entering and a list of other stuff. If we can get his parole officer to find him drunk, with a gun, or over the state line, then he’ll go back to jail – out of our hair.” She looked over at the floating object. “Is he asleep, in a coma, or what?”

Cori thought she could control him completely now. She shut her eyes for a moment then opened them. Marty’s eyes opened, too.

Cori looked to Ben and Megan. Their hands were intertwined. Huh, was there a little romance there already? In only two days? She hadn’t realized Ben was such a player. She blinked and turned her attention back to Marty.

"Stand up, fat man," she said, waving her hands. Like a puppet the body obeyed, but the motion was stiff. His boots barely touched the floor; she made him shuffle to the left and then the right. His eyes stayed open but unfocused.

Megan whispered in Ben's ear, "She can make him walk out of here then we can drive him to Ohio and call the police anonymously."

"I can hear you, sweetie," Cori purred. "I've got a better idea. I've got some stuff in my coat we can put in his pockets, then we, or rather I, just walk him to the neighbor's house behind us and make him break in." She nodded her head as if agreeing with herself. "And when their alarm goes off, the cops come, and voila. No more fat man. Larceny, possession of over the legal amount of a certain controlled substance . . ."

"What if the alarm's not on?"

"How do you know they have an alarm?"

Both Megan and Ben had practical questions, but Cori acknowledged them with an eye roll. "I just know, okay? What time is it?"

"Almost ten."

"Good, it's a school night, it's dark . . . let's do this."

All three stood up. "Put his wallet back." Megan handed it to Ben.

Emily moved to the dining room when she heard the group coming up the stairs. There was a strange thumping and she heard a few awkward giggles from Cori. A shadow from the big man's bulk filled the entryway first and Emily pulled back behind the wall. She heard Cori swear and wish aloud that either Ben or Megan had gone up first.

"Emily!" Cori shouted.

Like a robot she involuntarily moved forward. She stopped herself and shrank back.

"Emily! Come open the door!"

How could she do that without getting close to that man? She fingered the knife blade, poked her thumb, drew blood.

"Do it, Emily! Come on!"

The door flew open, just missing the man's face. Emily pressed harder with the knife tip. Did Cori make the door open or did she?

Adam pulled around the corner and slowed the car. There was a tow truck with flashing lights directly blocking the driveway; a police car was parked in front of it. He continued on cautiously. His heart rate didn't go up at all; he was proud of his control. He patted the gun on the seat.

He drove around the block then out to the main road and looped around to another street. He came up the street from the other end. The cop was gone and the tow truck was pulling an old vehicle away. The driveway entrance was clear but Ben's car was there. He parked in the street, arranged his scarf over the gun, locked the doors, and walked to the side door.

Good evening, family, he thought as he entered. He tipped his Fedora at the others. Strange that they were all standing in the kitchen together at this hour. He put the hat on a peg, hung his coat, removed his boots, and took one step down. He paused when he heard a voice, a hoarse voice much like Cori's, that was telling Adam to wait.

He was Adam.

He turned and stared.

They all started talking at once. A burst of syllables. Nothing that he could understand. Except for the stupid one – she was crying. He understood her emotion. Ah, such relief. He reached his hand up to tilt his hat but it wasn't there. He touched his forehead instead, felt the wrinkles crunching his eyebrows downward. He kept his hand there, turned it into an awning, and shielded his eyes from the kitchen light.

"Nevermind, I'll explain it later," Ben was saying. Ben waved him off like he was dismissing him. *Go downstairs, Adam.* Or *go downstairs, Chuck.* Yes, that's what Ben meant.

He took another step. And another. The girls' voices were hushed, jumbled. He heard them say Adam; he heard them say Chuck.

He reached the bottom.
Safe.

Monday

Chapter 9

Monday morning dawned frigid. The drafts in the old house swirled around the floors and chased after Emily's toes. She used the first floor bathroom so Megan could get ready upstairs. Emily's routine involved little more than the basics; even so she needed forty-five minutes, especially since she felt like she was moving at the speed of a sleeping snail.

The last thing she did was to make five peanut butter and jelly sandwiches. She wrapped each one in cellophane and then realized she needed one more for Megan.

"Morning, Em," Ben greeted her as he came in to the kitchen, grabbed a cereal bowl, and opened the fridge.

"Morning." She felt him watching her as she smeared the jelly on another piece of bread.

"That's nice, Em . . . that you're making Meg a sandwich, too." Ben poured the cereal and milk and took his bowl to the table.

Emily tucked a strand of hair behind her ear. It felt smooth and silky and not at all like her hair usually felt. She imagined for an instant that she was just as worthy as . . .

No, no she wasn't. She wrapped the sandwich and set it in line with the others and went back upstairs for her satchel.

"Hi, Emily," Megan whispered as she came out of the bathroom. "Is it time to leave?"

"Five minutes," Emily answered. She scooted past Cori's door as it opened. She heard Megan give Cori the same greeting though in a regular voice, no longer whispering. There was a growled response. Emily was surprised that there was any response at all.

She grabbed her things and hurried back downstairs. Maybe if she got outside first she could snag the front seat.

"Is Meg ready?" Ben asked. He rinsed his bowl, picked up three of the sandwiches, and tossed one to Emily.

She nodded as she put her lunch in her bag.

"Hold on a sec," Ben said as he slipped past her and ran down the stairs.

Now she was stuck, obligated to wait inside. She moved back into the kitchen so Megan could put on her stuff. Ben came up, threw on his coat, and was the first one out the door, followed by Megan.

Emily pulled the door closed and turned to see Megan scrambling into the back seat. She didn't want to like her, but she couldn't help it. She got in and buckled up.

"Look," Ben pointed as he started the car. The headlights illuminated the single set of tracks that the fat man's feet had so delicately made in the snow. They led to the fence and beyond, into the neighbor's yard. "That's what the cops saw last night with their flashlights. They're not deep enough, though."

Megan leaned forward. "Should we trample them?"

Ben put the car in reverse and said, "Nah, I think we're good."

Emily leaned into the door, away from Ben. How could he think they were good?

"What's the matter, Em?"

She shook her head. "Didn't sleep," was all she said.

"Welcome to the club," Megan said. She leaned back and shivered. "It must be like zero degrees today."

Ben backed down the driveway and into the street. He changed gears, but didn't start to drive until he handed Megan a sandwich. "Here's your lunch. Emily made you a sandwich."

"Aw, thanks, Emily. You're so sweet."

Emily looked back at the house and wondered how everyone could act like nothing amazing happened last night.

Only Chuck had slept well. He rose half an hour before he had to leave, right as Ben's car drove off. He hated everything regarding the alternative school except the late starting time.

He found the last three sandwiches that pathetic little Emily had made and ate one for breakfast before Cori came down. When she grabbed one and headed out the door, jacket unzipped, book bag empty, he raced to follow her, snatched the last sandwich, the one Emily made for Adam, and thrust it into the side pocket of his new, larger pack – the one he'd need to carry all the guns to school.

He lit a cigarette before stepping out into the dark and icy morning. He kept the usual thirty yard space between them, ready to run to the rescue if she needed him. He stopped when she did, watched her zip up her coat, and then resumed his pace when she started walking. He turned his collar up on his neck, wishing he had that cheap wool scarf Emily had given him for Christmas. Where the heck was that thing? He puffed on the cigarette and took longer strides.

Cori stopped again at the corner two blocks before the school. She shook a cigarette out of the pack in her pocket and tried to light it with an empty Bick. No luck. She held the cigarette at arm's length and wondered if her newfound skills included pyrokinesis. She focused her thoughts on the butt end and willed it to light. Nothing. A quick search of her bag revealed no emergency matches.

She looked back down the street. A block away a plume of smoke was circling Chuck's head. She wouldn't need magic or special powers to propel Chuck to her side. She raised her hand and waved him over. He covered the distance in five seconds.

"Gimme a light, moron," she said. He obeyed, handing her his half-smoked Winston.

Rather than return the cigarette, Cori threw the butt into the snow and took a draw on hers. She blew the smoke at Chuck in lieu of thanks, turned, and stepped into the street.

She was jerked back and the cigarette flew from her hand as Chuck grabbed her arm and pulled her out of the way of a nearly silent vehicle that was rounding the corner. The driver gave a quick honk.

"You idiot!" she screamed. "Let me go."

"Yes, m'lady," Chuck intoned, he released her arm and tried to add a chivalrous bow to his impulsive response. He bent down to rescue the burning cigarette, but Cori was faster. Her boot snuffed and crushed it.

"Stay away from me," she snarled. She held out her hands, palms facing him, and tried to levitate him away.

Whatever special power she held over fat Marty wasn't working this morning on Chuck. But he did take a couple of steps back. That was fine, Cori thought, she didn't feel like going to school nauseated – boredom was bad enough.

That was *my* move. *I'm* the one who bows to ladies.

Shut up, Adam. Go away, I can do what I want. Did you see how she looked at me? She waved me to her side. She *needed* me.

Chuck bent again and retrieved the flattened cigarette. He sniffed the filtered end and ran it around his mouth. A trace of Cori's dark lipstick transferred to his lower lip.

She wants me.

She hates you. She only pays attention to *me*. That's why you tried *my* moves on her. Why don't *you* go away and let *me*–

Shut up! Shut up!

"Hey, psycho-boy, who ya talkin' to?" Two fifteen-year-olds, recent transfers to the alternative school, crossed the road and edged up to Chuck.

"Got any stuff on ya?"

"Yeah, what're ya takin'? Give us some."

Chuck barely heard them. Processing their sentences interfered too much; he could not keep the conversation going with his brother *and* communicate with these guys. How was he supposed to respond to these maggots?

Adam, where are you? Tell them to go away.

Oh, so now you want me to stay. How about tomorrow you bring the guns . . . take care of these insects and that history teacher, too.

Megan waited until Emily finished thanking Ben for the ride to school before she added her own thanks. "Don't wait for me after school. I won't need a ride back this afternoon," she said.

Ben cocked his head, "You won't? How come?"

"I, um, I have an appointment to see someone . . . and I'll get a ride to the house after. Be home around eight." Megan shifted her bag to her left shoulder.

"You sure?" Ben held the door and let Emily and Megan through first. He walked beside Megan as they passed first the chemistry lab and then the math classrooms.

"Yup. Every Monday, actually."

"What kind of appointment?" Ben asked. "See ya, Em."

Megan gave a little wave as Emily turned left toward her locker and she and Ben continued to the south wing. "Um," she looked up at him, "it's kinda personal. I'll tell you later."

Ben released the dimples, smiled broadly and asked, "Where's your locker?"

"By the Art room."

"Mine's up by the language lab." He kept walking with her. "What do you have first hour?"

"English with Mrs. Linden."

"Is that room 239?"

"Yeah," Megan said. She reached her locker and started tumbling the numbers on her lock. "What do you have?" She listened as he ran through his morning schedule; she started figuring out a new route from English to math so she'd see him. A spark of adrenaline shot to every cell as she realized that he was doing the same thing as she listed her classes back to him.

Emily stuffed her things in her locker and joined a rush of kids that came in from the bus entrance. She floated along with those who were heading toward the Art room.

There they were. Ben and Megan at Megan's locker. She passed by unseen. Heard them talking about classes. Going through their schedules.

She reached the end of the hall and turned around. She waited for two loud seniors to walk past. She trailed them and passed by Ben and Megan again. Now they were laughing and smiling. They looked like any of a zillion other couples in this school who were joined at the hip, oblivious to everyone else . . . in *love*.

Her eyes welled with tears. There's the girls' restroom. Duck in. Lock yourself in the stall. Find the razor. Cut.

Megan asked her teacher if she could use the restroom five minutes before the end of last period. Instead, she raced to her locker, donned her coat, and ran out the front door as the final bell rang.

Mrs. Beridon's car was parked in the circle waiting. Best social worker ever. Megan knew that this lady was on her side. If anyone could help her get back custody of Simon it was Mrs. Beridon. She always stayed with Megan through the visitations and kept elaborate records. She took photos and logged every giggle and smile that Simon gave his young mother.

The foster care mother kept vigil, too, but her attitude was negative toward Megan. She didn't want to like her. She wanted to adopt Simon into her perfect little middle-class family. Of course that wasn't going to happen. Megan's ex-boyfriend's parents wanted custody, too. Any judge was more likely to give Simon to blood relatives first. *She* simply needed to be first.

Mrs. Beridon smiled at Megan as she buckled up. "My, but you look perky today. What are you so happy about?"

"Um, Simon, of course."

"Right," Mrs. Beridon drew out the syllable, put the car in gear, and signaled left.

Megan looked back at the surge of kids she'd beaten out the door. She wondered if Ben was looking around her locker for her now even though she had told him she had an appointment. They had met up between every class today. Too bad they had different lunch periods.

"Good day at school?"

Megan grinned. "Yeah, really good."

"I've been in touch with your parents. They're willing to come to today's visitation, too, if you're okay with that." Mrs. Beridon kept one eye on the road and the other on Megan's body language. The ambivalence was palpable. "Or we could put it off till next time. Or schedule them for a different day from you."

"No, no, I don't want them to be with Simon unless I'm there, too. All right?"

"Sure, Megan, so . . . can I call them to come today?"

"Can I think about it?"

Mrs. Beridon turned into the new subdivision and answered, "No problem."

Megan relaxed and then tensed up again as the car pulled into the recently plowed driveway. The elaborate Christmas decorations were finally taken down, but three freshly made snowmen guarded the front lawn. Megan's heart leaped to her throat when she saw the foster mom standing at the front window. She was holding her son up to the glass, his tiny palms leaving moist prints.

Megan spoke fast, "What about the other grandparents? Brian's parents?" She hated saying his name. Brian had been the perfect boyfriend for all of two weeks. Now he was off at college, probably spreading his seed as copiously as he had in high school. He had only been unlucky once as far as she knew; Simon was the result of one unfortunate quarter hour of failed resistance. Some might call it rape, but Megan couldn't remember it that way.

Mrs. Beridon answered as she put the car in park. "They visited Friday. Once a week, same as you, dear."

Megan opened the door and cut across the yard. She noticed again how her boot marks weren't much bigger than the ones made by the foster family's two biological kids. That made it easier for her to hide her surreptitious visits. She wasn't a peeping tom, but watching Simon through the windows in the early winter evenings was probably just as bad and wouldn't get her any points with the judge.

If only her parents hadn't made things so hard.

Chapter 10

Cori signed in to last period and then left as soon as the substitute's back was turned. She sauntered away from the school as if she were entitled to an early dismissal, then ran the last block and slipped on some ice as she crossed the street. She went down hard on her right hip, cursed the winter, and limped to the kitchen door.

She headed straight downstairs to get the step ladder and a flashlight. She ignored the flutters in her stomach as she remembered the previous night's events. The unnatural was becoming natural. The utility room's light bulb was burning as usual and, on impulse, she pulled the string. It wasn't as dark as she expected. Just gloomy. There was a gray illumination from the small window; it was half blocked with snow. She spoke to the shadows, partly to break the death of stillness in the old house, partly to warn the ghosts that she, Corinne Adele Bish, was not afraid.

She pulled the string again and the light winked on. She located the step ladder, but not the flashlight. She'd have to check the kitchen for it.

Chuck's vacant stare sheltered the inner ramblings of two souls. One half-dead, one half-alive.

Sometimes Chuck forgot who he was.

Sometimes he remembered. His twin brother, Adam, dropped dead of heart disease on the very day that Chuck finally beat him in a race. It was the 6th grade field day, five guilty years ago.

Chuck gazed out the window seeing not the early bus, not the winter jogger, not the goth girl he loved who was ditching school. His lips moved wordlessly. Wretchedness and angry grief made him pitch his head forward and down onto his arms.

Cori scraped the walls of the narrow staircase to the second floor as she man-handled the ladder upwards. She set it up under the attic entrance and rushed back down to find a flashlight. She found one, but of course the batteries were dead. She considered the living room lamps, but none had a cord long enough.

A candle, she thought. She took the stairs two at a time and barged into Emily's room; the useless little whiner had left it unlocked. The pine candle and a book of matches were in plain view. She snatched both.

Balancing on the top step of the ladder she pushed the attic door aside, then she lit the candle and stuffed the matches in her pocket. As her eyes adjusted she found a spot to set the candle and then she pulled herself up and through the small opening. She sat with her legs dangling through the ceiling until her eyes fully accepted the shapes and outlines of the low attic.

There were boards loosely set across beams to provide sections of flooring able to hold boxes, bins, and trunks. She hunched over and picked her way around a few objects, trying to decide where to start. If she had any luck at all, there would be something of value here that she could pawn. If she wasn't lucky she could at least make a trade with some jerkoff at school.

She ran her hand over the most promising item: a leather trunk the size of a dog crate. The dust was thick. She wiped her fingers off on her leg and then played with the clasp. She couldn't see well enough and quickly got frustrated. She rubbed the sore spot on her hip and wished, or rather cursed, for better vision.

There were tiny specks of light at various points in the haphazard flooring where ceiling fixtures below were allowing pinpricks of daylight through. They reminded Cori of the tips of white Christmas tree lights.

Not as stupid as they think! She lowered herself back down through the opening and trespassed again into Emily's room. *Yes.* Two strings of Christmas lights were wound up and sitting in a box in the bottom of the closet. *Perfect.*

Cori plugged them in an outlet behind her own bed and ran them up the ladder. She placed them up and over as many objects in the attic as they would reach, then sat back and allowed herself a bit of smug self-satisfaction. Then she pushed aside the leather trunk and dug instead into the largest box, using a handful of the little lights to illuminate the treasures.

Photo albums, sequined purses, yellowed papers, and . . . pay dirt: an old jewelry box. She lifted it out and snapped it open. She was expecting to find it filled with gold and silver charms, rings, necklaces, cameos, and brooches. Instead there was a single pin, still wrapped in its original packaging. She kept feeling around the edges of the box's felt lining. Nothing. But under the upper shelf she felt some tape and pulled. A double ring fell out. A diamond engagement ring and wedding band, soldered together, sparkled faintly in the low light.

Cori wasn't curious about its past. It only meant money to her. The sooner the better. But how much? If the ring was super old it might be worth more. She squinted at the yellowed documents and scanned for dates. The 1960s. Pretty old. She stuffed the rings along with the wrapped pin into her pocket.

She sneezed twice as she looked around the attic. Now she could see the sides to an old crib leaning against the far wall, a Christmas tree stand sat beside it, and a child's rocking chair. And something else. She rose up to as tall as she could with the limited head room. There wasn't a way to reach the item without balancing on the rafters. She was smart enough to know that if she stepped off the boards she'd crash through the ceiling. She needed to move a couple of boards, stand on one, and move another in a crab-walking effort to reach the other side.

She'd leave it for later; her hip was throbbing some more. She returned her attention to the leather trunk. She pushed it closer to the edge and then lowered herself to the ladder and struggled to get the trunk down without crashing.

In the light of her bedroom the age of the chest was apparent. The corners were worn, two of the five clasps were broken, one hinge dangled, and the leather straps hung frayed and tattered. It was at least a century old.

She unclasped the outer buckles, but the middle one was locked. The small keyhole challenged her. She tried paperclips and safety pins, but without success. Prying it with a kitchen knife failed. Kicking it with an angry boot was also ineffective.

New girl, she thought. The new girl had found a way into Mrs. Kremer's room, Ben's pretend Mrs. Kremer, that is. Ben was trusting Cori with a secret. Could Cori trust Megan with one? She glanced at the ladder and Christmas lights. Well, she'd unplug those and close the closet door and only let Megan see the trunk. She'd better wipe it down, too. She smirked to herself; Emily's pajamas would make a nice dust cloth.

Cori heard the kitchen door slam. Crap, she'd used up a whole hour. She needed to get to the tattoo parlor or Jason would be furious with her. She could skip school, but skipping work had worse consequences.

Mr. Felker drove down Elm Street late Monday afternoon and stopped to see how Megan was doing. He had an important looking letter for her from the County Courthouse. His mail was already being forwarded, but this arrived special delivery this morning. No one answered his knock at the kitchen door so he lifted the metal top of the mailbox and put the letter in.

Megan left Simon in the arms of his foster mother and followed Mrs. Beridon to the car.

"You okay?" the social worker asked as she started the engine. The wipers smeared away a coating of light snow.

Megan sniffled a yes and kept her face turned toward the house.

"I'm sorry. That didn't work out the way I'd hoped." Mrs. Beridon turned on the heat and the defroster. "But your folks mean well. It sounded like they want to make amends . . . patch things up between you. Didn't you think?"

Megan swiped a gloved finger under her eye and gulped. "I hate my life."

"Simon seems to like them," Mrs. Beridon ignored the comment, "and I'm sure they didn't mean to make what they said come off as a threat."

"Whatever."

"Come on, Megan," Mrs. Beridon tried her best to be encouraging, "let's look at the bright side. If you can go back and live with them, you have a better chance of gaining custody."

"Why? I'm doing great on my own. I have a job. I get my school work done. My new place is awesome . . ." her voice faded away as she thought of the not-so-awesome night before.

"Oh, that's right. You changed places. I was heading back to your friend's house. Which way do I go?"

"Just go to University Drive and I'll tell you where to turn."

"All right. Well, anyway dear, having your folks there for half the visit wasn't so bad and it's a step in the right direction. You'll see; things always work out for the best." She smiled with her voice. "And remember this: child care is expensive. If you get Simon back how will you afford sitters for him while you're at school and work? You'd hardly see him any more than you do now."

Megan sighed. Some supernatural help would be preferable to turning to her parents.

"Turn right on the street past the next light."

Mrs. Beridon drove away one-handed. She couldn't waste a moment; the others would want to know the change in the status of her number one project: Megan.

"Hello. Hey, can you call the others? Set up a meeting for this week? I think we need some extra support on this case." She listened to her friend's response as she braked at the intersection. "You know what? Maybe we better meet tonight. These things can get out of hand so quickly. I sensed a real susceptibility tonight."

She headed south on University. "No," she laughed at his comment, "we will not be needing garlic. Very funny."

The conversation retrieved its somber tone. “Right, I’d prefer that. Thanks. See you soon.”

Megan’s entrance through the kitchen was met with Adam’s solemn bow.

“Oh, hi Adam. Am I the last one home?” She kept her hand on the doorknob, ready to turn the lock.

Adam swung his head left to right a single time, but said nothing.

“Okay, then, I’ll leave it unlocked. All right?” When he did nothing more than stare she whispered the answer to herself.

The kitchen held no after dinner smells though the sink was piled with dishes; perhaps Monday was the cook’s night off. She wasn’t hungry; she was grateful for the fast food her parents had brought to the visitation. Maybe Mrs. B was right and her mom and dad were trying to make amends.

She took her bag to the dining room and flung it on the table. She had math and English homework, but with all she had on her mind now doing the dishes was a better option.

She turned around and thought *why not?* Adam was still standing like a statue in front of the sink so she asked him to move, found the no-brand dish soap, and ran the hot water.

Standing at the sink, looking out the window at the brick house next door, and washing the gunk off the cheap stoneware was preferable at this instant to doing anything else. She needed time to think about the visitation, the problem with her folks, Mrs. B’s advice . . . life was hard. Maybe thinking about nothing at all was what she needed.

She could see Adam’s reflection in the window; he was standing with his hand on the knob of the tallest cabinet. Good chance that’s where the potato chips were.

She focused through the reflection back to the neighbor’s house where an upstairs light blinked on. She leaned forward to see better, both hands working underwater on a crusty bowl. She could clearly see someone walking around their room. Was she so visible to the neighbors when she was in *her* room?

Megan bent her head to her task, rinsed the bowl, and set it in the rack. Too bad these old houses didn't have dishwashers. She stuffed the dishrag down a large glass that had a lipstick mark. Cori's, no doubt. She spoke over her shoulder to Adam, "Hey, where is everybody? Are we the only ones here?"

When he didn't answer right away she rinsed the glass, set it down, and turned.

A single nod up then down gave her the chills. Hadn't Ben said Chuck was the nutcase? Maybe Adam was just as crazy.

Maybe this *was* Chuck and he was wearing Adam's hat, acting like Adam, and not talking so he wouldn't give away the deception.

A little cough helped straighten out her heartbeats. Wild.

Maybe he was lying about nobody being here. She started on another plate and watched the neighbor's light switch off. It was pretty quiet here. No TV. No washing machine. No other voices, but Emily could be shut up in her room.

A pair of headlights flashed across the window. Maybe Ben was arriving.

No, they went on by. She finished the plate and started on a pan.

And in the reflection she saw Adam. His hand was still on the cabinet, but both feet were *off* the floor.

Megan spun around holding the pan like a weapon.

"What!? How?!"

Adam's entire body was arched between ceiling and wall.

And he moved. Like a spider. Across the ceiling.

Megan ran out of the kitchen and into the dining room. She sprinted to the front entry and lunged at the door. She got the deadbolt turned, but Adam's hand reached out from above and pushed against the top of the door. His legs were splayed between the walls of the tiny foyer, blocking her retreat.

Megan shrank to the floor.

Carla Beridon looked at the people who so devotedly helped her even on the spur of the moment in the dead of winter: two nurses, three teachers, and a day care worker. The seven of them all bonded together for one supernatural purpose.

They joined hands before they did anything else and stood still. No chanting, no incantations or strange spells, no summoning devilish spirits, though devilish spirits were foremost on their minds.

Megan looked up at Adam's snarling face. She closed her eyes against the evil she saw, but she couldn't close her ears. A raspy growl strained his vocal chords then a second sound emanating from deep within matched her thick scream with a demonic shriek.

She felt for and found the handle of the frying pan. She whipped the heavy pan up and over her head in a hysterical motion. She hit Adam's arm and then his head, but still he snarled and shook and quivered above her like a chained and rabid dog.

The urge to fall back and submit to whatever mauling the demon-possessed Adam was set to launch pushed at the edges of her panic. A smell like rotten eggs assaulted her nose and drew a groan from her lips. She had to fight.

She swiped at his head again and screamed. "Get back!" The pan connected against his ear and he screeched louder, more in anger than pain. Then the growls stopped abruptly and the unexpected silence was accented by a far away horn.

Megan threw the pan at his head and reached up to pull his leg down, hoping to unbalance his attack. For an instant he froze in the air, much like Cori's victim of the night before. Then his body flopped down unto her and pinned her to the floor.

"Help!"

She thrashed and pushed and wiggled her way out from under the dead weight.

"What's wrong with him?" Emily asked from a safe distance.

Megan started to laugh and cry. She *wasn't* alone.

"What's wrong with him?" Emily repeated. "Is he having a fit?"

Megan looked from Emily to Adam. He was frothing at the mouth and his whole body was experiencing a seizure. Epileptic?

"I don't know," Megan whimpered. "Adam attacked me . . . from the ceiling."

Megan looked up at Emily and held her hand out for help, but Emily simply stood and stared. "That's not Adam. That's Chuck." She tucked her fingers up her sleeves.

"From the ceiling, Emily! He could walk on the walls and the ceiling!"

Emily tightened her elbows to her body. "The seizure's over. He's probably okay." She turned and headed back to the stairs.

"Wait!

Carla Beridon's group of seven finished their "service", trusting that all was well with Megan Blakeney, the girl that Carla had presented to the group for supernatural protection.

"Anything else we can do, Carla?" one of the nurses asked.

"Just the usual. I have to do a little more intelligence gathering first. This new place where she's living is kind of off the grid as far as foster homes and the like. I wish she could have stayed with the other family or, better yet, move back with her parents."

The day care worker nodded her head. "Yeah, that'd be ideal. Sure would." She paused and then decided to share a story about a six year old. The others listened intently, wondering how such a delicate situation could be handled. They circled up again.

Ben beat Cori home by half an hour. He carried in two bags of groceries, noticed the clean dishes, and set the bags down on the counter. He went into the dining room and saw a new assortment of textbooks on the table, must be

Megan's. He crossed to the living room, shoved the front entry rug back into place with his foot, and tossed Adam's hat onto the table. Then he heard a sniffle and hoped it meant a runny nose and not a sobbing girl.

"Em? Meg?"

He went to the den and there sat Megan at the computer, a pile of used tissues on the floor.

"Hey, Meg, what's up?"

She wiped at her eyes and leaned aside so he could see the screen. "This . . . I almost called an ambulance."

Ben peered at the site she had on the screen. "Epilepsy?"

"Adam . . . or maybe it was Chuck . . . attacked me and . . . Ben, he was crawling on the walls and ceiling. And then he had a seizure and Emily saw that part and didn't think it was any big deal." She blinked hard. "Has this happened before?"

Ben pulled the side chair up, giving himself a moment to process the rush of information. He sat next to Megan. "No, not that I know of. Maybe it's a reaction to his meds."

"What meds?"

"Um, stuff he takes to, uh, control his . . . problem."

Megan waited a second to see if he'd explain more and when he didn't she told him, "When he came out of it he acted like himself, well, like Chuck. He said to me, 'Hi, how ya doin', Megan' and then he got up like nothing happened and went downstairs."

Ben stared at the screen and didn't meet her eyes.

"Ben, he walked on the *ceiling*. It was like what Cori did to that guy only *he* was in control. And . . . he was *really* scary. I was afraid he was going to kill me."

Ben reached his hand out and touched Megan's wrist. He felt awkward, but he ran his fingers up her arm and squeezed her shoulder. She leaned toward him and he was unsure how to respond. He gave a little squeeze and dropped his hand. "It'll be okay," he lied. "What do you want to do? Call the police?"

"Yeah, right, after they were here last night. They'll investigate this place and I have a feeling Mrs. Kremer isn't going to check out too well." She took in a deep, shuddering breath. "Is she?"

Ben shook his head. "Look, Meg, I don't know why all this stuff is happening. I can't explain it. But . . . if you think Chuck should go, then I . . . I guess I could get him into some kind of facility . . . maybe."

"And Adam, too?"

Ben touched her hand again, took hold. "Megan, Chuck and Adam are the same guy. That's his problem. He's schizophrenic. There's really only Chuck."

Megan pulled her hand away and used both to cover her mouth. "Oh, no." Her eyes welled up again. "He doesn't have anywhere else to go, does he?"

Ben shook his head, took both her hands when she dropped them to her lap, and pulled her up. "Come on, we can talk to Emily about this. Make a decision."

"No." Megan dropped back into the chair. "Maybe nothing really happened. Except the seizure. I had a bad day. I might have imagined the attack."

Ben sat down. "You had a good day, I thought. You seemed happy between all your classes. Did your . . . appointment . . . go bad?" He wished he hadn't said that as soon as it was out of his mouth. Megan's face fell and the sobs began. Ben had no idea how to respond to her outburst, but he didn't have to. A double ringing of the doorbell was immediately followed by pounding at the front door.

Ben jumped up and fled the room. He could see through the front window the outline of a police cruiser in the street. He stage-whispered back at Megan, "It's the police."

Could this day get any worse? Megan grabbed all the tissues and dabbed at her eyes with the dry ends as she sneaked into the kitchen to listen.

Ben opened the door and invited the officer in. She heard the cop stomp the snow off on the rug and close the door behind himself.

"Are your parents home tonight?" the officer asked. *Is that what Ben told him last night? That he lived here with his parents?*

"No, sir, sorry. It's just me and, uh, my girlfriend."

Girlfriend? Was that creepy or sweet?

A sweet but necessary lie, she decided. Megan could imagine the policeman scanning the two adjacent rooms for her. She should probably make her presence known.

"Uh huh, well, I'm here following up on what happened last night. The guy's locked up and he won't be out for a while. He was working alone, but if you see anything suspicious don't hesitate to call 911. Tell your parents that, too."

Megan shifted her weight and persuaded herself to go into the foyer. "Hello." Her voice was meek and she could feel the officer's eyes examining every inch of her.

"Evening, miss. You all right?"

"Uh huh, I'm fine." She should explain her reddened eyes, but Ben was holding out his hand and if she was supposed to be his girlfriend then she should grab it. As soon as their fingers were intertwined Ben grinned at her and she smiled back. Her eyes were most certainly shining.

"All right, then. You kids take care. And keep your doors locked." The policeman let himself out and Ben locked the door as soon as it was closed. He reached for Megan's hand again and led her into the living room and onto the couch.

"Sorry about that," he said, still holding her hand.

"What?"

"About lying. You know, that you're my girlfriend, that I live here with my parents, that stuff." He squeezed her hand.

Megan let herself be mesmerized by his eyes. She couldn't help but tilt a fraction of an inch toward him and then he matched the movement until their lips touched. Gently at first and then with a little more force that matched the pressure of their clasped hands.

She felt the euphoria, felt her body responding to his warm lips. She liked the heat from his cheeks and his breath. She kept her eyes closed and enjoyed the scent of his cologne, how their noses kept touching, and the softness of his lips.

From her nest at the window Emily had spied on the wintery world, watching and waiting for Ben's return. When he finally arrived she slipped down the hall and started down the steps, stopping when she heard him greet Megan in the den. She perched on the fifth step and listened. The door at the bottom was ajar a good five inches and she could hear them clearly.

When she heard Ben tell Megan that Chuck was schizophrenic and there was no Adam she put her head on her knees and clasped her legs tightly. She could barely take in the information. Why hadn't Ben shared this knowledge with *her*?

She thought back to when she had explored Chuck's room. Now she knew why he kept the field day certificate from so long ago.

They were all damaged. It was no wonder that she had nightmares. No wonder Cori could levitate people. No wonder Chuck was walking on the ceiling, attacking. Having seizures.

No wonder Ben was lying.

She heard him ask Megan what *she* wanted to do. If *she* wanted to call the police.

Emily closed her eyes and prayed. The police. The police. The police.

A knock at the door. Her eyes flew open and she glimpsed Ben passing the stairs. He whispered back at Megan a phrase with the very words Emily had chanted.

The police were here.

She came down two more steps after she saw Megan slip by. She listened to the lies. Why did the policeman think Ben lived here with his parents?

Girlfriend? Megan was his girlfriend now?

Emily's head was throbbing. She descended the last few steps and touched the knob when she heard the front door close. She stayed stiff, unmoving, and listened to Ben and Megan settle onto the couch. A few words: an apology, a question, an answer. Then a sheltered silence.

She pushed the door wider, a sixth and seventh inch, enough to peer through with both eyes and see down the hall and into part of the living room. Their knees were touching, their feet toe-to-toe, but she couldn't see their upper bodies.

Too quiet.

She pushed the door all the way open, stalled, then stepped through and closed it with excessive harshness.

Too loud.

"Em, is that you?"

Tuesday

Chapter 11

Megan sat in the backseat on Tuesday morning. All three of them were quiet on the way to school. It wasn't completely awkward, but if the drive had been much longer she would have brought up the fact that Cori had pounded on her door late last night. She had finally fallen asleep after lying there for an hour thinking about Simon, her parents, Ben's kiss, the police, and most of all Chuck's attack and epileptic fit. Then Cori had jiggled the knob and slurred a demand that Megan help her pick a lock. What was that about? Megan had merely rolled over and ignored Cori, who gave up and stumbled off more quickly than Megan expected.

"See ya later, Em," Ben said as soon as they all got out of the car.

Megan noticed how he was slighting Emily who wouldn't answer him at all, not even to give him her usual thanks. Megan tried to smooth things over by calling after her, "Have a good day, Emily." There was no response, only a quickening of her pace as if she were late for a test.

Megan turned to Ben. "She's upset."

"Did she have another nightmare?"

"I don't think so. I think she's upset about what she saw last night."

They entered the school and Ben gave a nod to a couple of kids who passed by. "Chuck's seizure?" he asked.

"No," Megan looked back at the kids he had acknowledged and then at Ben, "no, that didn't seem to bother her when it happened. And I don't think she believes me about him . . . you know . . . walking on the ceiling and attacking me. She's upset about you."

"Me?"

"She's got a crush on you, you know."

"What? Emily? We're just friends." Ben began to blush and smile, the dimples fluttering in and out like they were nervous, too.

"I think she saw us." Megan was direct. They turned down the next hall and one of Ben's teachers passed by and greeted them both.

When they reached Megan's locker Ben leaned against the next one and whispered, "You mean . . ."

"Yeah, and she's jealous and I feel a little like I'm betraying her. I only just moved in and, well . . ."

"I like you Megan." Ben's eyes were only inches away. She held the edge of the locker door and would have swayed with it if he moved any closer. Secret mirth rose from her belly to her lips and spread across her face. This was what it was like to be normal.

Emily let the numbness blot out the screaming rage within. Drops of blood stained the inner edge of the toilet bowl before they streamed down and were diluted in the water. She cut herself again, felt nothing, and watched with suitable appreciation as the pink tinge swirled and thinned.

No one else came in the girls' john except a single cheerleader, easily identified by the super white shoes with the blue initials of the school along the heel. The wall between Emily's stall and the adjacent was open at the bottom and high enough that she could see the girl's thin ankles and smooth fake tan up to the middle of her well-developed calves. Since it was Tuesday this would be a JV cheerleader and not one of the Varsity girls who were known to be aggressive with girls like Emily.

Still, she was wary. She grabbed some toilet paper and blotted her wounds. The first warning bell rang and she knew she had five minutes to finish up and get upstairs to first hour.

The cheerleader flushed, took her time adjusting her clothing, and finally left the stall. She spent another couple of minutes in front of the mirror and Emily watched from the crack where the door would swing. *Hurry up. Hurry up. Hurry up.*

When the outer door finally swung shut Emily came out and threw her satchel on the damp counter. She wet a couple of paper towels and tried to blot out the red stains that had formed while she spied on the cheerleader.

The one-minute bell rang.

Two girls burst in and Emily crumpled the paper towels and dropped them into the basket, turning her back on the girls as she did so.

"Oh, this is cute," one said.

Emily turned back to see the girl holding up her satchel.

"Where'd you get it?"

Emily snatched at it, thinking not of its contents – the broken ipod, the rarely used hairbrush, two textbooks, a razor blade, the useless cell phone she couldn't pay for – but instead she thought of the last birthday she had with her mom when, for a dollar, her mom had bought this at a resale shop. She tugged at the bag, but the other girl didn't let go.

Her earlier rage pitched her forward and she scratched at the teen's face. The girl screamed, released the bag, and slapped back. Emily struck at both girls and pushed between them. She raced out the door propelled by the vocal abuse. She hit the stairwell and joined two boys who were trying to beat the tardy bell by running up the steps. As they reached the top landing the bell rang and the boys put on a burst of speed that got them through a class door before the ringing faded.

But Emily slowed down. Her class was at the end of the hall and to enter now meant all eyes would be on her. She headed instead to the second floor bathroom.

Her mother would be so mad at her for skipping class. She should be severely punished.

Adam donned the Fedora and smoothed his plain black t-shirt. Chuck would have worn a sweatshirt today because it was cold outside, but Adam preferred short-sleeves. All the better to show off the guns and roses tattoo he got from that prick his brother's girlfriend worked for.

Poor Chuck, Adam thought, he must be delusional to think that a gorgeous girl like Cori was his girlfriend. She treated him like dirt. Maybe he should teach her a few lessons on how to respect his brother.

He heard her plod down the stairs. He bowed and swept his hat to the floor as she entered the kitchen.

There, that should teach her something. He grabbed a tuna fish sandwich from the counter and went out the side door. Coatless. The snow crunched under foot as he walked unhurriedly to his car. He started it up and sat there eating his sandwich. The car heater took ten minutes to warm up, the same amount of time as it took Cori to eat breakfast and leave.

Adam lifted his hat in salute as she walked down the driveway and passed the front of the idling car. He put it in gear and aimed at Cori's back. She stepped aside, as he knew she would, with barely inches to spare. He braked sharply at the stop sign; the gun slid out from under the scarf and onto the floor of the passenger's side. Adam watched Cori in the rear view mirror.

"Asshole," she yelled as she reached the corner. She stepped up to the sidewalk and continued on the route.

Adam saw her look back at the house. *She's watching for you, Chuck.* He turned the corner and sped up. When he reached the end of the block he pulled up into someone's driveway and turned around. *I'd be doing you a favor, Chuck, if I just ran her over.*

He parked and watched her stop to light a cigarette. *Stupid bitch, you'll die of lung cancer. Better to put you out of your misery now.*

No, Adam, please, no.

You're a good brother, Chuck, so I'll let her pass this time.

Adam reached for the scarf and wound it loosely around his neck. He put the gun back on the seat.

Ben was conscious of his knuckle-cracking and tried not to surrender to the habit when he was around Megan. He ducked into the john after lunch and ran a comb through his dark blond hair, checked his teeth for food, and worried over a pimple that menaced his dimples. Then he popped every knuckle and cracked his neck. When he came out and joined the crowds that flowed from the cafeteria he noticed Emily in front of him. At least he thought it was Emily, same stringy hair, satchel on the left shoulder. Did she have this lunch period all semester and he never noticed?

He stepped around someone and tapped her shoulder. She jolted and withered to the right, ready, he thought, to duck into the nearest classroom.

"Em!"

Her head swung at the sound of his voice and he saw panic and fear fade from her eyes before she shifted her gaze to the floor.

"How's your day goin'?"

She barely hesitated, "Okay. Yours?" She angled her body away from him though they were still moving with the flow.

"The usual." He walked along side of her looking for obvious signs that Megan was wrong, that Emily did *not* have a crush on him. She acted no more interested in him than the fire alarm box they just passed. He didn't see the flirty sparkle in her eyes that made Megan so attractive. He didn't catch her stealing glances at him or staring openly like Megan would. Emily was . . . was just Emily. Sorry, little, pathetic Emily who needed compliments. "Hey, lunch was good."

"Thanks. I thought that since, you know, you bought the cans of tuna and the bread last night, so . . ." she still didn't look at him. "I thought that's what you wanted today."

"You're the best, Em. Catch ya later." Two compliments should do it, he thought. He veered off and turned to fall in step with Megan as she headed toward the cafeteria. Megan smiled up at him. He wouldn't have heard Emily's response even if she had made one.

"What are you doing? You can't skip class," Megan beamed at Ben. She let him take her hand and they rounded the corner and went through the double doors back into the cafeteria.

"It's just Econ and there's a movie. That's the great thing about split lunch. Mr. Haley will have the video ready to start and the lights off as soon as the bell rings. He won't even think of taking roll again." He squeezed her hand. "Where do you usually sit?"

Megan let go to motion toward a table of junior girls, hoping that option wouldn't appeal to him. A jealous bone was making itself known to her; she didn't want to share him.

"Maybe we could try someplace else, though," she said. She twirled her hair in her fingers, silent laughter circled her heart with a pleasant warmth.

"My car?"

"What about the parking lot attendant? Doesn't he patrol the lots all day?"

" Sometimes, but at lunch he stays down at the exit, checking for early dismissal passes. Let's take our chances. What's the worst that can happen?"

Megan's face clouded at that expression. She had heard it before from the father of her baby. *Come on, what's the worst that can happen? What are you so afraid of? Everybody does it*. She faked a smile and shook off the memory.

"Okay." She placed her hand back in his and they wound their way past dozens of noisy tables and two teachers who were unlucky enough to have lunch duty. They ducked into the hall and out a side exit.

The noontime sun hit their faces, but the freezing January temperatures begged them to run to the car. Megan nearly dropped her sandwich as Ben pulled her along. The blacktop was icy or wet depending on where the snow had melted. He used the remote to unlock the doors when they were twenty feet away and then he opened the door for her and ran around the car.

"I'll start the engine. We'll be warm in no time," he said as he closed his door.

Megan unwrapped her sandwich and took a bite.

"Oh, man, I didn't give you a chance to buy a drink," Ben gave himself an exaggerated forehead slap. "I'm sorry. I can run back in and get you something. What'd'ya want?" He put his hand on the door handle, ready to leap back out.

"That's okay, I'm fine. I usually go to the drinking fountain after I eat anyway, so . . ." She gave a little cock of her head and took another bite. "Mmm, Emily should be a chef. Did she put nuts in the tuna?"

"Yup, you're not allergic are you?"

Megan shook her head.

"Good. Emily should have asked, though." He smiled at Megan.

"If we ever do this again you better save your lunch to eat with me. I can't stand your watching me. Here, you want the other half?" She held out the remaining half.

"Nah, that's okay. Sorry, I won't stare." He looked out the front window. "So . . . do you have to work tonight?"

"Yeah, five to nine."

"I'll drive you."

"I don't mind walking, really, and it's not that cold."

Ben twisted in the seat and faced her again. "I have to be somewhere at five," his mind's eye flashed on his mom's face, "and then I'll swing by at nine so you don't have to walk in the dark."

Megan smiled. "Okay, thanks." She took another bite and stared at him while he pretended to be interested in the rear view mirror. She wondered why he didn't already have a girlfriend. He was so cute. And so nice. Why was he paying so much attention to *her*? As soon as he turned his head back toward her she blushed and glanced away.

"Look!" She stopped chewing to point at Chuck's car as it crept through the lot. "Is that Adam? I mean, Chuck . . . Chuck wearing that hat? What's he doing here?"

"This can't be good." Ben's voice was low; an adult tone colored the words.

Adam eased the nose of the car up to three garbage bins, clearly in defiance of the over-sized no parking signs posted on their sides. He looked toward the windowless double doors that were an emergency exit from the cafeteria. He had run out those doors on his first day of high school.

No, that was *me*. *I* ran out those doors. Yes, Chuck, you're right. You told me all about that day and now I remember it like it happened to me. I will avenge you.

Adam looked down at the box of doughnuts that sat tilted over the gun's handle. When had he bought those? He opened the top and stared at the three remaining ones: glazed, chocolate, jelly. He couldn't remember eating nine doughnuts. Had he shared them with someone? With Chuck?

He pushed the box away and fingered the barrel of the gun. So smooth.

He unwound the scarf from his neck and placed it in his lap. He settled the gun on top and turned it until the angle suited him. He knotted the scarf and flipped the package over and knotted it again. Now he had a bulky present that would be appropriate for . . . for . . .

What were their names, Chuck? Did you ever tell me their names?

Adam raised his head and focused on the red letters of the sign. The car idled and the heat blasted and an insistent knocking emphasized the pounding in his head and the slow beating of his heart.

Ben kept knocking on the car window.

"What's wrong with him?" Megan was at his elbow, peering into the front seat. "He's like a zombie. Is the door locked?"

Ben tried the door, but nothing happened.

"Chuck!" he pounded again, faster, hoping he wouldn't break the window.

Megan moved around him and waved her hands in front of the windshield. She yelled, "Adam! Hey, Adam!"

Adam's head moved slowly to the right and Megan circled the car to the passenger's side while Ben kept up his battering.

"I think I've got his attention," Megan called over the hood. She shivered and grabbed the passenger door handle and jiggled it. Locked. "He's staring at me. Ben, it's the same look he had last night. What if he has another seizure?"

Adam broke his gaze. He moved like a snail, scooting himself to the center of the bench seat. He placed the "package" on the dashboard and lifted the doughnut box to his lap, all in the slowest slow motion. He stretched both arms out to the sides and held his fingers above the door locks.

"That's right, Buddy, open the doors," Ben implored.

The lock buttons rose to meet the tips of Adam's fingers. He felt the power of the action and pulled his arms to his chest with the suddenness of a striking snake. His head struck the back of the seat and his mouth fell open.

Ben flung the door open and lunged into the driver's seat, but Megan stared through the window.

"It's okay, Buddy, it's okay. I'll take you home. Everything's gonna be fine." He motioned for Megan to open the door, then instead hit the window button and rolled it down. "Hey, I'm takin' him home. Can you go turn off my car? And, uh, drive yourself and Em home after school?"

"He never said a word. He didn't have a seizure, but somethin' *really* weird is goin' on with that guy." Ben shook his head.

Emily stood in the entryway and listened as Ben explained to her and Megan what happened next.

"It's like he had his tongue cut out or something. He tries to speak and then it's just a garbled mess. He goes from angry to tearful to nothing in five seconds. Then he stares."

Emily was mute. Welcome to my world, she thought.

Megan handed Ben the keys and moved on into the dining room to set her books down. Ben turned his back on Emily and followed.

Emily stepped up into the kitchen, felt invisible. Felt . . . angry.

Felt the pressure on her chest that only came with nightmares. She wanted to run up to her room, but she could hear Cori up there moving furniture or something. She didn't want to pass her room.

Maybe she could do something for Chuck. She didn't mind Chuck . . . or Adam. Well, now that Megan had revealed the secret on the way home that they were one and the same she considered him to be as equally outcast as she was.

Was he as stupid, too? She felt like an idiot that she'd never put two and two together. When had Adam and Chuck eaten dinner together? Never. When had they both watched TV at the same time? Never.

So many lies and secrets from Ben. The only good thing was that Ben looked out for all of them and kept their secrets. Well, not anymore.

She listened for a second to Ben and Megan's conversation in the dining room. Their voices were lowered and there was a lighter attitude. They weren't talking about Chuck any more. They wouldn't notice if she went downstairs.

She took each step cautiously. This was a big deal for her. She never reached out to others. She hadn't been particularly friendly with Chuck ever and pretty much ignored him with the same heartless indifference that she knew most people had for her.

She was half-way down the stairs and felt a twinge of dread that she might soon find herself rebuffed by a schizo. Her good intention folded in on itself; she felt her goal wither and cramp.

She paused. Something changed. Her heart was leaden and the pressure was spreading to her limbs. All she could see ahead was the bottom step and nothing beyond.

The basement shouldn't be this dark. There was no laundry room light bulb. She glanced back up the stairs and couldn't see the window in the door. Her vision narrowed until she could no longer see even her hand in front of her face.

I should yell, she thought.

Her lips moved, but air skipped past her vocal chords.

She felt along the wall and turned toward Chuck's room, found the door knob, and froze. The pressure knocked her to the floor. She saw nothing. Could not scream. Could not feel herself rise up, stiffened, frozen mid-air exactly as she remembered the fat man. Was it Cori? Was she doing this to her? There was no way to control the fear.

Mute, blind, paralyzed.

Emily panicked to the point of passing out.

Chapter 12

Cori strode into the dining room with a purpose. "Hey . . . Megan. Need your help. Come upstairs." She turned with the confidence that her command would be obeyed though she expected Ben to say something inane. This ridiculous little romance was tiresome, but she could endure it if Megan could unlock the treasure trunk. "Bring that lock pick you had to get into Mrs. Kremer's room." She thought of turning back to wink at Ben when she said "Mrs. Kremer", but she smirked to herself instead.

She didn't hear Ben's whispered question to Megan, but she heard her little minion obediently following her, though she paused at the den door for some reason. Cori hurried up the stairs first and waited at her door.

"Right this way, new girl," Cori oozed sweetness, fake though it was. She closed the door behind Megan and dropped the friendliness. "That thing. I can't get it unlocked. Lost the key. Can you pick it?"

"Me? I don't know how to pick a trunk lock." Megan kneeled down to take a look at the trunk. "What's in it?" She stuck the metal pick she had retrieved from the den's doorframe into the large hole.

"NOYB."

"Enno why bee?" Megan looked straight at Cori, studied her piercings, noticed the blue-ish black of her dyed hair.

"N. O. Y. B. None. Of. Your. Business." Cori grabbed at the pick and jiggled it. "That's too little. Have you got something else?" The pick clunked on the floor boards where she dropped it.

Megan sat back on her heels and put her hands on her knees. "Maybe. But you've got to tell me about this trunk first. It looks old. Was it your grandparents' or something?" Megan held Cori's stare, read the meaning in her gaze, and backed off. She lowered her eyes without saying another word and reclaimed the pick.

Five minutes passed as she struggled with the lock. Megan asked for several items that Cori fetched with the enthusiasm of an annoyed sloth. A nail clippers, a ball point pen, a paper clip. Ten more minutes passed and then fifteen.

Megan's persistence was the positive counterpart to Cori's stubbornness.

"Hold this right there," Megan said. She used both of her hands to work the tube from the pen in tandem with the straightened end of a paperclip.

"You got it!" Cori's reaction was the closest to a warm response that Megan had heard from her in the short time that she had lived here. They flipped the lid up jointly and laughed at the first thing they saw.

"Holy cow. How old are those?" Megan leaned back and let Cori lift out the sheaf of yellowed drawings. They were nude sketches that would have been given a PG-13 rating for their chasteness. The artist had hidden the private parts with objects held by the model.

"Old," Cori answered, forgetting to be rude. There were seven in all. The old paper was ragged and crumbling. The charcoal drawings were smudged in places and had imprinted themselves faintly on the backs of each other.

"Look. They're signed." Megan pointed at the faint signature of one. "Robert Joseph Kinton. Sounds familiar. Maybe it's some famous dude and you've got some original artwork worth millions." Megan tried for a smile from Cori, but it didn't work. The single moment of shared discovery had evaporated.

"All right, you can leave my room now."

Megan stood up. "Aren't you going to thank me?" She couldn't resist putting her hands on her hips as if she were scolding a child for ill manners.

Cori uttered something unrepeatable and Megan was tempted to kick the trunk. From this vantage point she could see the edge of a brown board revealed beneath some other objects. The trademark symbol and name at the top caught her attention.

"Is that a Ouija board?"

Ben rummaged around the kitchen wondering what the heck Cori was doing with Megan for so long. And where was

Emily? She usually helped him on Tuesdays while he prepared his customary salad and frozen family-size lasagna. He switched on the oven according to the package instructions and got out some dishes.

From the basement there suddenly blasted Chuck's music as if he had opened his door wide.

Feet charged up the stairs and Ben stuck the pan in the oven before it finished pre-heating and quickly backed away, prepared for Chuck to run through. He had been bowled over before, though it wasn't the ceiling-walking attack that Megan had depicted. He doubted that things truly happened as she described. That was entirely too weird. But for some reason he could accept Cori's levitating abilities. That seemed like yoga or something. Wasn't there scientific proof for that?

Chuck checked himself at the top of the stairs, turned and ran back down. Ben figured he had forgotten something or was simply Chuck being Chuck. Then he heard loud choking gasps. Was Chuck strangling himself? He stepped to the entry and looked down.

"What's the matter, Buddy?" he called to Chuck's back. His dark shadow was as still as a brick.

Ben took a step down, pulled his foot back when the oven beeped that it had reached the set temperature, then said, "Chuck? What's wrong?" He continued to ask in as smooth a voice as he could muster all the while slipping down step by quiet step.

When he was close enough to reach out, he touched Chuck's shoulder. The tensed muscle felt rock hard and Ben's contact didn't budge him. Without warning Chuck crumpled to his knees and the scene that his silhouette had hidden shocked Ben. Emily!

"Emily!"

He ran to the floating figure and wrapped his arms around her, tugging her to the floor. "Emily! Wake up!" Her body was cold and stiff and Ben wasn't sure she was breathing. He felt his pockets for his cell phone, pulled it out, and punched in 9. Emily's eyes opened and she groaned.

"I'm calling 911, Emily. What happened? Did Cori do this to you?"

"No, no, don't call." Emily shrank away, sat up, and looked beyond Ben to Chuck's body on the floor. "What's wrong with Chuck?"

Ben scooted over, his finger still hovering over the keypad, ready to hit the next number. Chuck was now prone on the concrete and sleeping like a baby, breathing normally, and smiling like the Mona Lisa. Ben felt for a pulse in his neck and found a strong heart beat.

Chuck moaned, opened his eyes, and sat up. "Dude."

"You okay?"

"Dude . . . Emily. What were you doing?"

The guys turned their attention back to her and she cowered. "It wasn't Cori this time." She paused, stuck her fingers up her sleeves, and scratched at her cuts. "It was demons."

"I did not," Megan protested.

"Yes, you did," Cori barked. "I could feel you pushing that thing. It's supposed to move on its own."

"It is. It keeps spelling the same thing. Look, it's pointing to the same letters: B and J again."

"That doesn't spell anything, Einstein." Cori lifted one hand to push back a strand of hair and unconsciously brushed her fingers over the most recent piercing. The Ouija board was intriguing, even if it was hokey and looked like it was a hundred years old.

Megan lifted her hands, too, and used them to accentuate her words. "Think. They must be initials. Who do you know with the initials BJ? It's not Ben. Billy Joe? Bobbie Jean? Bobby Joe?" Megan's hands flew to her face.

"What?" Cori tried to dampen her interest by folding her arms in an appropriately defiant gesture. "You know a Bobby Joe? Old boyfriend?"

Megan grabbed for one of the nude sketches and read the signature again. "Robert Joseph Kinton! Bobby Joe! The murderer. The guy who killed his mother and sister . . . it must have been right *here* . . . in *this* house!" Megan looked towards Cori's closet. "This is from the attic, isn't it? You went up there."

Cori started to give a rough answer then caught her breath as the planchette began to move around the board on its own.

It stopped on *YES*.

Megan sucked in her breath. The air in the room abruptly felt like it had been routed through hell. "The pointer is on the YES! Yes, you went up into the attic – it's answering my question." She saw Cori give a nod. Megan stared back at the board, moved the planchette to the center of the board between the numbers and the letters, and asked, "Are you Bobby Joe Kinton's ghost?"

The little wooden piece spun around twice and then wobbled toward the corner. It landed on the *YES* again and Cori's expletive overpowered Megan's exclamation. They stared at one another, trance-like. Finally Megan spoke, "We should tell the others. This may be why Emily has nightmares and why you can levitate things and . . . why Chuck can walk on the ceiling."

Cori's eyes widened. "And you," she said.

Megan frowned. "Me? What about me?"

"I saw you. You were sleeping mid-air. Floating."

"Huh?"

Cori completely lost her gruffness. "I got home late Saturday, well, it was early Sunday morning, I guess. I was stoned and I picked your lock and I saw you there. I didn't think it was really happening, but . . ."

Megan nodded her head, remembered waking up half off the mattress, her door open. "Let's show the others. Come on." She grabbed the board and pointer, not expecting a protest from the usually obstinate girl, and not hearing one.

Emily wavered between enjoying Ben's arm around her as he helped her up the stairs and worrying about running into Megan when they reached the first floor. He guided her to the living room and sat next to her on the couch. Chuck had trailed them and settled himself into the corner chair.

Cori and Megan just happened to come bounding down from the second floor a few seconds later.

Emily tensed and pulled away from Ben when she saw what Megan carried.

"Oh, good, you're all here." Megan sounded happy, but there was a strange catch in her delivery. She plunked the board down onto the floor at Ben and Emily's feet. She and Cori sat on the floor and Chuck slid off the chair and folded his long legs as well as he could to get close to the Ouija board.

"Wait a second," Ben left Emily alone on the couch and sank down next to Chuck. "Uh, Chuck and I just found Emily floating in the basement. Did you do that, Cori?"

"No way. I was with new girl, up in my room. You knew that."

"I told you," Emily whispered, "it was demons." She shuddered.

"I can believe that," Cori pulled roughly on Emily's hand. "Get down here. We're all gonna sit around this thing and see what the problem is in this house."

The five of them sat still. For a few seconds the room was normal, as if five teens had decided to play a simple board game on a wintry afternoon. Then the spectrum of light changed, imperceptibly at first, and then slowly the room reddened. Megan placed the planchette in the middle of the board and left one finger balanced on the end.

"Everybody, put your finger on an edge. What should our first question be?"

Megan had hardly voiced the last word before the pointer rose beneath their hands. Even the guys gave little gasps, but everyone kept their hands engaged as Cori announced each letter aloud that the pointer passed. After every few letters Megan repeated the word that was spelled.

"What . . . is . . . in . . . the . . . trunk – oh, my gosh! I asked what our first question should be and it answered that we should ask what's in the trunk."

"Weird," Ben said. He pulled his finger away first, thinking of what he had in his car's trunk.

Cori and Megan lifted their fingers, thinking of the trunk in Cori's room that they hadn't finished searching.

Chuck pulled back his hand, wondered if Adam had hidden more weapons in his car trunk. He slowly pulled himself up off the floor. "Stupid," he said and left the room.

Only Emily's finger remained on the planchette. She whispered to the Ouija board, "Do you mean the trunk in the basement? The freezer?" She kept her finger lightly touching the top of the pointer as it began to slide to the far side of the board. She had to lean to reach that far if she wasn't going to let go. It was heading toward the *NO*. Her sleeve caught on the edge of the board and it was drawn back. She reached with her other hand to pull the material back down, but not before Ben yanked her wrist and twisted her hand over.

"Em, are you hurt?" He reached for the edge and folded the cuff back, revealing a series of slices criss-crossing back and forth from her elbow to her wrist. "Em, no . . ."

Without thinking Emily whispered, "Cori did it."

Ben and Megan together took hold of Emily's arms and raised the sleeves on both arms as high as they would go. Emily stayed unresisting like a toddler getting his shirt changed.

Megan looked from the wounds to Emily's face to Ben and then to Cori.

"I didn't touch you, you lying creature!" Cori had no reason to conceal her anger; her pale complexion tinged to scarlet in an instant. She lunged forward over the board and Ben and Megan closed ranks over Emily and pushed Cori back.

"How do you explain these cuts?" Ben held his hand in front of Cori's face.

"She's a cutter, you idiot." She raised her timbre a couple notches. "Psycho-girl . . . haven't you noticed?" She glared at Emily who brightened rather than faded.

"You did it," Emily claimed again, eyes down.

"Liar!" Cori picked up the board and pointer and rose to standing. "She was right the first time when she said 'demons'. Obviously she's possessed."

Emily's lips quivered. She didn't want to smile, had nothing to smile about, was ashamed at herself for lying, yet she had no more control over the smile that stretched her mouth than she did over the words that she had uttered. Maybe she *was* possessed.

Ben got up when the kitchen timer beeped. He left Megan to comfort poor little Emily while he dished up the lasagna. It should be an interesting family meal. Quick, too. Everyone had jobs to get to. He plated the sixth piece when Megan came in.

"She's gone up to her room," she said. "Hey, why the piece for Adam? We all know now that he doesn't exist."

Ben handed her a plate. "All of us except Chuck. Do you want to be the one to tell him his brother is a figment of his imagination?"

"Ben . . . this is all so screwed up. What are we going to do about Emily? And Cori? And, and everything?" She followed him into the dining room. They sat at adjacent corners and picked at their food.

"I think," Ben began carefully, "I think our brains are accepting this stuff little by little. It's like there's a whole new reality . . . weirdness . . . that we can accept or reject, but we're slipping into acceptance. I'm not sure I'm making the right decisions anymore." He took a bite and gave her an opportunity to comment. She didn't. "Things were so clear-cut when I came up with my big plan."

"What big plan?"

"Now, looking back, it wasn't the smartest thing I've ever done." He looked at her eyes, got a lump in his throat, and couldn't tell her the truth. He switched subjects. "About Cori and Emily . . . I think she lied. I think Em cuts herself as a way to cope. We haven't been able to find her mom and brother."

"So you don't think she's possessed?"

Ben shook his head no. "I have an advantage over you – a little more perspective on her problem. I don't get why she'd lie about Cori, though, unless it's to get back at her for a bunch of little things. Cori has bullied her from day one."

"But she's got to know that Cori will retaliate even more." Megan put her fork down. "You know, I was sort of getting along with her up in her room. She's not a total bitch."

They heard Chuck come into the kitchen, grab a plate, and retreat.

"But the demon thing . . ." Megan let the thought hang for a second. "It would explain the levitation, Chuck's attack, the Ouija board, the smells."

"What smells?"

"Oh, well, maybe that's just my imagination."

Soft steps, another plate claimed, another retreat, but this time it was Emily.

Megan lowered her voice, "Somebody once told me that there's a lot of demon possession in other countries, but not so much in America, because it's a Christian nation. Well, supposedly. But anyway, people like Emily would be susceptible to it because they're so fragile . . . and don't have any faith." She watched Ben give a little nod of agreement and then she asked, "What faith are you?"

"Me? Uh," he put his fork down and started cracking his knuckles. "Oh, sorry, habit. Um, I guess I'm Christian. My dad took us all to church when I was little." He smiled at the memory. "My mom's family wasn't anything, but my dad and his parents, my grandparents, were . . . are Christians. We prayed all the time. My dad prayed with me before bed and I remember that we would go to these fellowship dinners and I got to run around the church basement with some other kids. It was fun."

"Sounds nice," Megan said. She took her last bite of the lasagna.

"It was. And I went to Sunday School. I don't remember anything about demons, though."

"Talking about me?" Cori burst in from the kitchen, slammed her plate down on the table and pulled out a chair at the opposite end. "I didn't cut that little twerp."

Megan waited until Cori sat down. "We didn't think you did. She's got serious problems. Be nice to her."

Cori closed her eyelids to the involuntarily eye roll, shoved a forkful of lasagna into her mouth. She chewed as if she were in a competition and scarfed down half of her dinner before Megan and Ben took their dishes to the kitchen.

They were standing side by side at the sink when Emily came in with her empty plate and spoke to Ben. "I forgot I have to work tonight, Ben. Can you drive me?"

"Um, sure, Em. When do we need to leave?" He glanced at the kitchen clock.

"Now."

Ben shrugged at Megan and said, "I can make it back in time to drive you like I promised or-"

"You don't have to. I told you I can walk. No big deal." Megan smiled.

"I was going to add . . . or . . . you can come now and we can talk some more after we drop her off." The dimples spread wide and deep and Megan nodded.

"Just give me one sec." She raced upstairs.

Emily put her coat on and bolted out the door. It had begun to snow again and there was nearly an inch on the ground. She got into the back seat of the car – it was where she belonged now. She saw the way Ben and Megan looked at each other. A troubling image formed in her memory; she squeezed her mind shut to the thought. She stared at her wet shoes, watched the snow slide off onto the floor and melt into the carpet. She encouraged her soul to embrace the ache that wept in her heart. It wasn't hard. The new cuts on her thighs were ready reminders, tingling still.

She thought about her lie, the one she told about Cori cutting her. She had felt sanctioned for a brief moment when the others had believed her. Her second claim was weak and forced and did not intensify the pardon as she had hoped. And then her secret was out, her lies interpreted. The worst part was how Ben's gallant protectiveness collapsed into pity.

The car doors opened and the two lovebirds got in without a word to her. Ben started the car and then the wipers. She watched him from the corner of her eye as he got back out and brushed the snow from the windshield with his coat sleeve. She bowed her head and let her hair fall over her face. What good would praying do her now? She was hopeless. She would never pray to God again.

The short drive to the main road took forever; Ben drove slowly on the slick snow-covered street. The main road was much better, but still he was cautious. Emily waited for them to say something, even if it was merely to have their own cute little personal conversation, but they were dead quiet. The swish of the wiper blades and the slushy sound of the wheels on the snowy pavement had no rhythm. Her own breath came in shallow puffs, amplified by silence inside the car.

The farther they went, the lighter she felt.

As he pulled up in front of the store she knew she could work a four hour shift without a problem.

"Pick you up in four hours?" Ben asked.

"Yes, please," she said in her smallest voice, sad, contrite, withering.

She walked away without a word to Megan.

Megan watched Emily go into the store. "That was weird," she said. "Do you think she'll be all right?"

"Not really," Ben signaled left and pulled out into the main street traffic. He drove with a more anxious determination, hurrying to get to the Steak House Grill.

Megan held the seat belt strap away from her chest, an old habit, and ran her glove up and down the edges. She turned her whole body towards Ben and watched him concentrate on his driving. He had to put the wipers to their fastest speed to keep the snow from accumulating.

"What should we do about her?" Megan's voice reflected the genuine concern that she felt.

"We?"

She smiled, engrossed in the right side dimple that appeared when he said the word. "Yeah, I feel like I belong at 328 Elm. We should help one another . . . right?"

Ben didn't answer right away. He cut over to the right lane and to the road that led to the back of Megan's restaurant. He found a parking spot and pulled in, noting the time on the car's clock. "We have forty-five minutes to spare. You're stuck here with me until your shift." He turned off the wipers but left the engine idling.

A nearby lamppost's light threw a beam that caught the sparkle in his eyes. Megan's eyes fluttered from his eyes to his dimples to his lips and back around again. She released her grip on the seat belt and unbuckled it. "I wouldn't say I'm *stuck* with you," she teased back, "more like *assigned*."

"Huh?"

"Like we have a group project and we're partners. Our goal is . . . wow, our goal is a tough one: number one – get help for Emily. Number two – get help for Chuck."

"I see where you're going with this. Number three – get help for Cori. Right?"

Megan nodded.

"And number four . . ." Ben undid his seatbelt, reached for her hand, and pulled off her glove, "number four is get help for Megan." He squeezed her fingers and leaned forward to kiss her.

Megan didn't miss an instant of the kiss. She brought her arms around his neck and let herself sink into his warmth. "Yes," she breathed when their lips parted for a moment. The second kiss was longer still and both of them heightened the potent energy between them with anxious gasps.

Suddenly Megan pulled back, straightened herself in the seat and looked out the passenger window.

"What's wrong? What did I do?" Ben's voice harbored an honest plea.

"There's something you should know about me," she sighed.

Chapter 13

Ben watched her face, tried to keep his own from twitching. The wrong reaction now would spoil things. When he had written the letter as Mrs. Kremer inviting Megan to live in a supposedly adult supervised rooming house, he had no idea that he would become so infatuated with her. This was not part of the big plan.

"Go on," he said. He reached for her right hand again and held it with his left.

"I made a huge mistake. Um, the end of my freshman year I started dating a senior. I thought he was going to ask me to prom, but . . . anyway, I was stupid. I, uh, got pregnant."

Ben rubbed his thumb and fingers over the back of her hand, hoping he was giving her the right signals. He wanted to tell her that he knew some of it, knew she had a baby, knew she was trying to get custody.

Megan didn't draw her hand away. She continued, "I kept the pregnancy secret until I started showing. My parents were furious." She took a moment to think what she wanted to say next. "I . . . we, uh, we had a huge argument. I'm not pro-this or anti-that but my parents wanted me to get an abortion and I positively *couldn't* kill my baby. I called the guy, Brian, and told him and he said it couldn't be his and he told me not to bother him again. He was off to college, up at State."

"Wow," Ben interjected, "that was harsh."

"Yeah," Megan glanced at him and then stared at their hands, "I guess."

"So? What happened?"

"Uh, I told my mom I wasn't going to get any financial help from the baby's father . . . my parents are far from rich, by the way, and all of a sudden I found myself out the door. Literally – pushed out the door!" Her voice got a little higher pitched as she struggled with some old emotions. "I went to a friend's and snuck back the next day for my clothes and some stuff. Then I went to Brian's house, to talk to his folks.

Simon's their grandchild after all and I thought they might help me."

"Simon?" Ben said the name with a little tilt of his eyebrows and a slight smile. It was getting darker in the car as the snow covered the front and back windows.

Megan grinned. "Yeah, you should see him. He's ten months old now and he's absolutely adorable. People say he looks like me."

"Does he have freckles?" That got a laugh out of her and Ben was glad.

Megan covered her nose with her left hand. "No, silly, babies don't have freckles."

"I know," Ben laughed with her, "so . . . where's Simon now?"

Megan let out a huge sigh. "In foster care. You see, what happened was . . . even though Brian didn't want to have anything to do with the baby, his parents did. They let me live with them, paid all the medical expenses, drove me to school and stuff, and then, when Simon was born they wanted to *buy* him from me . . . and adopt him."

"But . . ."

"I know, but they have money. They got a lawyer. Everything got really weird, really fast."

"What about Brian?"

"That was the worst part. I'd be there when he came home from college and he'd swear at me and call me names whenever his folks weren't around. But when they could hear him he was all nice and everything, but insisted the baby wasn't his and that they shouldn't try to get custody--"

"Well, that's what you wanted, right?"

"Right, but then Simon was born and they thought he looked exactly like Brian when he was a baby and then they insisted on a paternity suit and when I checked the lawyer websites online it seemed like a good idea . . . because then I could get child support." Megan's knees started to shake and she pulled her hand out of his and slipped her glove back on.

"Are you cold?" Ben turned the heater up to the highest notch. "Or . . . I could put my arms around you . . .?"

She scooted closer and gave him a shy smile. He wrapped his arms around her and pressed his cheek against hers and whispered in her ear.

"I already knew about your baby." He felt the smallest shift in her posture and hugged her more tightly. "I'll help you. But . . . there's something you should know about me, too."

"You could have picked me up. It's a blizzard out there!" Cori stomped and shook the snow off her coat as soon as she entered the tattoo parlor.

Jason twirled in the client chair and laughed. "Babe, I had a customer. It was a $300 job with an awesome tip." He waved a wad of twenties at her. "Besides, who's gonna watch the store? Can't just lock up for ten minutes."

Cori dropped the plastic bag she was carrying and took off her coat, hung it on a peg. "Let me see the appointment book." She stepped to the counter and ran her finger down the page. "Shit. I've got a five o'clock and a six o'clock and whaddaya wanna bet they both cancel because of the snow?"

Jason stuffed the money in his pocket, got up and stood behind her, groped her, and chuckled. "They're only ear piercings. Big deal. They'll be back tomorrow."

Cori turned around into his embrace, gave him a peck on the lips, and scrunched her nose at the sourness of his breath. She put her hands on his shoulders and shoved him away. "I need money," she stated. "And I've gotta find another place to live. That house is too crazy."

"Babe . . . too crazy for *you*?" He kept his hands stretched out, wiggling his fingers as if he were enticing her back into his embrace. Cori ignored him and picked up the plastic bag. "What's in the bag, babe?"

"Stuff. And I'll give you first crack at buying it and then I'll try the jewelry store down the block and maybe the antique store. And if they don't bite I'll look for a pawn shop or sell these on E-bay." She held up a large antique ring. "Whaddaya think?" She tossed it to Jason.

"Cool." He slipped it on his middle finger and off again. The stone was similar to a cat's eye marble, but dull. There were engravings along the sides in a foreign language that Jason couldn't determine. Three symbols were deeply cut on the underside. "What else ya got?"

Cori lifted out a heavy book. The title was *Astrology, Chiromancy and Physiognomy*. She placed it on the counter and carefully opened it. She put her nose an inch from the yellowed page and sniffed the staleness. It made her think of her grandmother's musty shelves of old paperback books – a memory from her nicer life. "It's very old. Look at the date." Jason's eyes widened upon seeing the numbers in the middle of the page: 1549.

"Dude! You probably shouldn't have carried it in a snowstorm. This has got to be worth some serious cash. What's chiromancy?"

Cori shrugged.

"And physiognomy? Isn't that some class in high school?"

Cori shrugged again. "I'll check on the internet later."

Jason smirked and slipped his phone out of his pocket. "No time like the present. It's not like we're busy here." He checked the window. Snow was falling thickly, cars were creeping by. He googled chiromancy. "Dude, it's palm reading, fortune telling."

Cori flipped gently through the pages. "I thought so, look at these charts." She held it open to a set of drawings that showed right and left hands with lines, symbols, numbers, and definitions. "Maybe we could add palm reading to our list of services: ear piercing, tattoos, and Madame Corinne's fortune telling."

"Yeah, and you don't have to only be a palm reader you could be face reader, too," Jason said, still studying the screen on his phone. "According to this, physiognomy, or however you pronounce it, is figuring out someone's personality by the lines on his face, how heavy his brow is, if he has a square jaw, small or large nose, and so on."

"Well, this book is full of astrological charts, lists of symbols, pictures and stuff. It's a gold mine of fortune telling information. Do you believe in horoscopes? I'll bet half this town does. Maybe we could sell star readings, too."

"I think that's more of a girl thing."

Cori screwed up her face then relaxed it. She realized she was feeling light-hearted. It was so much better here than in that house where things were happening that she couldn't explain. She had almost brought the Ouija board. Should she tell Jason about her new skill? She was half tempted to hold her hands out and try to levitate him, but she didn't want that dark affliction to dominate her now; she was happy.

"Here's another book," she said. She opened the bag and presented him with *Manuale Exorcismorum.*

"What's that about?"

"Exorcism." She chilled as the word passed her lips. Was exorcism something that needed to be done to psycho-Chuck, nightmare-Emily, floating-Megan . . . or . . . herself? The light mood was growing heavy.

Jason set the book down, stepped around her, and opened the bag to see what else she had brought. He scooped out more jewelry and placed the items on the counter: pentacle beads, charm bracelets, goddess pendants.

"I'll give you a hundred bucks for the lot."

"Somehow I think I'll get more somewhere else."

"How about a hundred twenty-five? . . . and you can live here with me."

"Let me think about it," Cori said. She started putting everything back into the bag, tried to feel light again, and checked the wall clock. She had enough time for a smoke even if her appointment showed up early.

Chuck drove to work for a change. The snow was blowing hard, but it still only took him two minutes to get to the video store. Twice as long as it took the owner to hand him his paycheck and tell him that his hours had been cut back. Way back. He only needed him on Saturdays. Chuck left without responding as to whether he'd come in on Saturday or not. Maybe he'd send Adam in his place, he thought. Then he could stay home and watch after Cori. Follow her to work, wait for her, see that she got home all right. Then watch over her. *Over* her. Literally.

He hopped back in the car and sped home, deciding that since he had the house to himself this evening he could work on his project, maybe add some footholds in the passageway so he wouldn't have to scrape himself so badly to squirm up into the attic.

Ben took a deep breath as he put a little more space between them. He turned the heater down a notch and began.

"It's not totally bad, but it's not good, either."

"What is it? That you're not actually on the honor roll?" Megan kept her face as serious as possible though there was mischief in her voice. She was so relieved by Ben's reaction to her having a baby that she could have laughed or cried or both.

"Did you check?" Ben's eyes flashed.

"Not yet, but I will."

"Don't bother. I messed up my grade point when I started playing hockey at midnight. But maybe my name will be there next semester." Ben dialed down the heater another level and asked Megan if she was still warm enough. Then he began.

"I haven't told you the real truth about myself, actually. I told you my dad was killed in Iraq and my mom was in rehab. Half true. My dad *was* killed there, but my mom isn't in rehab, though I think she should be. I have a home, a big one, in a really nice subdivision, where I live with my step-father and my mom." He started to slow his speaking. "She's great, but she does have a problem. It started after my dad died. I guess she's an alcoholic because she can't control it.

"Anyway, she remarried the year after my dad died and my step-dad turned out to be a real jerk. He takes her out drinking and doesn't do shit, pardon my French, he doesn't do *anything* to help her with her problem. He's an enabler, I guess. I asked him once if he didn't think she should go to rehab and he told me to go to hell. He's rich and arrogant and about as opposite from my real dad as you can get. I don't know why she married him."

Megan removed her gloves again and put both hands over one of Ben's. He turned the corners of his lips up, but not enough to earn her a dimple. She had a question already. "Tell me about your real dad. How did he die?"

"Helicopter crash."

"How old were you?"

Before Ben could answer there was a pounding on his window that made both of them jump. A beam from a powerful flashlight pierced the interior of the car. Ben hit the wipers and an inch of snow flew both ways. He could see someone standing near the front of his car, another man right at his window. He rolled down the window and the man shined his light back on his own jacket just long enough to make his badge sparkle.

"What are you doing here, son?" the officer asked.

Ben recognized the cop from the night before. "Hello, officer. I'm just dropping off my girlfriend. She works here at the Steak House."

"You've been parked here for quite a while." He cast a beam on Megan's face and she squinted. "You all right?"

She nodded.

"What school do you two go to?"

They both answered at the same time and the officer smiled, satisfied. "All right. You know you're parked in the bank's lot? Next time pull in the restaurant's lot or parallel park on Main."

"Yes, sir," Ben said. "I'm sorry. We had a bunch of time to kill so . . ."

"It's all right, son. And be careful on these roads. We're gonna get six inches tonight. If you're lucky you won't have school tomorrow." He winked and left.

"So . . . where were we?" Ben said.

"Um, I want to know why you're living on Elm instead of with your mom."

"Well, technically I *am* living with my mom. That's part of what I wanted to tell you. I go back and forth between places."

"And your mom and step-dad don't care?"

"Well, they don't know . . . in fact, the house on Elm is owned by my step-dad's company and I, uh, I sort of rented it under the fictitious name of Mrs. Kremer."

Megan's eyes narrowed unconsciously and she drew back both of her hands.

"What are you thinking?" Ben pulled one of her hands back into his own.

"I don't get it. Why would you do this?"

"Lots of reasons. For one, I'm kind of screwing with my step-dad. Renting this under his nose is kind of perfect. And I wanted a place to bring my mom to if I can ever get her into rehab and make her realize she should leave Ed. I also needed a place I could store some stuff I inherited from my dad that I didn't want Ed to get his greedy hands on." He felt her hand relax into his. "And I knew some kids who needed a place, too, and I thought this might be a great college essay that would get me into a good school . . . with a scholarship maybe."

"I really like you, Ben, but this is all so complicated. I don't want to mess up getting custody of Simon."

"How can this mess it up? You're proving you can live on your own. It's like you'll have a support system . . . me and Emily anyway. I guess you wouldn't want to put Cori or Chuck on a resume," he tried to laugh it off.

"I've got to get to work." Megan reached for the door handle.

"Hold on. I'll take you right up to the door."

"Don't bother." Neither one added a smile to their goodbye.

Ben sat there a while longer thinking. Maybe, if his mom wasn't too drunk, he could get the advice he needed.

Chuck walked over the pile of dirty clothes that was accumulating on the floor totally unaware of the faint odor; laundry was something he had Adam do once a week. He opened his closet and pushed aside several hangers. Two months ago he had pried away some boards, looking for a place to hide his weapons, and discovered what he first thought was a laundry chute. Further exploration negated that theory. The narrow shaft went to the attic with spy holes conveniently drilled near the floors and ceilings of Mrs. Kremer's bedroom and Emily's bedroom. If there had been a mechanical or useful purpose for the passageway, which must be as old as the house, he couldn't figure it out.

He started climbing, slithering in spots or using his feet and hands for leverage. He didn't bother to stop and spy this time, there was nothing to see tonight. He made it to the attic and pulled himself up between the crib and the child's rocker. He took the candle he had left in the crib, a little tea light that Emily had set out at Christmas, and lit it. His eyes adjusted to the gloom; the single flame was sufficient to get his bearings.

The square lid that he'd pushed off two months ago lay against an old Christmas tree stand, bent nails protruding at three of its corners. He set it out like a table across the arms of the rocker and put the candle on it. Three eight-foot boards were sandwiched between adjacent rafters. Chuck picked one up and started to lay out his path to Cori's ceiling. He usually stretched out over her light fixture. There was a neat little hole right on the brass plate that gave him a view of her entire room. His favorite thing was to watch her wake up on the weekends.

He set the first board down and carefully carried the other two to its end. Then with the second board he bridged several more rafters. Finally he placed the last one and stood on it. He noticed that the group of boxes that had been spaced around the attic trapdoor appeared rearranged. Had he moved them that time he hung down head first into her closet? That had been a close call. If it hadn't been for Adam's warning he wouldn't have pulled himself up in time and gotten the door replaced.

Something was missing. Wasn't there a trunk here before? Chuck's memory felt hazy, blurred. He remembered arguing with Adam about looking in the trunk. Adam won. They left the trunk and boxes alone and even put the boards back – Adam's insistence. What a pain it was to have to make this walkway every time.

You should thank me, Chuck. Look, she's been up here. She took the trunk out. See? The attic door is sitting next to the opening. Be careful you don't fall through. And look, she draped Christmas lights over everything.

Chuck stepped carefully around the boxes and reached for the door lid. He shoved it back into its spot though the string of lights kept it from fitting back entirely.

No, you idiot. Now she'll know you were up here.

Shut up, Adam. I'll do what I want.

Chuck settled himself lengthwise on the board and peeked down into her room. He saw the trunk open on the floor, the Ouija board next to it, the planchette scuttling from letter to letter on its own.

He felt Adam kneeling on his back, stretching out the length of his body and pressing harder against his frame, as if he were trying to steam-roll himself right into being Chuck.

Get off!

. . . no . . .

Snowplows were already scraping the main streets and Ben followed one until he had to turn into the subdivision of his legal residence toward the luxury home his step-dad was so proud of. Already the maintenance crew that tended all the lawns in the summer had several well-bundled men out shoveling sidewalks while the crew boss plowed the driveways. They would undoubtedly be back when the snow stopped to re-plow and charge double. Ben wondered how long before his step-dad canceled the service and demanded that Ben himself do the job. He parked in the street, hopeful that the city plow wouldn't get to the subdivision until morning. The signs looked good for a day off from school tomorrow. He couldn't think of a better way to get to spend some time with Megan. They had a lot of talking ahead of them; he worried about her reaction to his confession.

"Hola." He waved to the guy who was finishing his porch. That was the extent of his Spanish vocabulary other than to order at Taco Bell.

"Mom?" he called as soon as he opened the door. "I'm home!"

He hoped he wasn't too late. The Molly Maids came on Tuesdays and his mom hovered around them all afternoon, watching, directing, following them as they cleaned and scrubbed and vacuumed a house that was barely lived in. She didn't pour herself a drink until they were out the door.

"Mom?"

"Oh, Ben, I thought you had hockey tonight. You're home?" She came toward him from the kitchen. Sober footsteps. Fashionable pant suit. "You'll never guess what I did this morning." She smiled and threw her arms around her son for a warm hug.

Ben sniffed for booze, but smelled only the rich flowery scent of her perfume.

"What, mom?"

"I interviewed for my old job. I'm pretty sure I'll get it, too. Isn't that great?" Her dimples were a close match to her son's, her short hair several artificial shades lighter. She stepped back and waited for his congratulations.

"Great, mom, but . . . you know . . . you'll have to stop drinking."

"Ben! Don't be silly. Why do you keep saying stuff like that? I drink because I'm bored. As soon as I go back to work I'll be happy as a clam. I'll have some focus." She pinched him on the shoulder and added, "You don't need a stay-at-home-mom to drive you to school and hockey practice and the dentist anymore. This'll be good for all of us."

"Sure, mom." Ben followed her toward the kitchen. "What's for dinner?" His stomach had already forgotten the small square of lasagna he'd had earlier.

His mom took some steaks out of the refrigerator and set them on the polished granite counter next to the glass of wine she had poured before he came home. "Porterhouse steaks. We're celebrating. If I start next Monday I'll be getting up early like you and we can have breakfast together."

Ben tensed, turned toward the family room, and stared out the picture window at the snow. An automatic light blinked on next to the sofa and turned the window into a mirror, reflecting back a conflicted boy and a woman with a wineglass at her lips.

He was glad for his mom; a job might help her a lot. But breakfast every morning? He'd have to spend less time at the rooming house and confess to the others what he had told Megan.

He turned back around and watched his mom as she prepared salads. He started re-thinking his plan. There were a lot of "ifs". If only his mom could keep a job, if only she could stop drinking, if only she could leave Ed, if only she would move into the rooming house, if only she could help him with all the problems there . . .

"Does Ed approve of you going back to work?" Ben neglected to phrase his question correctly, but his mother allowed the hint at her marital oppression.

"He knows I had an interview. He didn't get mad at all this time. I think the company is stretched a little thin and any money I can earn will help around here." She gave a little laugh as she tore the lettuce. "I don't want to give up the Molly Maids, let alone this gorgeous house."

"I liked our old house," Ben stated. He was taking a risk reminding her of the little ranch house where he was born, where he had played in the fenced yard with his dog, where they had received the devastating news about his father.

His mother stopped chopping carrots and took another sip of wine. "I know," she said softly. "We were so happy then."

"Mom," Ben pulled at his thumb knuckle, "do you believe in ghosts?"

She took another sip before answering. "I think I see your dad sometimes . . . but . . . no, I don't believe in ghosts. Neither did your dad, so . . ." She left the implication hanging.

"Well, do you believe in extra-sensory stuff like mind-reading or levitation or, like, demon-possession?" Ben slipped in the last part with an accentuated finger-quoting gesture.

His mother's short laugh and raised eyebrow preceded another sip of wine. "You need to talk to your grandma and grandpa Kinlaw about that stuff. I know your dad believed in every part of the Bible and he told me once," she paused, remembering, "he told me about an experience he had with a crazy man they came across in a cave in Afghanistan. He thought the man was demon-possessed. He told me that it reminded him of the stories he learned as a child – that every where that Jesus preached he would cast out demons." She turned back to finish up the salads and mumbled, "I really should read the Bible."

"So, you think it's possible? Nowadays?" He took one of the bowls she handed him and set it at his place on the kitchen table.

His mother placed the other two salads down and shook her head. "I'm awfully sorry that we didn't keep on going to church after I married Ed. You should call your grandparents, Ben. They'd love to hear from you and they can answer all your demon questions a lot better than I can."

The rumble of the garage door opening announced his step-father's arrival. His mother instantly became agitated and outwardly frantic as she hurried to put the steaks on the indoor grill. Ben noted her fear – that heavy, passive fear that had driven her to drink.

Cori's second appointment called to cancel and Jason offered to drive her home after she mentioned that no one else would be in her house for a couple of hours.

"Shit, there's a car here," Jason exclaimed as they pulled up to the curb.

Cori promised him that Chuck had walked to work; they'd still have the house to themselves. Chuck's car was fast getting buried by the snow, the tracks from his arrival were invisible.

"Exactly where does this Chuck kid sleep, anyway?"

"Downstairs, in the basement. Jealous?" Cori reached over and stroked his thigh, the gesture reeking of sexual innuendo.

Jason parked the car, turned off the engine, and took advantage of the dark night to enfold Cori in his arms and challenge her with kisses. This was the softer side of Jason that she liked. They hadn't been drinking, or smoking anything, and the clear-headed excitement was pleasant and unhurried. She didn't mind the slightly stale taste of his mouth. They didn't break apart until the confines of the car and the cooling temperature moved them both to reach for their respective door handles. They laughed and caught handfuls of snow off the ground to hurl at one another as they dashed for the side door.

"Oh, I left my treasures in the back seat," Cori said, "Don't let me forget to get them before you leave." She pushed the door open and Jason trailed after her. The entry and basement stair lights were on. They left their coats and boots in a heap and Cori stepped up to the kitchen, but Jason descended the stairs.

"Where're you going?"

"I'm checking up on this Chuck dude," Jason said over his shoulder. At the bottom of the steps he turned and stood in front of the open door of Chuck's bedroom. "Dude's a slob," he stated. Cori was at his back, peering in, too.

"I told you, he's not here."

"Why's the light on?"

"We're kids. We leave lights on. Come on." She pulled at his sleeve but he didn't budge.

"That mattress looks kind of comfortable."

"Ew, don't be gross. Chuck sleeps there. Those sheets have probably never been washed." She pulled at him again and this time he let her lead him up two flights of stairs.

Chapter 14

Dinner with Ed Rose was the very first thing on Ben's list of things he hated to do. Ed complained that Ben's mom hadn't bought his favorite salad dressing. Then he criticized that his steak was too well done. He hated the vegetables and carped about the water spots on his glass. There was no end to his grumbling, as he found fault with everything his wife did. He was no less appreciative of Ben's efforts to be pleasant at dinner. He denigrated the boy with verbal abuse; he disparaged his manners and scorned him when he defended his mother.

Ben's anger stewed in his belly and nearly rose to his mouth, but a quiet look from his mother cooled the heat he felt. He couldn't fully take on Ed yet. His plan to shelter his mother, whisk her away to safety, needed more time and more money. Treachery and violence filled his mind, but his heart was patient.

Ben stood to take his plate to the sink. "I've got to go, Mom. I do have hockey tonight and I'll be late."

"Hold on there, son, you're not going anywhere. There's a blizzard out there." Ed Rose knew he was irritating Ben by calling him 'son'. He tested the teen further by adding, "I forbid you to go out and drive in this weather."

Ben rinsed his plate. He weighed his options. He could be submissive and agree. If he called Chuck, he might be able to get him to pick up Emily and then Megan, but Chuck was not completely reliable. He could be defiant – just go out and leave as soon as Ed settled into his office or in front of the TV. Did he want the consequences that would come later? He could beg his mother to let him go. She would cave in; she'd drunk enough to be easily persuaded. But then she would earn the consequences.

He opted for the truth, laced with flattery. "Um, Ed, could you drive me? I'm supposed to pick up some kids and, uh, well, their folks aren't as cool with stuff as you are. I don't want to leave them stranded, you know?"

Ed must have been thinking of an insurance payout on the kid if he should wind up in a car accident on this wintery night. He said, “You know what, son? I’m going to let you get some good old-fashioned experience in driving in the snow. Be careful and keep your cell phone on.” He gave a phony smile. “But you’re paying the deductible if you get in an accident.”

Ben produced a doomed sigh. “Okay. Thank you, sir.” He kept his dimples flat, but it took effort. They appeared only after he was half way up the stairs headed to his room where he would mess up his bed and bathroom to maintain the deception.

Jason wanted to look into the other girls’ bedrooms, but Cori pulled him into hers, flipping on the light switch and pulling the shade on the single window. She felt a tinge of guilt for what she was willing to do, but as she stepped over the Ouija board the guilt evaporated, replaced with shameless power. She spoke to Jason in a husky whisper.

“Why are you whispering if there’s no one here?” Jason eyed the trunk and the board. His voice was as low as hers.

Cori spoke again, her words still ancient and unintelligible.

“What are you saying? I didn’t catch that the first time either.” Jason looked her in the eyes, waited for a clear response, felt himself begin to float. His heels clicked back on the floor and he wobbled. “Did you feel that? Was that an earthquake? Michigan doesn’t have earthquakes.”

Cori shrugged her shoulders. He pulled her to his chest and kissed her with all of the passion and impatience of a self-centered Neanderthal. She moved against him with her hips and knees and breasts as if she were dancing some weird alien tango. Then she shuddered and twitched as she dropped to the bed, her eyes watering. The effort to levitate him left her raw. She swiped a finger across one eye, smearing her mascara and smoky black eyeliner into dark streaks across her temple. Jason yanked off his shirt and fell on top of her.

The bed creaked, creaked again as he rolled to his side and grabbed at her clothing. A nearby tapping noise caught his attention and he bolted upright.

"What the –" he looked over the bedside to the Ouija board and watched the pointer move from *D* to *I* to *E*. "Cori!" He grabbed her by the elbow and wrenched her forward.

They both stared unmoving for a second until Cori spoke. "Why are we staring at the Ouija board? Do you expect it to move on its own?" She was speaking coherently; the trance of a moment ago gone.

Jason rubbed his thumb across his heart, tracing the skull tattoo that was there. His vision started to blur; he heard a thrumming from above the light and turned his face upward. He squinted and swore. "If you have bats in your attic, they snore," he tried to add a laugh, but the sound was more of a choke. He jumped to his feet on the mattress and reached for the ceiling with tattooed knuckles. He pounded. The noise stopped with a final snort.

Cori waited, motionless. Her heart beat fast in her chest, a reassuring clock that ticked the message that she was still alive. Somewhere. She broke into peals of sharp and horrid laughter.

Jason fell to his knees on the mattress and shook Cori hard. If she had taken some drug that made her act like this he was not aware of what it was.

Adam snorted and wobbled on the thin plank; he woke up disoriented and off-balance. The attic was dark. The tea light was flickering, ready to going out.

Chuck, you idiot, he thought. Spying on this chick again, falling asleep, and leaving me to get your ass out of this situation.

He put his eye to the peep hole, saw the ugly and pierced face of the man he had paid to tattoo his arm, and, beneath him, his brother's love interest rocking with shrill laughter as if she were possessed. The man shook Cori with callous force.

Adam, do something. He's hurting her. What do you expect me to do, Chuck? Pop down through her closet, bow, pull out a sword and fight him off?

Let me call to her.

Adam acquiesced. He drew his legs up under his chest and rose up to howl like a wolf toward the roof. He opened his mouth to let Chuck call out however he wanted, but the sounds that came from his throat were unearthly.

Jason was a half a second away from slapping Cori's face. He had seen hysteria before, knew he could let it run its course, but felt a violent urge to hit her. Then the sound from the attic stopped him cold. The shriek was three-fold, a demonic chord that shivered through the air and entered not only his ears, but all his senses.

It affected Cori likewise. She stopped laughing, clung to Jason, and gulped in as much air as her lungs could hold. Both of them stared upwards, waiting for a second sound.

Ben was amazed at how much snow had fallen while he'd been inside. He took the shovel one of the workers had left on the porch and stuck it on the floor of his back seat. With this much snow he'd probably have to shovel his way up the driveway at the rooming house.

The streets were horrible in the subdivision and not much better when he got out to the main road. Traffic was light but slow. Cars that had parked on the street were plowed in with snow stacked to the door handles. He chuckled at one man who was trying to kick the snow away with his boots and shovel it with his hands.

He knew he had plenty of time to pick up Emily, but there was a fender-bender ahead. Traffic stopped. He watched the colored lights on the police cruiser come up behind him and pass, wondered if it was the officer from earlier. As he waited he sent a text to Emily to warn her that he might be late. She was probably getting used to his tardiness. Poor Em. It was too late to cut down a side street and go around since he was hemmed in by a Hummer and a couple of SUVs.

Shortly after the tow truck appeared things cleared up and the cars started to creep along again. The Hummer was bolder, faster than the rest, and Ben slid in behind it and passed the slower cars.

He pulled in parallel to Emily's store and watched her work behind the counter. She was ringing up a large order for a woman. He could see that the lady was chatting away at Emily's blank face, probably wondering why such a nice store had hired a shy girl who exhibited the antithesis of fashion and friendliness.

The woman handed Emily her credit card. Emily finished with it, handed it back, and then the woman handed her something else before she lugged her purchases to the door. Ben considered jumping out of his car and getting the door for her, but the store manager appeared from behind a display and did the job. He watched the lady remotely open the trunk of the car parked in front of him and stow her packages. She must have been shopping for quite a while because her car was engulfed in the white stuff. An earlier plowing service had scraped the road snow right up past her hubcaps.

Ben got out and pulled his shovel out of the back seat. Without a word to the lady he started to shovel out the driver's side. She closed the trunk, stood back, and pulled her scarf up over her face.

"Thank you so much, young man," she said as he finished. He asked her if she had a snow scraper and he did all her windows and lights for her, too. "You are a life-saver," she said. "Let me give you something."

"No, no that's all right. I'm just picking up my friend," he nodded toward Emily.

"Oh," she said, accenting the single syllable with a strange look. "Here, take this." She held out a card and Ben accepted it. "If I can do anything for either of you, please call that number. Thanks again."

Ben gave her a wide dimpled grin and nodded politely. He put the shovel back and climbed in behind the wheel. He turned the dome light on to read the card. It was postage card-sized and had writing on both sides along with a logo, an address, and a phone number. He gave an involuntary grunt when he read the back. He set it on the dashboard and leaned back to think.

"What was *that*?" Cori finally said. Her grip on Jason was hardly romantic and she started edging toward the foot of the bed, closer to the bedroom door. The shrill vocal sound that had filled their ears was both more and less than human.

"Is there a third floor? A way into the attic?" Jason asked.

"Through my closet."

Jason hopped off the bed and opened the closet door. The step ladder was crushing most of Cori's black clothing; the end of a string of Christmas lights fell loosely from the ceiling and draped over the ladder.

"Are you going up there?" Cori sounded nervous, incredulous. "Plug those in first."

Jason took the end and found the outlet. He took a moment to watch Cori's reaction as he asked her, "What are you hiding?"

As soon as the lights blinked on in the attic Adam backed off. This is *your* problem, brother. I'm outta here.

Chuck felt his brother leave. He sensed that he was lighter, as if he were a twelve-year-old again with no worries, no problems. Then he saw the access lid move aside, a square of light shined heavenward. He tip-toed across the boards, blew out the tea light, and threw it in the crib. He took the cover board and rested it next to the opening, then slithered down his escape hatch. The last thing he did was to reach for the leg of the child's rocking chair and pull it close, trying to position the board over his hole while angling the rocker to hide the space. The lid dropped into place with a hollow thump.

"I'm not hiding anything," Cori said, a lump forming in her throat. "That scream was unreal!" Her vision kept blurring, she felt the beginnings of nausea.

Jason stuck his head up and looked around. The little lights spread enough illumination that his eyes immediately caught the movement of a small chair, rocking ghost-like on the other side of the attic.

He nervously tapped his tongue stud against his teeth then whispered down to Cori, "You might have a raccoon or rats or something up here."

"What do you see?"

"There's a chair and a crib and a bunch of boxes. Is this where you got that stuff from?"

Cori was impatient. "Yeah, yeah, do you see anything else?" The pain in her skull was a constant thumping, tattooing itself into her brain.

Jason climbed all the way up. He looked back down at Cori after he pulled his feet up. "I'll walk over and check it out."

"You can't. You'll fall through the ceiling. You have to put boards down."

"There are boards. There's a path to the crib."

"What? No, there's not."

She heard creaking; Jason's voice was farther away. "Nothing over here, just a crib, a rocker, and a tree stand. It was probably my imagination that the rocker was moving. You spooked me out, girl." He crossed back and stuck his foot through the opening, felt for the top step, and descended. "Probably a coon got its paw in a mousetrap and lit outta here like a bat outta hell."

As soon as he was out of the closet Cori started up the ladder.

"Hey, babe, where're ya goin'? Let's get back to business."

"I wanna see for myself. See if it's gone. I'm not sleeping here until I'm sure--" She saw the boards, the path zig-zagging across the rafters. She swore with all the vehemence and anger she could produce. "Somebody's been up here!" She slid back through the opening and Jason caught her, carried her to the bed.

"What are you doing? Get off me! Don't you get it? One of those dweebs I live with has been in my room." She furrowed her brow. It couldn't have been Megan or Emily, they had left before her. Ben could have come back, but she doubted it. "Chuck! I'm gonna kill him!"

Emily pulled open the door and bent down to stare vacantly at Ben before she got into the car. She slipped in without a word. Ben gave her a pleasant greeting, but she neither replied nor looked his way again, refusing to answer his several questions with even so much as an eyelash flutter of acknowledgement. She concentrated on the stupid lyrics of the song on the radio.

The salt trucks had been out and the roads were slushy. He had plenty of time to drive the relatively short distance home and then pick up Megan, but Emily was going to make it feel like hours by ignoring him. She knew he couldn't stand it. She kept her knees tight against the passenger door and leaned her forehead on the window. She had glimpsed the same card on the dashboard that she had in her pocket. Ben must have put that lady up to it. How else would she know to ask her those particular questions?

Ben passed the street where he should have turned and Emily lifted her head for a moment. She checked the clock. This was ridiculous. He had more than enough time to drop her off. Why was he taking her along to Megan's restaurant?

She wondered if the window would smash if she started butting it hard with her forehead.

Ben pulled into the plowed lot of the bakery on the next corner.

And parked.

"Okay, Em. What's up? Why are you ignoring me?" He set the emergency brake and turned off the radio. "Talk."

Emily shifted slightly, straightening her knees.

"Em? Did something happen at work?"

Her hand shot out and pushed the card off the dashboard. "Why did you send *her*?"

"Send who?" Ben picked up the card and turned on the dome light. "That lady?"

Emily's lip quivered. "You're getting rid of me?"

"What? I am totally confused. You're not making any sense." The silence stretched. "Look, I cleared off that lady's car and she gave me this. It says 'Carla Beridon, social worker'. I assume that's her, but she's a stranger to me, Emily."

Emily loosened up. "She said . . . she said she could discern a bad spirit around me."

"Discern? Like see?"

Emily shrugged. "I thought she was rude." She talked at the floor, still not meeting Ben's eyes. "But then she explained that she's a social worker and helps teen girls all the time. And . . . and has a special support group to deal with, uh, bad stuff." Emily couldn't bring herself to say the words.

Ben flipped the card over. "You mean like what it says here? Eating disorders, self-esteem problems, pregnancy, bullying?"

"Read the next line."

"Addictions, self-mutilation, witchcraft, devil-worship, demon-possession. Yeah, that kind of struck me the first time I read it." Ben fanned the card, set it back on the dashboard, and reached over to pat Emily's hand.

"Take me home, please," she whispered, tucking her hands under her armpits. He had read that second line so fast she knew he had missed the point.

"Wait, tell me what she said to you. Honest, Emily, I didn't send her."

A sigh. "She said to call her if I wanted out. She could help me."

"If you wanted out of what? Our house?"

Emily's voice pitched down in impatience, her tone took on a reedy quality. "Yes," she lied. Her heart sank; lying was always punished, but lying to Ben would be punished twice.

Cori intended to race down two flights of stairs and ransack Chuck's room, but Jason caught her on the fifth step and yanked her arm.

"Chill out, woman! What's your problem?"

Without a conscious thought she turned, anchored herself with one arm wrapped around the stair banister, and thrust her left hand up into Jason's face. She mentally pushed him away. He tumbled upwards like an astronaut in a rolling ascent. He screamed at first and then choked to silent terror, the silver bead on his tongue caught between his teeth. He floated between the steps and the ceiling, arms and legs balled in tightly, head jerking back and forth.

Cori dropped her hand and Jason fell, somersaulting to her feet. He leaped up and drew his fist back, aimed for her jaw. A gush of profanity preceded the violence, but she stopped him again. He could move his mouth, but not his hands.

"You're a witch!" Jason yelled. "And you're fired!"

She held him there as she descended backwards, dark eyes keeping him still. At the bottom she released him. He ran to the side door, grabbed his coat and fled from the house shirtless. She waved him on and threw her own special oaths at his back.

She flung more curses after him as he drove away and she remembered the books and jewelry she left in his car.

Another set of headlights rounded the corner and Ben pulled up to let Emily out. Cori narrowed her eyes and watched the little wretched form try to walk in Jason's footprints, the snow halfway up her legs.

She cursed again and went to the stairs. She locked the stairwell door behind her.

Twenty minutes later the card on the dashboard caught Megan's attention as soon as she got in Ben's car.

"Hey, what's that? I know that logo." She didn't show signs of being annoyed with him anymore. She examined the card.

Ben twisted toward her and relaxed. "Some lady I helped gave it to me."

Megan slapped it back down on the dashboard. "Small world! That's my social worker, Mrs. B. How did you help her?"

Ben explained as he waited for her to buckle up.

"That was nice of you." A promise of a smile fluttered at her lips.

"Thanks, but Emily was totally freaked out. The lady, your Mrs. B., gave her a card in the store and told her she could help her *get out*."

"Get out of what?" She smoothed the seatbelt and left her thumb tucked under the strap near the buckle.

Ben moved into the left turn lane and answered as he checked traffic in both directions. "Get out of the rooming house, I guess."

"Why would she say that? How would she even know where she lived? She probably meant she'd help her get out of her behavior problem – that cutting thing she does. Mrs. B. can spot trouble like you wouldn't believe." She pulled the card off the dashboard again and tried to read it in the colored light cast from the traffic signal. "Uh, self-mutilation, here it is. Wow, demon-possession, too. I have a little white business card of hers and it doesn't say any of this stuff. Huh." Her harrumph echoed the muttering sound Ben made.

Ben turned, fish-tailed and recovered, and spoke in a penitent's tone, "You still mad?" He didn't know her well enough to read her without watching her facial expressions so he kept glancing back and forth from the snowy road to her face.

"No, I wasn't mad, I was . . . you know, concerned." She didn't look at him, stared instead at the huge flakes that were dissolving on the windshield. "I thought a lot about it at work and . . . you're right. It shouldn't be a problem that I live without adult supervision. I *am* the adult, right?" She laughed.

"One of us has to be." Ben focused on the road. "I think we're gonna have a day off school tomorrow."

"Good. I need a snow day."

Chapter 15

Chuck slid down the chute and came out in his closet. He could hear Cori's screams, blanched at the fighting he heard, jumped when Jason slammed the door. Good riddance. Maybe he'd start his mission at the tattoo parlor and then head to the school. Yes, he'd put that place on his list. Maybe he'd need special bullets to kill that ugly rat-faced moron. Silver bullets.

You don't have any silver bullets.

Oh, great, so now you're back. You got any good ideas, Adam?

Sure, why don't you scrape his name into a couple of shells. Or, better yet, put *our* initials on all the bullets. That'll show'em.

Chuck sat down on the bottom step, his back to the kitchen door above. He didn't move, not even when, a moment later, Emily came in.

He didn't hear her pound on the door to the second floor. He didn't feel the house shake as she slammed the bathroom door.

He sat motionless and stared.

He was still hunched there when Megan and Ben let a blast of cold air and snow blow in with them a half an hour later. Nothing broke his trance.

Megan gestured down toward Chuck with her thumb as she stepped out of Ben's way.

Ben gave a little groan. "It's gonna be hard to get my hockey bag past him."

"You're going out tonight?"

"Yeah, I've got a practice, but I think I'll call first. The last time it snowed this hard it was canceled and I didn't find out until I got there."

Megan flipped her hair around a few times, but the snowflakes had already melted in. She ran her fingers through it and then rubbed her damp hands on her jeans.

"Are you feeling a strange vibe here tonight?" she asked.

"Yeah, no TV blaring. That's strange."

"I'm just gonna use the bathroom." Megan glanced in the dark living room as she turned into the hallway. The bathroom door was closed; a thin light shone along the floor. She tapped on the door. No answer. She touched the knob. Locked. It would fit Cori's personality not to say anything. She went to run upstairs, but the door to the second floor was latched from the other side. That wasn't something Emily would do. Again – Cori. But then, who was in the bathroom?

She heard Ben on his cell phone calling the skating arena. She had a few choices: she could use the metal thing she had put back above the den doorframe to open the bathroom door, she could use it to try to lift the latch on the stairwell door, or she could go downstairs, jump over Chuck, and use the boys' john.

She felt along the doorframe right as the bathroom door opened and Emily walked out. She was deathly pale.

"Emily, are you all right? You look awful." She helped her to the couch in the living room, turned on a lamp. "Ben, come here. I think Emily is really sick."

Ben finished his call and cut through the dining room, setting his phone on the table as he passed it. "Whoa, Em, you could be cast as a zombie." Wrong thing to say, he thought, as soon as it was out of his mouth. "Uh, sorry. You just really look white." He sat down next to her and she leaned against him.

Megan sat across from them on a chair and studied the two. Emily's body language would have been considered seductive if she were anyone else. But she was simply sick, and sad, too, and lost and lonely and pathetic. Megan's heart went out to her at the same time as it filled with respect, admiration, and awe for Ben. For the most fleeting of moments she wished that he were Simon's father. Then Cori unlatched the stairwell door and kicked it open.

"What're you lookin' at?" Cori was ready to stare down all three of them, but Emily didn't even look her way and the other two turned their attention back to Emily as if the interruption wasn't the least bit startling. Megan got up and moved to Emily's other side, forming a protective enclosure together with Ben.

Cori slowly growled. "What's wrong with *her*?" Her blood churned to levitate the little nobody and smash her face against the ceiling a few times. That should put some color in those cheeks.

She clenched and unclenched her fists, moving closer by subtle increments. She rarely spoke directly to the little mouse, but since neither Ben nor Megan answered, she had to. "Emily, look at me! What's wrong? Feeling *guilty* about something?" That got a reaction.

She took another couple of steps, stopped three feet away, and asked, "Did *you* go in my room?" She could just as easily take her anger out on Emily if she had trespassed. Maybe she had misjudged things and the culprit wasn't crazy Chuck, but sneaky Emily. A certainty filled her; she was sure that she could control them all with her new power, laced as it was with passion and anger.

What? They had been speaking. But she hadn't heard a thing. Their voices were low, whispering into Emily's ears from either side. Ben, then Megan, then Ben again, making reassurances, comforting the little brat. She didn't hear them. Her heart was pounding fiercely in her chest, in her ears; the drumming thudded an evil tune.

"Did you go in my room? Did any of you go in my room?"

She heard their answers this time. Three *no's* that sounded true.

"Is Chuck back? I thought I heard him come in."

Megan pointed, but Cori didn't take the hint. She closed the gap and raised her hands out in the air and tried to push the two aside from Emily, expecting to levitate them away, force them into a fetal position and hang them like suspended disco balls.

But nothing happened. Her hands trembled inches from their shoulders. She spun around and dropped to her knees, twisting back to face them. Three pairs of eyes widened to see Cori cast her reddening eyes down, large tears streaming to her chin.

Ben couldn't stand all the tears. Maybe they were all getting their period at the same time, maybe there was a full moon, maybe they were . . . possessed. That card was on the counter in the kitchen; he could call that lady.

He patted Emily and looked out the window. The snow was incredible. Would a social worker make a house call in a blizzard?

Emily's body shifted toward him as Megan got up from the couch. He watched her settle next to Cori to try to console her. Megan was amazing. He knew she couldn't possibly give a crap about Cori and yet she was generously trying to comfort her.

He kept his head bowed, all the better to listen, but his eyes caught the furtive movements of Emily's nervous hands. She was rubbing at a red smudge; there was a dark stain spreading on her upper thigh. Was this what the guys in the locker room laughed about, an accident? He didn't pay attention to all that girl stuff – headaches and periods and tampons. He suddenly wanted to switch places with Megan. Being on the floor with an apparently kinder, gentler Cori was preferable. Time out. He needed a time out.

He heard the ring tone from his cell phone. If he could have jumped out of his skin, he would have. He moved so quickly that Emily folded over onto the cushion, then drew her legs up to lie completely flat, keeping both hands tightly pressed against her legs.

Ben read the text: hockey canceled. Too bad, he thought, maybe he should say he had to leave and just go home. Yeah, it probably would be smarter to wake up at his own house tomorrow rather than have to explain to his mom and Ed where he was all night, especially if they called off school. He could come back here—

Another ring, new text from the same hockey teammate: school already canceled for tomorrow, pick-up game at noon if roads clear. He turned his back to the girls.

"What is it, Ben?" Megan asked.

He didn't try to analyze the sad note in her tone. Split second decisions were coming more easily to him; he kept his voice solemn as he spun around, "I gotta go. I'm late. Can you handle things here?"

He thought she took too long to answer. He nearly told her there'd be a snow day tomorrow. No, better to let her find out the usual way or she'd be suspicious about hockey.

"Sure," she answered, not looking up. "It's no big deal. Catch ya later."

Megan was two seconds away from calling Mrs. Beridon for help, but then she thought of all the possible consequences. She was still on the floor with Cori. She watched Ben's headlights sweep across the living room, the lights diffused by the thick swirls of snow, struggling to cast their beams far enough into the darkness.

Ben had left too quickly, she thought, and he didn't go downstairs for his hockey bag. Perhaps it was already in his trunk. She pictured Chuck sitting on the bottom step, hoped he wasn't still there.

"Are you all right now, Cori? 'Cause we have to get Emily up to her bed. Can you help me?" She spoke with the same lilting, smooth tone she used on Simon – her mothering voice. She encouraged Cori to rise with a mild hand on her arm.

Cori was placid now and strangely preoccupied, but she gasped and cried out, "Look! Look at the blood!"

Emily's hands had fallen forward and thick red stains of blood were seeping through her jeans.

Megan grabbed Emily's arms and pulled up the sleeves. There were no new cuts. She looked back at Cori and said, "She's cutting her legs now. Help me get her pants off."

They fought against the awkwardness of undressing a limp and unwilling Emily.

"Sorry, Emmy, sorry," Megan crooned as the pants were peeled away, re-opening some of the scabs that had dried to the material. "Oh, no. Look, Cori, do you have any antiseptic and bandages or band-aids or anything? Maybe we'll have to use pads or panti-liners. Oh, sorry, Em, sorry. Oh, why did you do this to yourself?"

Cori lumbered off to the bathroom without a word, but she returned with supplies and more than a few words to say. "You're an idiot, Emily. Why would anybody cut themselves like this?"

Megan shushed her. "You're one to talk. Why would you tattoo yourself? Pierce your body like that? Are you insane?"

"Look who's talking . . . *mama*." Cori rolled the word off her tongue with all the snake-like venom of the dark creature that slithered behind her eyes. Then, like a dropped mask, her face changed. She looked at Emily to see if she understood the secret she had just revealed.

Emily groaned as Megan dabbed her wounds with peroxide. "At least they're not too deep," she said. "Emily, you have to promise to never do this again." She gave her a little shake on the shoulder. "Okay?"

Emily's voice was weak. "I just want *out*."

"You don't think we *all* want that? Life is hell. We all got problems . . . look around." Cori handed Megan the band-aids and continued, "Why do you think they invented drugs and alcohol?"

"Cori! Shut up!" Megan glared at her. "Go get her some pajama bottoms before Chuck wanders in here."

"No, I can . . . walk . . . upstairs," Emily rose to her elbows and looked at her thighs. It was not a pretty sight. Facing this humiliation in front of Cori and Megan was going to require more punishment.

She felt a little dizzy, heard Megan tell her to lie back down. Heard Cori go upstairs to get her pajamas. Heard Megan say she'd put her bloody jeans in the washing machine.

She thought about the lady. Wondered if the lady could help her find her mom and brother. Panicked when she thought of the lady's card in her jeans. Please, Megan, please check the pockets.

She realized her eyes were closed. So sleepy. Felt something on her toes. Something moving up to her knees.

Heard Cori's raspy voice telling her to lift her hips. Felt a blanket being tucked around her.

She opened her eyes when Cori lifted her head and stuck a pillow underneath it. Saw the streaky black lines on the face that could be pretty if it smiled. Saw a little smile on that face. She let her eyelids droop, blinked them open again when she heard the gruff question concerning her comfort. That outlandish smile or smirk or whatever made another brief appearance before she groaned a positive response, closed her eyes a final time, and fell asleep.

Chuck came out of his stupor on Tuesday night when Ben went out the door. The closing sound, the draft of cool air, and Adam's echoed voice all reached his inner self and he rose, stiff and confused. He walked into his bedroom and began a methodical cleaning and sorting of all of his possessions.

He heard Megan come down minutes later and start the washing machine. By the time he heard the machine buzzing after the final rinse cycle he had a reasonably livable space – neat, if not clean. He had a pile of laundry that needed to be washed, but it was an unwritten rule that you did not mess with someone else's wash. Girls were weird about it. Some of their stuff had to be dried on hot or warm or tumble only or not even put in the dryer but hung up. They used the cotton settings or the delicates or normal wash. Chuck didn't bother with any of that. He left the machine on whatever cycle they had last used and threw his clothes in. If he remembered, he added detergent.

He waited and waited for Megan to return to do whatever she needed to do to her wash, then he would do Adam's work and start a load himself. Finally, past midnight, he heard her creep down. He quickly doused his light and spied from the edge of the door, near the floor where no one ever looked, and followed her quick steps to and from the laundry room. When he was sure she was all the way back up to the second floor he carried his dirty clothes and sheets to the machine.

When his stomach growled he stole upstairs and found a half-empty box of Cheerios. He ate them by the handful as he looked out on the snow storm first from the kitchen window, then the dining room, and finally the living room.

He crunched away until the box was empty, still staring out the front window, alone in the dark. Or so he thought, until he heard a whimper from the couch. He bent low and stared into the slumbering white face of Emily. Sweet Emily. Ugly Emily. Useful Emily.

He picked up the edge of the blanket that was slipping off her feet and rearranged it, tucking the back part into the cushion.

What was wrong with Emily? Why was she lying here?

She moaned in her sleep and gave a little cry.

Chuck wondered if Adam knew what was wrong, but Adam was as quiet as a flake of snow.

Chuck took the empty Cheerios box back into the kitchen and grabbed his winter coat. He planned to use it as a blanket for himself. He sat down in the chair opposite the couch and kept vigil for as long as his eyes would stay open.

Wednesday

Chapter 16

Ben woke up at six a.m. and stared at the clock for a full minute until his brain cleared away the strange dream he was having. Then he turned the radio on to listen to a long list of school closings. It was absolutely official – no school. The weather man announced that six inches had fallen in the city with some neighboring areas receiving as much as eleven inches of the powdery stuff. Ben wondered how many days off school eleven inches would get you. Still, one day off was good enough.

He stretched and cracked and yawned. A pang of remorse followed as he remembered how abruptly he left the girls last night. No, he wasn't going to feel bad. They didn't need him there, they could handle that girl stuff better without him. They'd be okay today, happy for a day off.

He switched on the bedside lamp and rolled to one side to study the shelf of pictures. It looked like the maids had put them back in order this time or else they forgot to dust the shelf. The middle picture was the one his eye always rested on the longest – his dad in uniform, young Ben at his side looking up, the dog nuzzling his knee. There was no holiday or activity connected to the photo, it was simply a picture taken in the back yard on a summer morning of an ordinary day. It didn't have any special memory attached to it like the photo on the far right did – the last picture taken of his dad, the one that showed a tearful family minutes before being split up for what they thought would be six months. Six months sounded like forever then. And it was.

He returned his gaze to the middle picture and concentrated on remembering all the good things about his dad.

Megan woke at nearly eight o'clock to a lifelessly quiet house. The silence was so complete that she wondered for a second if she was alone, wondered if she had been wrong to turn off her alarm clock, sure that school would be called off. Then she remembered how late she had stayed up with Cori, watching over Emily's restless sleeping from where they sat in the dining room. They talked in whispers, seriously debating all sorts of things, finally agreeing to disagree. They lapsed into a comfortable silence for a while and then Megan asked Cori about Ben. They laughed softly and fell into an easy conspiracy that matched any two girlfriends' secret boy-talk. By midnight they decided that they would leave Emily on the couch and Cori went upstairs first while Megan tip-toed downstairs to take the blue jeans out of the washer and hang them to dry.

Megan hadn't latched her door. In fact, she had left it wide open so she could hear if Emily called out. She listened hard for any sounds, but heard nothing. She got up and looked out the window. The neighborhood was so thoroughly blanketed with snow that it looked like a calendar picture. It was beginning to get light, but there was no movement anywhere. The streets weren't plowed, no one was outside shoveling, and it was too early for little kids to start building snowmen. The stillness was creepy, the few faraway traffic sounds muted.

She padded to the bathroom, then to the stairs. As she passed Cori's room, she saw that she, too, had left her door open, though only a couple of inches. Maybe there was hope for some civility, maybe they could start caring for one another and get along. There was a glow from a lamp, but no sounds of stirring. Megan listened for a rhythm of breathing, but any noise Cori was making must have been muffled by a pillow or blanket. She hesitated a moment longer, vacillating between knocking or moving on. She moved on.

She treaded softly down the steps and reached the open door at the bottom. A little farther and she could see what she expected: a soundly sleeping Emily lying on the cushions of the couch, blanket to her chin. And then, in the chair across from her was what she never expected to see.

Cori awoke early and lay staring at the ceiling. She thought of her violent episode with Jason, his firing her, and her attic treasures stolen away. She puzzled over her conversation with Megan. It had felt like the times in junior high when she used to have lots of friends, was invited to birthday parties and sleepovers, and talked endlessly about boys with girls who were a lot like Megan. She had giggled with Megan over something stupid, something about Ben. She couldn't remember the last time she had felt so . . . so normal. Their tête-à-tête had begun with a dispute then morphed into apologies on both sides. They had differences in their opinions, nothing that would change the world, so they agreed to be tolerant of one another.

There had been a silence during which Cori mulled over how to explain the staircase incident with Jason without sounding positively insane. Already she was questioning that it had happened – perhaps she was losing her mind. Drugs did that to you. She didn't get a chance to say anything about it to Megan because that was when Megan asked about Ben. Their hushed laughter was its own drug; Cori drank it in. She started to feel some sympathy for Emily as they periodically checked on her. By the time they decided to go to bed Cori was free from her earlier anger – hadn't even thought about the attic trespasser.

But now she did. She sprang up in bed and fumbled for the lamp switch. She plugged in the Christmas lights and scrambled up the ladder.

The attic smelled mustier than usual, but not as cold, the quilt of snow on the roof was insulating the old house. She plucked up the end of the Christmas tree lights and dragged the line after her as she followed the planks along the path, the rough wood cool on her bare feet. She reached the crib and rocker and tree stand. She wadded up the end of the string of lights and used the extra illumination to inspect the items. It occurred to her that Megan might be interested in two of these items – for Simon.

But something was tugging at her memory. She left the lights on the chair and walked back to look at the things from her original perspective.

It was different. There had been a fourth item before. What was it? Something squarish. Another box? She wasn't sure, but she could feel her stomach starting to twist in anger. The thought that someone – it must have been Chuck

– had come into her room and up into the attic totally unnerved her.

She stared at the scene until the lights blurred and her head began to pound. She pressed her hands to her eyes and bent her head. When she released her hands she felt a little dizzy and there were more spots of lights from the pressure on her eyes. Lightheaded. She kept her head down.

And saw a pinprick of light coming up through the ceiling of her room.

She knelt on the board and put her face to the hole. The crumpled sheets on her bed stared back at her. She could clearly see the indentation her head had made on her pillow. This was a spy hole!

Her pajamas all of a sudden felt thinner, the air colder. The hairs on her arms stood stiff beneath her sleeves.

No, this couldn't be what she thought. This was just . . . just normal electrician stuff. The brass connector plate was only missing a screw, that was all.

She stood back up and looked across the attic floor, imagining where the other bedrooms' lights would be. She saw no other holes. Of course, if their lights weren't on . . .

And then there was a new yellow stab of light where the bathroom would be. The boards didn't pass that way and Cori wasn't eager to spy on Megan anyway, but she listened to be sure. And then there was a flush.

She froze, remembering that her bedroom door was slightly ajar. She moved toward her closet and put her head near the opening. Held her breath. Listened.

Finally she heard the fourth step creak on the staircase; Megan was going downstairs.

Cori looked back at the crib and wondered again what was missing. She decided to inspect the area once more.

Megan stared at Chuck sleeping in the chair, covered by a coat, and looking like he was as uncomfortable as if he were sleeping on a bed of nails. The bones of his neck seemed to have surrendered; his head had flopped back in a super-relaxed way. Like he was dead. But not at peace.

Emily, however, did look peaceful. She appeared warm and serene and tranquil.

Megan backed away and went into the kitchen. She looked out the window for Ben's car but there were no tracks anywhere. He hadn't come back.

She heard a thump downstairs.

But if Ben wasn't here and Chuck was in the living room and there wasn't any Adam. Who . . .?

She thought of Cori, the idea forming that she had risen earlier, left her door ajar and gone downstairs to do laundry.

She lifted her hand from the sink counter where she had been gripping the edge. She ran her fingers through the snarls in her hair, wiped some crust from her eyes. She was glad Ben wasn't here to see her. He must have stayed at his parents' house after hockey. That was probably smart, but it was going to be a long time before he showed up here by the looks of the snow. She leaned forward to catch a glimpse of a neighbor's car thrusting itself through low walls of snow. Ben didn't have four-wheel-drive so he'd have to wait until–

She heard a grumble overhead. She squeezed the edge of the counter again as she tried to interpret the meaning of the sudden tumble of angry footfalls down the stairs.

"You bastard!"

Cori was yelling.

"You asshole!"

She swung through the kitchen and would have pushed Megan aside if she had moved into her path.

"I'm gonna kill you!"

"Stop. What's wrong?" Megan reached out, but Cori shoved past and bolted down the basement steps.

Megan heard a groan from the living room and then a snort from Chuck. Let him babysit Em, she thought. She hurried after Cori.

Chuck came awake with a start. His neck cracked as he brought it forward and stared at Emily.

"Huh? Did you say something?" he asked as Emily moved onto her elbow, scanning sleepy eyes around the dreary room.

Rumors. They were only rumors. Right, Adam? Gossip and lies and blather and nonsense.

His knees scraped against a metal threshold. Two more feet and he could rid himself of this bile.

Is that you, Adam? When did you put this blanket on me?

Chapter 17

Ben's subdivision hadn't been plowed out yet. He ate breakfast by himself then hid out in the living room while his step-father, Ed, fumbled around the kitchen cupboards. Twenty minutes later Ed went out to the garage and backed his SUV down the driveway, leaving deep ruts. Ben went to the window and watched him slip and slide and fish-tail down the street. If the SUV was having a hard time, Ben didn't stand a chance in his little car. He'd have to wait for the professionals. He couldn't hope to get to Elm Street before mid-morning.

He needed something constructive to do to pass the time. He had an idea as soon as he saw the neighbor kids emerging in snowsuits and boots, throwing snowballs at each other, and laughing loudly enough to be heard through the double pane windows.

Mrs. Beridon looked out at the trouble and work that waited for her. Every inch of her long driveway needed shoveling. Her husband was out of town, her son was at college, and her daughter was too sick to lift a finger, let alone a shovel full of heavy, wet snow. She thought of the nice young man who had brushed off her car last night and wished he would magically appear and offer to help her. She needed to be to work in an hour and it would take almost that long to do the shoveling.

She set her coffee down and sighed. The phone rang.

"Yes . . . all right, I didn't expect a decision yet." She tapped her nails on the side of the coffee cup, tried to envision her calendar, nodded in agreement. "Oh, really? In the mail? Well, she moved, so maybe she didn't get it. . . Okay, I'll let her know. . . Tomorrow at nine a.m. I'll make sure she's there. Thank you."

She hung up and went in search of her planner, checked the date, marked the appointment, and thumbed through the pages looking for Megan Blakeney's number. She didn't have it. The only way to contact her would be to drive to the new place where she was staying. Maybe on her lunch hour. Thank goodness she knew where Megan lived now. She didn't have a good feeling about such a sudden decision by the judge, but maybe this would work in Megan's favor. Maybe not.

Ben rummaged around the storage room in the lower level of the house looking for any old winter things he could use, hoping his mom hadn't thrown the stuff out or given it to some charitable organization. He found a pair of boots of his mom's that were hardly worn and thought that Emily might like them. Then he hit the jackpot when he discovered a dented cardboard box with the words 'winter' written in black marker on the side. He pulled open the tattered flaps and dug through items that were at least ten years old. At the very bottom he found three sets of winter boots. He laughed to himself as he set aside the small pair that was decorated with cartoon heroes – his favorites from long ago. The man's boots, his dad's, were still a few sizes too big for him, but he could take this second pair of his mom's boots to Megan.

He heard distant beeping. At first he thought it was the microwave and his mother was up early. Then he heard it again and reevaluated the sound. Cement trucks beeped like that when they ran in reverse. So did other heavy machinery, like city snow plows.

He stuffed the things he had pulled out of the box back in and closed the lid. He took a quick look around the storage room and spotted his old sled, imagined himself and Megan wrapped together on it, flying down the toboggan hill at the park. Then he spotted something better peeking out from behind the sled.

Megan left Cori to stew in her room and went back down to get Emily. She found her coming out of Chuck's room.

"What happened?" she whispered.

"He threw up. I walked him back to bed . . . covered him up." Emily sounded stronger and definitely possessive towards Chuck.

Megan took a quick look in the bedroom, watched the blanketed form rise and fall with regular breathing.

She followed Emily up the stairs. "And what about you, Em? How do you feel?"

"*Emily*. Call me Emily." Her tone held unusual force, with a measure of resentment.

Megan waited for an answer, but Emily said nothing until they reached the kitchen. She turned to Megan then, her eyes contrite, her mouth downturned. "I'm okay. Thanks . . . for last night."

"You should see someone," Megan began. She reached on top of the refrigerator and pulled down the card she had removed from Emily's jeans the night before. "Here. This was in your pocket. I know this lady. She can help you . . . you know . . . with your problem. You should call her."

Emily took the card with both hands and played with the edges, keeping her eyes down, mumbling, "Sure, okay." She started moving away. "I'll . . . I'll just pray that she comes over. My, um, my phone doesn't work."

Megan ignored the remark and continued, "Em, uh, Emily. You should give me your razors, okay? Will you give me your razors?" Her voice rose in the gentlest of ways, coaxing, as if she were speaking to a child.

Emily tilted her head, strands of hair sticking to the corners of her mouth. She brushed them aside, wiped at her eyes, too, and answered. "If you leave." She left a stunned Megan standing alone in the kitchen, quite taken aback. Emily hobbled to the first floor bathroom and locked herself in.

It took Ben twice as long to make the short drive, but it wasn't so bad that a school bus couldn't have run its route. If the district had only delayed the opening of school by two hours they could have had most of their classes. The city was quite efficient in clearing away the excess snow, though there were great piles down the center of Main Street, making the left turn lanes non-existent. Traffic moved slowly even where it didn't need to.

He parked in front of the house and got out, laden down with boots, skates, and the shovel. He left the shovel outside but tossed the other items down on top of the mess of shoes and boots at the kitchen entryway.

"Ho, ho, ho," he sang out as he entered. "Santa is here." He hung his coat on a peg and entered the kitchen to find Megan coming in from the dining room. He gave her the biggest smile ever; it was easy – as soon as he saw her he felt good.

She smiled back and then her face grew grim.

"How's Emily?" he asked. He crossed the kitchen and the two of them gravitated to the living room as they spoke.

"Better. She slept on the couch. You'll never guess who stood guard over her all night."

"Cori?" Ben was incredulous. He sat on the couch and Megan sat next to him, her left leg curled underneath, her knee touching his.

"Nope, though Cori and I stayed up late talking. She's not so bad."

"So Chuck watched her all night?"

"Uh huh."

"That's unbelievable. Maybe there's hope for him yet."

"That's debatable. Cori discovered a secret passageway that Chuck has used to go from his room up to the attic. She thinks he's been spying on her from there."

"What!" Ben half rose from the couch. He was ready to check out Chuck's room for himself.

"Wait, sit down. I'll show you later. He had a . . .an episode. Not the epilepsy thing, but Emily said he threw up. He's sick or something."

"And where are Emily and Cori now?"

"In their rooms."

"So . . ." Ben leaned back, grinned. "We need some stress relief around here. Wanna go skating?"

"Oh my gosh, Ben, besides the fact that I don't own any ice skates, how is skating going to solve any problems here?"

He sat forward, grabbed her hand. "Come on. I'll show you. I brought you some boots and some ice skates. Hopefully they'll fit." They both stood up. "We can walk to the park and that will give us time to talk out the problems. Then we skate and have fun. Come back . . . fix the problems . . . voila. Everything's back to normal."

His innocent desire beamed like sunlight. He squeezed her hand and leaned forward, bent closer and kissed her gently. Her lips were the softest he had ever felt. He opened his eyes and drew back a few millimeters, enjoyed her breath on his wet lips, and then kissed her again. She squirmed her hand out of his and put both arms around his neck. He, in turn, encircled her back with his arms.

This is good, he thought. He put a little pressure on her back, wanting to tug her down to the couch, but she stood firm.

"Ben . . ." she whispered.

"Huh?"

"I've never skated."

"Never?"

"Never."

He pulled back and grinned. "This is gonna be fun."

Emily knew the moment that Ben returned. She watched him carry some things to the house, heard the door close; she smiled when she heard him call out that Santa was here. He did that once before, in early December, insisting that she accept the gift he held out, not wanting her to wait until Christmas to use the mittens he knew she needed.

She went toward her door now, wondered what he had brought, and then heard Megan's voice below. Oh no, he probably brought something for *her*. She scuttled back to her nest by the window and stared outside, was still staring fifteen minutes later when she saw them walk down the street, Ben shouldering a shovel like a fishing pole, his other hand knotted with Megan's.

She touched the skin on her arms, lightly at first, making it tingle. The image of Ben with Megan multiplied across her mind in broken mirrors, a repugnant picture that reflected her own self-loathing. She scratched at her scabs, felt the pricks of pain force away the tickling. How ticklish she used to be. She pinched her eyes closed, tried to remember her brother's face, his laugh when she would tickle him under the arms or grab his foot and threaten to run her nails along his sole.

As quickly as the image appeared in her head it vanished, replaced by a vision as real as any she'd ever had: she saw Megan in Ben's arms.

When she opened her eyes she saw a figure standing at her door. Her first thought was of the fat man that Cori had levitated, but this faceless intruder was smaller, and growing smaller as she blinked.

"Who– ?" she started, but the figment waned to less than a shadow. Still, though, there was something at her door. Was this some dreamy fear come to haunt her waking hours? To taunt a rejected Emily?

She rose slowly and held her hand out, tracking it back and forth as if she were swatting away invisible spider webs, feeling for a wisp of something real. Had she caught Chuck's illness? Had some infection spread from her bloody razor cuts to her mind?

The image returned, barred the door with its shadowy presence. Its face was more womanly now, friendly, motherly. Yes, she knew this face. Its pearly white skin so shocking against the ruby lips, the stringy hair a match to her own. Her mother. The woman who had abandoned her. The woman who had left town with her brother and told Emily she was on her own. The woman who gave her a hundred dollars and told her good luck.

She stretched her fingers toward the face. It wasn't so motherly now. She hated that face. So full of lies. But Emily herself wasn't much different. She had invented crazy lies and told them all to Ben. So many hours he had wasted with her, searching for a family that Emily knew they'd never find, not anywhere near here.

The hallucination faded then sharpened. The eyes began to blaze as she came too close. She drew her hands back to her own face and slapped her cheeks. *Why is this happening? What's wrong with me?* Her mother's eyes were scorching through to her soul, the light behind the eyes reflecting the red flurries of hell. The rest of her face was too white, the lines hard like drawn wires. The delusion grieved Emily; all around her fluttered a longing.

And a deadly fear.

"Mom?" Emily sank to the floor and watched the face change to a silhouette, fogging away with a Cheshire grin, and then, at last, evaporating.

"There," Ben announced when he finished shoveling a small area on the park rink. They were the only ones there, but their privacy wouldn't last for long. The sun was out, the snow sparkled, and the temperature was a few degrees above freezing. Every kid in the area would be here before long. No wind, no wind chill – a perfect winter day.

Megan was waiting on a bench he had brushed off with his gloves. Two pairs of skates, laces tied together, leaned against each other on the edge of the ice. Megan shivered, more with excitement than the cold.

Ben planted the shovel in a mound of snow and motioned Megan to join him.

"Don't we need to put on our skates first?" she crinkled her nose and cocked her head, swaying a few strands of hair that stuck out from under her knitted hat.

"This is how my dad started me out. Boot skating. It's simple and you'll get the feel for slipping and balancing and all that. Come on."

Megan's first cautious step onto the ice was met with a huge grin on Ben's part though she didn't see it. She kept her eyes down, took a few more steps, and looked up.

"Piece of cake," she said. One more step and she slipped backwards. "Ow!"

Ben was at her side immediately with apologies and strong arms. "Are you okay?"

"I guess so." She let him lift her to her feet. "Maybe this isn't such a good idea. I can be pretty clutzy."

"I can't believe you've never skated."

"Oh, I've roller-bladed, but this is so slippery." She leaned into him and let him lead her around the rink.

"Well, if you've roller-skated then you probably have the balancing skill already. It'll just be the slipping and sliding that you'll have to master." He began his instructions, reaching back into his happy memories to teach her little tricks he'd learned. When he thought she was ready they returned to the bench and put on their skates.

Ben knelt down in front of her to lace her skates as tight as possible. "They're a little big, aren't they? We should have brought extra socks."

"They'll be fine," Megan smiled. She held her arms out like a child waiting to be lifted up and Ben offered a strong and steady arm.

She caught on faster than she expected, but she never let go of Ben. From clutching his arm to holding his hand to letting him push her with both of his hands on her waist, they soon found the small area he had cleared was too cramped. He encouraged her to keep practicing while he shoveled off a larger area. Neither of them noticed Cori when she tromped down the middle of the street on her way to town.

Emily was still on the floor, her back to the window, when she heard the chimes. It took a moment for her to realize that the ringing was the front doorbell. Someone must have trudged up the sidewalk. Kids, most likely, wanting to earn some money by shoveling porches and driveways.

The bell rang again followed by insistent knocking. Not kids.

Cori was probably going to ignore it and Chuck, well, Chuck wasn't going to get out of bed today.

Three more knocks.

It was up to Emily to go to the door. She tried to control her steps down to the living room, swayed and leaned and almost bent over double before she reached the front door.

She could see the back of a brown hat through the window. And then the lady turned.

And saw Emily.

It was the lady from the store, the one who gave her the card, the lady that Megan knew. Emily suffered two disconcerting emotions before making a deliberate decision.

She opened the door.

"Oh, hello! I recognize you," the lady said. "Do you live here, too? I'm here to talk to Megan. May I come in?"

Emily stepped back and allowed the smiling steam roller of a woman to stomp forth.

"Well, I'm Mrs. Beridon and like I said I'm here to speak with Megan." She pulled her gloves off. "Are you all right, dear?"

Emily inched back further, answered with an ambiguous shake of her head. She strained for an honest word.

"Is Megan here now? I know there's no school so I was sure I could catch her. They didn't call her in to work, did they? That doesn't seem likely." Mrs. Beridon droned on. Her words buzzed out of her mouth like sharp teething grinding on bones, her eyes flitting around corners, seeing through walls.

Emily's slow denial didn't faze Mrs. Beridon. The woman kept speaking, "I have some news for Megan. It's important. Is she here?"

"No. Gone." Emily's elevated gaze fixed on the snow outside the dining room window.

"Oh . . . well, does she have her phone with her? I don't have her number." She started digging through her purse for paper and pen, "Maybe you could tell me her phone number?" She found what she needed and waited for Emily to rattle off the numbers.

Emily put her index finger between her teeth and chewed on a nail. Her sleeve slipped down a tad. She dropped her hand and tucked both fists under her arms. "I . . . don't know her number."

"Hmm. Well, is it written down somewhere?" Mrs. Beridon took an optimistic step forward, looked toward the kitchen.

Emily shook her head with troubled detachment, the corners of her mouth drooped and her eyes remained dispassionate. She saw Mrs. Beridon move toward her, drop her purse and use both hands to hold her up; she heard the subdued tones of reassurances, but they were phrases that meant nothing to her brain. She could not translate the syllables that tumbled from the woman's mouth, yet she knew they were spoken in her own language, not some foreign tongue. But not a single word made sense.

Not a single word. . . but now she felt, for an instant, the strength that squeezed her shoulders. The woman was pulling her and making her stumble toward the living room. She focused on the winter coat, the third button, the four tiny holes, the frayed end of a thread. She was seated now, felt a shaking on her arms, knew her head was bobbing, but she saw nothing. All was black. All was silent.

Mrs. Beridon prayed for help. If only she could remember the girl's name. She rolled her eyes to the ceiling and imagined the name tag clipped to the clerk's shirt. Emily!

"Emily!" She shook her harder. "Emily! Stay with me." She grasped her arms harder and looked around at the dingy green walls, wondered who else lived here. She called out for help, but the hum of the refrigerator was the only answer.

Megan fell into the snow bank laughing. This was the best day of her life. The. Best. Day.

Ben skated away as if he were chasing a puck. He weaved and dodged around imaginary opponents, skated backwards, stopped so sharply he sent flares of ice chips flying, and then raced back to where she sat beaming at him.

He flashed a one-dimpled smile back, tried not give her the full grin, and then twisted himself as he plopped down into the snow next to her.

"Wow," she fawned, "you should play professional hockey."

The full grin escaped. "Yeah, right. I'm not even good enough to make a college team."

"I think you are." She crinkled her nose at him, no longer self-conscious of her freckles. She wished he'd move closer and he did. Pin pricks of exhilaration danced through her body. He was going to kiss her again. Each time today that he kissed her she had willed away the old stabs of fear, evicted them by design, and allowed herself the carefree thrill that erased all thought. Each time the kisses had multiplied, the brief interludes had lengthened, and the excitement had added to the glorious day.

He kissed her.

Time stopped again. His touch warmed her, spiked her erratic pulse, and melted her fears. His lips brushed hers with no more insistence than a feather and yet there was a restless pleasure that electrified her and stirred more than one emotion. The cold silence framed them in a motionless picture.

Ben pulled back and gave her a toe-tingling smirk.

What? she mouthed. He pulled her into a hug and whispered in her ear. She memorized the unexpected words: *you are the best thing that's ever happened to me*. His breath was like licks of flame on her neck, potent and completely unnerving.

She pulled back and looked in his eyes; one pesky dimple made another brief appearance. She was completely smitten. She realized how much she cared what he thought, how important he had become to her, and how much what he had said meant. She stared into his eyes and wondered if he could see to the very depths of her soul, too.

She whispered back the same phrase, he was the best thing in her life, too, and then shivered at the realization that she had so quickly and easily put him above Simon.

"Are you cold?" Ben wrapped his arms around her. "Maybe we should skate some more. Come on, one more time. You're getting really good at this."

Chuck pushed himself up from the mattress when he heard the doorbell. The chimes were at the top of the steps; he heard them clearly. His stomach roiled; he stretched back out until the bell chimed again. Unrelenting knocking followed.

Get that, Adam, will ya? It's not for me, buddy, you get it.

Chuck shook himself, swallowed hard, and left his chilly room. He climbed the stairs, heard a woman's voice ask about Megan. Heard Emily give a couple of one word answers. He paused at the top of the stairs.

Then . . . what? Is that a scuffle? Adam, what should I do? Where are the guns?

He crept through the kitchen. Heard the woman call out for help. What was she doing to Emily? Why was Emily so quiet?

Take that knife, Chuck. There, on the counter. Use that knife.

Chuck picked it up without a sound, bent low and crawled to the hallway. He held the knife to his face, saw his eye reflected back flat and colorless, turned the knife over and saw Adam's silvery eye. He winked. He put the knife at an angle near the floor and out into the hallway. The tiny reflection revealed the scene in part. A large woman, hat and coat still on, was seated on the couch, her back towards him.

He pulled the knife back and stuck his head around the corner. He spotted Emily seized in the woman's clutches. The walls and the windows huddled around them.

Words. Strange words. Was the woman swearing at Emily? What lord? Whose lord? Devils? Demons? Soul-whores?

He ran his finger along the blade, grasped the knife's handle in his fist, raised it up, and swept it back in an arc. Still low to the floor he fixed his attention on a pile of crumbs that trailed from old linoleum to dirty carpet.

Attack her, you fool! She's hurting Emily. Don't listen to her words. She speaks nonsense. Don't listen! Chuck, Adam, one of you stand up and get her out of here.

The things that woman was saying! *That* name! She said *that* name! My *God*!

Chuck put his fists to his ears, the sharp end of the knife pointing heavenward.

Resist. We must resist.

"You're doing great, Meg," Ben called out. He was skating backwards in front of her, swerving left and right, ready to catch her if she hit a rough patch again. She'd never make the Olympics in a million years, he laughed to himself, but she showed determination and grit. She didn't whine once about all the spills she had taken the first hour. She had improved dramatically as soon as some kids had shown up to skate. Now they shared the shoveled area with a couple of them while another one was borrowing Ben's shovel to make a spider's web path for a game of tag. Meg wasn't ready for that, but he suspected she would stubbornly want to try it.

"Getting tired yet?" He slowed and let her glide into his chest. As soon as he had her in his arms those predictable heart-stopping rockets went off in his chest. He leaned in and kissed her forehead. He controlled their balance as they coasted to a stop.

"Yeah. I think my ankles are going to break." She tilted her face upwards. Her action was obvious and he brushed her mouth with his lips and would have kept on kissing her if a pair of young voices hadn't started in with high-pitched mocking.

"We have an audience," Megan grinned. "I liked this place better when we had it to ourselves. And now look," she pointed over his shoulder to where a group of middle schoolers were heading their way.

"You want to go into town and get something to eat?"

"Sure, but I didn't bring any money."

"Not a problem." Ben patted his pocket. "Hey," he yelled to the kid with his shovel, "I'll be back for that in half an hour. Okay?"

He helped Megan to the bench where they changed back into their boots. He laced the skates together, flung them over his shoulder, and grabbed Megan's hand.

"So," he said, "we can walk and talk and figure out our problems."

"What problems?" Megan began, "Oh, yeah . . . I forgot. *Those* problems." He didn't need to analyze the flat note in her voice.

"So . . . of the three of them, Cori, Chuck, and Emily, which one do you think needs the most help or needs help the soonest?"

Megan mulled it over as they came to a partially shoveled sidewalk. "Well, as far as dangerous goes . . . I can't decide. Emily attacks *herself*. Chuck attacked *me*. And Cori, well, what she did to that fat guy was positively unbelievable." She stretched out the last couple of words with weighted meaning. "Have you ever seen anything like that?"

Ben shook his head. "I gotta believe it's what magicians do when they create those illusions on stage. There's some higher power or energy or something that can be controlled with brain waves."

"Do you really believe that?" Megan cocked her head his way, watched him give a noncommittal shrug, and continued, "Because I know what I saw, and . . . I keep thinking of Mrs. Beridon's card and the phrase 'demon-possession'. If someone like her believes that's possible, then . . . I don't know, I guess it's possible."

"Hmm," Ben said, "so you think Cori is possessed?"

It was an effort to affirm such a crazy assumption, especially in the middle of a bright, white day, but Megan nodded. "Yeah, maybe. And Chuck and Emily, too. I mean, think about it, Chuck goes into trances and talks in two voices and . . . honest, Ben, he walked on the ceiling and attacked me."

"I believe you." He squeezed her hand. They stopped at the corner before crossing and Ben added, "Maybe demon possession mimics the symptoms of other things, like schizophrenia."

"Yeah, or epilepsy."

"Right."

They came to the alley behind the stores and followed some tracks to the back entrance of a coffee shop. Ben held the door for Megan and they stomped their boots on the inside rug.

The room buzzed and the atmosphere was sharp and pungent with tension as Mrs. Beridon called forth every phrase that had worked for her before. She commanded authority. She pronounced her words with conviction to rule over the demon. She trusted that she was in the right place at the right time to do exactly what she was doing. Emily convulsed. The hefty woman fought to capture Emily's flailing arms and arrest her spasms.

She knew the only thing that would work and it wasn't holy water or consecrated oil. She wouldn't recite any incantations or touch her with a silver cross or yell jumbled up ecstatic words of nonsense. There was only one name to which these demons responded and only if the speaker had the proper belief, authority, and faith. Carla Beridon did.

She spoke the command and prayed.

Emily was burning up. Her body was a fiery furnace, each cut in her arms and thighs a blazing flame. Her stomach was far from settled, she ached in every joint and her bones vibrated with a dreadful weariness from head to foot. A slower burn began to scorch her thoughts.

What is that woman saying?

There was an air of expectancy flavored with dread, but not her own. She, Emily, was hopeful. But the terrified pleas sent shivers up her own spine the instant she realized that the voice in her throat was of another world.

She forced her eyes open and saw nothing but the dull green walls. Then slowly, with a gradual and unhurried recovery, she could see the furniture, the windows, the ceiling, and finally the woman.

She heard the woman speak the sacred name, command the demon to depart, then bow her head in prayer.

With a sudden and bewildering jolt her own mouth screeched out a torrent of blasphemous curses more profane and wicked than anything Emily knew. But before the awful echo reached her ears the memory of it ceased. She was clean.

The blistering fever was gone.

Resist. We must resist. Chuck rose with the knife cold in his hand. No, close your ears. Do not listen. Run. Go upstairs.

The unsettling dissonance of Emily's shriek gave him time to dart through the hall, grab the banister, and pull himself up the narrow staircase. He made no sound. He moved as the breath of hell.

There. Safe. She was not speaking to us. The name means nothing. Do not listen.

Chuck entered Cori's room just as he heard the name again. It seared his ears with an intolerable off-pitch resonance, wrecked his balance, and cast him to the floor.

Get up. Get up. The devil and his children walk with earthly feet.

Get away! Climb. Hide.

He clambered up the ladder and scrambled across the attic boards.

Use your claws! To the hatch. Slide away. Away.

Chapter 18

Megan nibbled at the impossibly sweet dessert that Ben had bought her; a drizzle of hot chocolate syrup over the brownie satisfied her need for something warm. He had coaxed her out of the inexpensive hot chocolate, the traditional after-skating drink she expected, and persuaded her to try this pricey item as soon as they finished their hamburgers. Meanwhile he sipped on a frozen Coke. She teased him for ordering the icy drink on a 'snow day' no less.

"Come on, take a taste," she tempted. "It's so good."

"It's more fun watching you enjoy it. Do you know that you hum at the beginning and end of each bite?"

"I do?"

"Yeah, it's cute."

They smiled at each other. It was time to get back to serious business. They had talked about skating while they waited for the waitress to bring them their order. Neither one was anxious to talk about demons as they related to Cori, Emily, or Chuck, but they had to.

"So, tell me about Chuck. Where are his parents?"

"Believe it or not, they only live a couple of blocks away. I think he does the same thing I do, lives in both houses off and on. I offered him a place to stay last fall because his folks kicked him out when he went kind of berserk on them."

"Were you guys friends?"

"Uh, not in a long time, but I knew them, Chuck and Adam, in elementary school. They weren't totally identical, by the way, you could tell them apart." He took a sip and moved his feet, putting them snug against Megan's.

"And does he go to the doctor for his, um, schizophrenia?"

"Oh, yeah, like once a month. He was institutionalized for a while, but I guess their insurance only covered so much and they had to let him out. Then he did some weird stuff that got him put in the alternative school. They can handle behavior problems better there, I guess."

"Maybe, um," Megan held a forkful aloft as she formulated her thought, "maybe the demons can mimic the symptoms of schizophrenia just enough to fool the doctors . . . or . . . maybe they can get into people who have mental problems to begin with. You know, because they're open to it." She took a bite, but didn't hum as she waited for Ben's response.

"That makes sense. And Emily was open to it because she's so sad and depressed and Cori is open to it because she uses drugs." He started to crack his knuckles then stopped when his phone rang. He checked the short text message. "Crap."

"What?"

"Oh, nothing, just a pick-up game I missed." He finished texting back and looked at her. "But I had better things to do."

He reached across the table and placed his hand palm side up next to hers and Megan slipped her left hand into his. Her heart did a little flip-flop.

"So," she said, "are we solving the problems?"

"Well, we're figuring them out."

"I wonder if they each have their own demon or if it's the same one and it makes each of them act different." She finished the dessert and added, "Maybe it *is* a ghost, the ghost of that murderer, Bobby Joe Kinton, who killed his mother and sister. That's what the Ouija board said."

"When?"

"When we were in Cori's room . . ." Megan frowned. "Oh, I forgot. When I asked the board if it was the ghost of Bobby Joe . . . that pointer thingy moved to the yes. And I said that would explain Emily's nightmares and why Chuck walked on the ceiling and how Cori could levitate things. And you know what she said? She said she saw *me* floating in the middle of my room when I was asleep."

Ben squeezed her hand, made her look at him, "It's not a ghost."

"I didn't believe in them before this week, but now I'm not so sure. Maybe I'm possessed, too."

He flickered a doubting smile and shook his head. "What about that lady, your social worker? She doesn't have ghost-buster on her card, but she does have demon possession listed. I, uh, I talked to my mom a little bit and I . . . I think we need to look it up in the Bible."

Megan almost let go of his hand. "That kind of shocks me. I didn't expect you to say that, but, huh, we can do a search on the internet a lot easier than flipping through ten thousand flimsy pages."

"Sounds like a plan."

"You know," this time she did pull her hand out of his, took her napkin and wiped her mouth, "I thought from the first that there was something odd about that house, but if the others moved in after their problems started, then it's not the house. I can see how they have some sort of mental problems going on, but what about me? My problem is a legal one."

Ben shrugged. "Demons are contagious?" It was easier to make a joke.

There were two demons tormenting Chuck as he slid down the chute. They closed his ears, blinded his eyes, and stilled his vocal cords. They filled his thoughts with ridicule, contempt, and hatred. Their rage seethed with a pounding frenzy that held no relief for him until he hit the floor in his room and crumpled to a mental oblivion. The void and nothingness of his stupor lasted only a few minutes and then he awoke to a headache so agonizing that he crawled to the mattress on his hands and knees.

No one shared guardianship of his movements, not even Adam.

Emily felt the lightness more as a physical buoyancy than anything else. Before today she would have cringed at the unbearable shame of having this stranger, this nice lady, witness her breakdown. She would have needed to ease the mortification with a razor, but the lady was holding her hands, her head bowed, her words mumbled yet clear and Emily's weightlessness was a joy.

"How do you feel, Emily?" Mrs. Beridon released her hands but held her gaze.

"Fine, thank you."

"You were having a terrible episode. I don't want to scare you, but this sort of thing is going to happen again. I can help you. Do you still have my card?"

Emily nodded.

"Good. We need to set up some appointments. This is going to be tough, but we can win." She touched Emily's sleeve. "May I look?" At Emily's nod Mrs. Beridon gently lifted the fabric and revealed several scars.

Emily looked, too. They were almost healed. She watched Mrs. Beridon's fingers trace a tickling line. She wanted to giggle. She felt elated, full of a happiness she hadn't felt in ages.

"You don't need to do this, Emily. You don't need to punish yourself for *anything*. Not ever. Okay? Do you understand? Think of it this way," she let go of the sleeve, "everything bad that you've ever done or ever will do has *already* been punished."

As they came out the back door of the café Ben smiled at Megan's complaint of feeling too full to try ice skating again.

"Didn't you have fun?" He looked around the alley and dropped the skates onto a ledge of snow as she answered.

"Yeah, I did, but it couldn't have been much fun for you . . . having to hold me up so much."

He took a final quick look around and blocked her way. He wrapped his arms around her and said, "It was the most fun I've ever had on ice. Especially the part where we did this." He leaned forward and pressed a kiss to her lips, a tender kiss that wrapped around both their souls and made their talk of demons seem like nonsense. Nothing was real except this sweet moment.

Cori pounded on Jason's door until she saw him come from the back room. He waved her off and turned away. She pounded all the harder.

"Give me my stuff!" she yelled. She wasn't leaving until she got what she came for.

Jason stomped to the door and twisted the deadbolt. He threw the door open to a gust of wintry air and stepped outside wearing nothing more than a rock band tee shirt.

"Get the hell away from here."

"I want my stuff now!"

He glared at her, waiting to see if she'd whirl him around in public with her magical powers. When she didn't, he huffed out a heavy sigh. "All right. It's inside – stay out here."

Cori ignored his order and pushed in behind him. "Don't worry, Jason, I'm not gonna hurt you. You're an idiot and I take pity on idiots." She sneered at him when he glanced back.

He found the bag where he left it and lobbed it at her feet. Several things plunked out including the ancient book on exorcism.

He squinted his eyes at her. "That's it, isn't it? You've been reading about this stuff and got yourself possessed. It's dangerous stuff, Cori, all that fortune telling crap . . ."

"Fortune telling? Yeah, right. In five seconds your phone is going to ring. Five, four, three, two, one."

Jason's cell jingled in his pocket. They both let the interruption stun them into a wide-eyed union. "So . . . who is it?" Jason pulled the phone out and waited while it rang two more times.

"I don't . . . uh, it's a woman . . . wanting to cancel an appointment."

Jason flipped the phone open and answered with doubt and suspicion in his voice.

"I can't stay any longer," Mrs. Beridon said. She gave Emily a generous hug and reminded her to call her soon. "Oh, I almost forgot the reason I came here." She got her pencil and paper out again and wrote a message for Megan. "Here. Please give this to Megan. It's extremely important that she read this today."

She folded the paper once and handed it to Emily who only nodded.

Mrs. Beridon gave her a parting smile and rushed out.

Emily watched the vehicle slog away. The overjoyed happiness of a moment ago was dissipating in chunks now. The depressed and forlorn puppy dog look returned to her colorless face, but there was no one to see it. She unfolded the note and read: *Megan, the judge is ruling tomorrow. You must be there. I'll pick you up here at 8:15. Don't go to school. Mrs. B.*

Emily refolded the note and set it on the dining room table, next to Megan's books. Then she opened one of the books and stuck the note inside. She thought about her action, felt the old guilt wheezing back into her chest. Mrs. Beridon had directed her to see that Megan got this very important note. Megan must see the judge tomorrow. She must show up or . . . maybe Megan would be sent away . . .

She pulled the note back out of the book. A thought flashed across her mind, a need to cut herself, but just as quickly it died. She wasn't going to hide the note; she was going to hand deliver this very important message. She tucked it in her back pocket.

Megan agreed to try to skate some more. After all, it was a snow day; the little bit of homework she hadn't done yesterday could easily be knocked off when they got back. She'd have plenty of time before work. She wanted to enjoy this special afternoon with Ben, but when they reached the rink it was crowded with skaters.

"I think I'd be a hazard to the others," she said.

Ben laughed. "No you wouldn't, but we can come back tonight and have it to ourselves again. If you want to, that is."

"I have to work."

"I know, I mean after work. There won't be any kids here then for sure and we can work on your stops."

"Won't it be too dark?" Her heart danced at the thought of spending more time with Ben.

"Nope. See that street lamp over there? There'll be plenty of light and if there isn't . . . you can hang on to me all you want."

That sounded more than great to her. "Okay. Guess I'll spend the rest of the afternoon doing homework then."

"What, you want to go home already? I thought we could help those little kids over there build their snowmen."

Megan snorted a laugh. "You want to know something else I've never done?"

"You're kidding. You've never built a snowman? How long have you lived in Michigan?"

"I'm kidding," she gave him a little shove that underscored her laugh.

"Come on, babe, I'm sorry. I didn't mean it when I said you were fired. Come on, let's make up." He moved closer, still unsure of Cori's reaction, until he was an arm's length away. "Babe? You're so special."

He was unsure if the look on Cori's face meant she was ready to relent or not. He inched even closer, puckered his lips and raised his eyebrows.

Cori thawed. "I'm sorry, too. I didn't mean to let it get so out of hand, twirling you around like that. I was just so mad that someone had been in my room." She stepped into his arms for a reconciliation that would blossom into something else later, he was sure. With her new abilities she should have a bedroom potential beyond hot. He felt himself growing restless at the thought.

Cori stepped out of his embrace and tilted her head. "So, what do you think of my new talent to tell the future?"

Jason tapped his tongue stud on his teeth. "Awesome. How long have you been able to do that?"

"About one minute."

He pulled her back into his arms. "What do you see in our future? Like in the next hour or so?" He ran his tongue along her neck.

Cori stiffened. "I see the police coming in here." She shook herself away from him. "Really, I do." She bent down and stuffed the items back into the bag and slung it over her shoulder. "I'll bring your shirt back later. I really feel like I need to get out of here now." She pushed on the door and turned back to ask, "Am I rehired?"

Jason nodded. "Be on time."

Cori's quick laugh was baffling. He watched her look left then head right, the opposite direction he expected. A couple of cars slowed for the traffic light and then a police car pulled up right in front of his store.

Cori saw the cop car coming and changed her intended direction. She went up the street and turned the corner. After a few seconds, when the cruiser didn't go through the intersection, she peeked back and saw it parked in front of Jason's store. She had a pretty good idea of what was happening in there now and it looked like she wouldn't have a job after all. What was she going to do for money now?

Her eye caught the glittering sparkle of jewels in the display window across the street. It was the store that sold estate sale finds and antique jewelry as well as the modern stuff.

She already knew what they were going to offer her. This fortune telling power was, like Jason said, awesome. Next she'd have to buy a lottery ticket . . . though she'd have to wait to redeem it on her eighteenth birthday. She could see the power ball numbers now.

She stayed frozen to the sidewalk a moment and sorted through all the thoughts that came to her, separating the fantasies from the clairvoyant insights. She had seen ads for psychics. Wow, she could have her own five dollar a minute phone line. Awesome. Who needed Jason anyway? She had thought they clicked, but now she foresaw that he wasn't right for her at all.

Emily finished her homework after lunch and sat staring at the snow outside the dining room. A pair of animated figures came into her view down the street. Ben and Megan. Ben and Megan holding hands. Ben and Megan, faces red from the cold. Faces smiling. Eyes seeing only each other.

Emily looked down, closed her eyes. Prayed to a new god.

Let the jealousy go.

Cut yourself.

No, I'm not going to do that anymore.

She took the note out of her back pocket, opened it, and read it again as the two figures came up the driveway. Megan *must* be there tomorrow. She must *not* go to school.

"Hey, Em." She heard Ben's voice.

"Hi, Emily." Megan remembered to use her full name. Only Ben could use the shortened version. Only Ben.

She sat still, considered looking up to greet them, too, but didn't.

"You okay, Em?"

She nodded.

"There were tracks on the front porch. Was somebody here?"

Her shoulders lifted of their own accord. Her body was lying to Ben. Sorry Ben.

"Hey," Ben waited for her to look up, "I got you some boots. They were my mom's and they should fit you all right."

"Thanks." A present. He thought of her. That was something.

Ben went on, "You should have seen Megan learn to skate. She's a natural." He kept talking, looking at Megan.

His Meg. Praising her.

Touching her hand.

Using all those glowing adjectives to ramble on and on with nauseating accolades.

Now Megan was talking. Saying how great a skater Ben was.

They kept standing there, above her, looking down on her. She was small. She was shrinking. They wouldn't pay attention to her much longer. She had the note in her hand and it was going to disappear with her.

But Megan *had* to be in court. The *judge* was ruling tomorrow.

Now Ben and Megan were heading through the kitchen to the den, talking about getting on the internet, searching out something.

Emily stuffed her textbook in her satchel, rose, and followed them to the den.

She stood in the hallway and held the note out. Take it, Megan, take it now. It's important. But Megan kept her eyes shut. Ben's were closed, too. They were standing in front of the computer, waiting for it to boot up as they passed the time so intimately.

Emily dropped the note into her bag. Held out the razor instead and entered the den, noting how the walls leaned in and the ceiling poised itself to tap her on the head.

She cleared her throat. "I have something for you, Megan," she said. She watched them break apart.

Megan held out her hand and accepted the razor. She clucked and fussed like a mother hen and commended Emily for making a brave choice.

Emily could not smile back.

Chapter 19

As soon as she was sure that Emily was upstairs and out of earshot Megan stunned Ben with the facts of Emily's self-mutilation.

"What? She's *still* cutting herself?" His disbelief spread across his face to flatten the hollows of his cheeks.

"It's bad. Really bad. She has cuts all up and down her arms and now she's cutting her thighs."

"I knew she was upset about not finding her mom and brother, but after she blamed Cori for the cuts I thought she'd stop." He sat down in the computer chair and Megan pulled up the other chair. "Why is she cutting her legs?" he asked.

"I don't know. Jealousy?" She raised her eyebrows high then pursed her lips.

Ben rested his elbow on the desk and put his head in his hand. "She's gonna need therapy and medical attention right away, isn't she?"

Megan nodded. "How are we gonna pay for it?"

Ben lifted his head. "We? It's not your problem, Meg. I'll figure out something."

"I want to help. Besides, it's not like we can float a loan from Mrs. Kremer." She gave a short laugh.

Ben put his fingers on the keyboard and typed in a website. Megan fixed her attention on the screen with a puzzled look.

"What's with the baseball cards?"

"Look at these values," Ben said, "they're anywhere from a couple of bucks to hundreds of dollars, a few are over a thousand dollars."

"So?"

"So I have two plastic bins in the trunk of my car full of thousands of these cards. My dad and grandpa were collectors. Whatever it costs to get Emily some help . . . well, I just have to put some cards up for auction on eBay and I'll have the money in a week."

Megan's admiration for Ben doubled. "Why would you do that?"

He waved off her astonishment. "Because she doesn't have anyone else."

Megan threw her arms around his neck and whispered in his ear, "You are the best."

Chuck set the knife down on the counter still wondering why he had been sleeping with it in his hand. His stomach woke him with growls that begged for food. He couldn't remember when he had his last meal. His headache was gone, but there was a fuzzy feeling in his brain like he was forgetting something important.

He stood by the refrigerator and stared at the door handle. He wanted to open it, hoped there were eggs and bacon on the top shelf, afraid there wasn't. He held his fingers an inch away, listened to the voices.

Interesting. Baseball cards. Plastic bins.

Did you hear that, Adam? Those plastic bins you saw Ben get from the freezer are full of baseball cards. Are you listening, Adam? Remember? It was early Sunday morning. You followed him upstairs, watched from the window. He put them in the trunk of his car.

Thousands.

Adam? Do the math. He must have twenty or thirty thousand dollars worth of cards in his car. Maybe more.

Cool.

Cori marched in the house hauling a bag that was bundled into a square under her arm. She took a moment to wipe her boots on the rug, but left them on.

"What're *you* lookin' at?" She whipped past Chuck leaving wet smudges on the floor.

Chuck stuttered, finally choked out an offer of bacon and eggs, but Cori was already in the next room.

"Well, well, the lovebirds are all cozied up in the den." She stood behind their chairs and opened the bag. "Megan, will you . . . please . . . look some stuff up for me?" She played on the little bit of camaraderie they had shared the night before.

"Uh, sure, what do you need?" Megan cocked her head at Ben as Cori pulled out the dusty Exorcism tome. Nothing else was in the bag. "Can you look up what this is worth? It's really old."

Megan took the book and opened it on her knees. "Is this from the attic?" When Cori wouldn't nod Megan went on, "It is, isn't it? It's not yours to sell, Cori. It belongs to the owner of the house." She glanced at Ben. "Whoever that is."

Ben grinned back. "I say 'finders, keepers'. If there's stuff up there of value like books, jewelry, art, whatever, then we can use that money for Emily."

"Emily?" Cori barked, "Why should she get the money? She's got a job. I don't."

"You lost your job?"

"Let's just say Jason's tattoo parlor might be closed for a while." Shc sneered. "Anyway, what's with Emily?"

"Shh, keep your voice down. We were just talking about her and all the strange stuff going on. Like you levitating people and Emily cutting herself," she gestured toward the computer screen, "and we're looking up stuff in the Bible about demon-possession because that seems to be what's going on here."

Cori scoffed at them. "The Bible? Really?" A strange look replaced the scorn on her face, she crumbled the bag in her hands. "That's full of prophecies, right? Well, you can add prophesying to my talents because now I can predict the future."

"What?" both Ben and Megan said together.

Cori tossed the bag in the corner and turned. "I just remembered something," she said over her shoulder, "I'll be right back."

Chuck walked on numb feet toward the den as soon as Cori went upstairs. His face was chalky white, his jaw slack. It took tremendous effort to walk all the way into the den and speak to Ben while ignoring the book in Megan's lap and the scriptures on the computer screen.

"Help me, too," he breathed. The color drained from his face, his cheekbones were sunken, his eyes dead. He took a step back.

"Sure, buddy," Ben answered.

Cori searched through the pockets of the clothes she had worn the first time she went into the attic. The wedding ring and the packaged pin were stuffed in the deep pocket. When Ben had mentioned jewelry and art she thought of these and didn't want to forget them. Finders, keepers. That's what Ben said. She didn't have a smidgen of guilt for selling the other things in town today; these would be next.

She hurried up the ladder and wrestled a few of the closer boxes down through the opening and hid them under her bed. She'd check them later for valuables. She thought maybe Ben would ask to go up in the attic today – she couldn't exactly foresee it though. But she did could predict that he wasn't going to find anything of worth.

She left her room and headed to the bathroom, then went instead to Emily's room, drawn there by the sniffling and sniveling she heard.

Cori was gruff as she pushed open the door. "What's your problem? Why all the tears all the time?" She stared at Emily, trying to get a read on her future, but saw nothing.

Emily sobbed out an angry response that included profanities Cori never expected to hear coming from Emily's mouth.

"Yeah, girl. That's the spirit. Get angry." Her attempt at levity was ineffective in raising a smile. She fixed her eyes on the pile of shredded paper that littered Emily's blanket nest. "What were you tearing up?"

Emily kept her head low, but looked out from under half shrouded lids. There was something ominous in her sudden calm. The small room filled with expectation and alarm.

Cori could see it form between them, an empty, hollow shape at first, and then a blackened corpse. It moved. It writhed in pain, gnashing its teeth and wailing soundlessly, moving charred limbs as if trying to free itself of tethers and chains. She wanted to scream, could see Emily's mouth wide and neck thrown back, but neither girl could force out a beckoning squeal. Even if they found their speech, who would they call? Who could save them?

Then Cori heard the screams, not just one voice, and not Emily's, but a cacophony of dissonant groans and grunts and howls and keening screeches. As if there were a million mouths agonizing a painful sorrow of eternal torture. As if they were being burned alive. As if their skin was being peeled away in careless ribbons.

As if they had seen glory once, but had no hope of salvation.

No deliverance.

No rescue.

No escape.

Emily awoke to a suffocating silence. Cori's body was stretched across her room, her left hand close to Emily's nest, reaching out. Not quite touching the blanket. Asleep.

The tiny strips of Mrs. Beridon's note were blown away, scattered throughout the room. Only two pieces were left in her lap, the simple words a message: *the judge . . . here.*

"I'm sorry, Cori," Emily touched the hand that was close. "I'm sorry. Wake up." She spoke softly as Cori raised her head, "You had one of my nightmares. I'm sorry. Really."

She twitched back as Cori exploded to her feet. She stood in front of Emily for a moment, opened her mouth to speak, then held her hands out as if to levitate the entire nest.

But nothing happened.

Emily spoke again. "Sorry. The memory will fade. It's fading already, isn't it?"

On an afternoon break Mrs. Beridon gave a quick call to one of her team members. Her guilt had mushroomed throughout the day as she thought about how fast she had left poor little Emily after her awful incident of violent shaking and cursing. She wanted to return, but her friend's advice was to wait until Emily reached out to her.

She wondered if Megan was part of the bigger plan to help Emily somehow, or maybe Emily would be the catalyst to get Megan to move back to her parents'. Things always worked out in strange and unexpected ways. She couldn't worry too much about it. Mrs. Beridon and her friend prayed together over the phone.

Megan observed Chuck as he held a patchy conversation with Ben. Her reaction to being this close to him surprised her. Perhaps it was Ben's presence that blocked any apprehension; maybe it was Chuck's harmless demeanor that eased her nervousness. His eyes were like chunks of lifeless coal, empty, yet full of despair. His face had acne scars she had ignored before, but now the paleness of his skin drew her attention to the spotty marks.

He wanted something.

Megan's thoughts wandered, she and Chuck weren't much different. They both were kicked out by their parents, then helped by Ben. But Chuck was sick, very sick. She had to forgive him for his attack on her.

He pitched back another step, then forward as Ben persuaded him to talk. The back and forth became a soothing rocking motion that lulled Megan's senses.

Yes, she could forgive him. Chuck was tall and lean, but his attitude and slumped stance totally erased the terror he had manifested the night he attacked her.

Still, there was something vaguely intimidating about him. She couldn't quite identify it, couldn't name the suspicion. There was just an inkling of . . . something.

The perception that he was shrinking as he walked away bothered her more.

"Where were we?" Ben smiled at Megan. "We keep getting interrupted. Do you think if I close the door they'll all leave us alone?"

"I don't think a closed door would stop Cori. She said she'd be right back."

"Obviously that was a lie." He scrolled through the page on the screen. "I'll check this while you go through that book. Let me know if there are any words you want me to look up."

"Okay. It looks like it's all in Latin and the writing is that old fancy stuff like calligraphy, but . . . oh, hey, here's something interesting."

Ben turned away from the online Bible and peered at the page Megan held open.

"I think I recognize some of these words. 'Remedia' would be remedy and 'daemones' looks like demons," Megan said.

Ben took the book, ran his finger down the page, turned to the next page, and scanned for any other familiar words. "Too complicated for me," he said. "Are you sure it's Latin?" He handed it back.

"Pretty sure. I'm in Spanish, you know, and my teacher said English and French and Spanish have their roots in Latin. I'm guessing that word is 'against' and don't these look like 'communion', 'medicine', and 'theology'?"

"Uh huh, but it'll take forever to look it all up. What's the title again?" Ben copied *Manuale Exorcismorum* into a new window and waited a second for the results. "Looks like you can get a scanned copy of this for around forty dollars. That should mean the actual book is worth more. Hope that satisfies Cori."

They were quiet for several minutes as Megan flipped through more pages and Ben searched online for Bible references to exorcism.

"Well," he finally said, "we've been dabbling in some risky behaviors, so to speak."

"Huh?"

"Ouija boards are a no-no according to this site. This guy says it's a gateway into the occult."

"I believe it."

"Also we should stay away from tarot cards and pornography and recreational drugs."

"I can do that." Megan gave a little snorty laugh. She looked up from her book. "What about kissing?"

Ben smiled back and leaned over. "Uh, that's a yes-yes."

A few moments later they broke apart and Megan asked, "Sounds like you found out how not to get possessed, but what about exorcism?"

"Oh," Ben straightened up, "must be some big church secret or else it's so simple I'm missing it. In the Bible stories Jesus just says 'come out' and the demon obeys. We could try that with . . ." he nodded his head toward the door, ". . . all of them."

"Come out? That's it?"

Cori stared at her face in the bathroom mirror. She removed each piercing on her nose and her eyebrow and the seven in her ears. She scrubbed every trace of makeup off her skin. She stared again. Who did she look like? Was that resemblance to her older sisters still there? Was that her mother's nose? Eyes?

She brushed her hair back into a ponytail and concentrated on each feature. Why was she trying to be so different? When had she become so angry?

She focused on her forehead, seeking a way to see into her own mind, but only succeeding in startling herself as her vision blurred her features into a bony skeletal mask.

Tears sprang to her eyes. What did she need to do? There was something . . . something pressing her to a decision . . . but . . .

When had she set her dreams aside? Why was everything so futile? Everything . . . pointless.

She compared herself to pretty Megan, then remembered that Megan was trying to get custody of her baby. What was his name? Simon? Well, she was better off than Megan. She wouldn't want to be in her shoes.

And Emily. She had seen her semester report card – perfect grades. Nice, but she wouldn't want to be that unhappy little mouse either.

What *did* she want? She couldn't put it into words, but there was a deep and profound longing for . . . *God, what is it!?*

Is it You?

"Well," Megan set the book down, "I guess Cori isn't coming back. And I've got to get to work." She smiled at Ben, was paid back in a pair of dimples. "This was the best snow day ever. Thanks."

"No problem. I'll drive you to work. And remember, we have a skating date tonight."

"Do you mind if we make that tomorrow night instead? I forgot about some reading I have to do for English class."

Ben stuck his lower lip out in an exaggerated pout. "You don't work on Thursday night?"

"Not this week, not unless they changed the schedule since yesterday, and that's not likely."

"Thursday it is, then."

Thursday

Chapter 20

Megan woke to the same eerie silence in the house that she had felt when she arrived from work last night. Ben had dropped her off at the restaurant and then called her there later to apologize that she'd have to walk home. He was in some sort of trouble, didn't want to explain, and was plainly embarrassed.

Megan had not only used the latch on the stairway door to lock the three girls in, but she, like Emily and Cori, had moved her dresser in front of her bedroom door. There was no conspiratorial plan, no whispered paranoia, no hushed panic. In fact, no one spoke. Megan had reached the top of the stairs and saw Emily's eye at her door. The door closed; the scraping of furniture followed. Then she heard Cori bar her door with something, heard a grunt and the sounds of heavy objects sliding across gritty wood. Had something happened with Chuck while she was at work? A flashing memory of his attack on her sent her scurrying to her room. She latched the door, moved the small dresser against it. There were sounds in the attic, but they were accompanied by Cori's usual curses.

Megan read until late then slept with the light on.

Chuck didn't sleep. He was thinking more clearly than he ever had. The voice in his head was his own. From time to time he asked Adam a question or made a joke, but Adam never answered and Chuck had no one except himself to humor.

He stuffed all of Adam's things up the chute and taped a poster over the hole. He made both beds and leaned the third mattress up against the wall. He sat on the floor with the wastebasket between his legs and meticulously picked up every crumb and scrap and speck of dust that was on the floor.

By morning his room was spit-polish clean, his back sore, his eyes red, and his plan completely in place. They wouldn't see him coming. The guns were loaded, the large bag ready, the field day certificate taped to his chest. He doubled his dose of meds, then stuffed a couple extra pills in his pocket. The tremors in his hands increased, his mouth went dry, the muscles in his legs began to spasm.

Time to go.

Sorry, Ben. You were cool.

Ben woke early, the anger flooding back into every vein in his body as soon as his eyes opened.

He hated Ed. What a jerk he was. Making his mother cry. Grounding Ben. Taking his car keys. Was it any wonder that he had to keep away from that idiot as much as possible?

The worst part was letting down Megan.

He showered quickly, intending to get over to the rooming house as fast as he could. The roads were good today, school was on, he had a skating date tonight. The eager anticipation coated the anger and calmed the agitation. By the time he went to the kitchen he wasn't so upset that he couldn't fake a contrite apology to Ed and beg for the car keys.

"What's wrong with taking the school bus? My taxes pay for that thing. Your driving to school is a waste of gas." Ed slammed around the kitchen looking ready to take Ben on again.

Ben didn't rise to the bait. "You're right. I should take the bus. But . . . I can't. If you haven't been riding it all year they won't let you on. Security, you know. Like I could be a terrorist or something. The bus driver doesn't know who I am." He stood next to the end of the counter, trying to be as small a target as possible. He expected Ed to take a swipe at him again.

Ed poured some milk on his cereal and set the jug down hard enough to make some milk splash out the top.

"Look what you made me do. Get me a paper towel."

"Yes, sir." Ben cleaned the mess up and stood back. "So, uh, I guess you'll have to drive me to school."

Ed gave a definitive shake of his head and dug in his pocket for Ben's keys. "I've got better things to do, you little pissant. Here. I have to check on one of my rentals on Elm this morning."

Ben caught the keys, but held back a gasp. How was he going to pick up the girls if Ed was going to the same street?

Cori was the first of the girls into the kitchen and almost ran into Chuck.

"Your face," he said.

"What about my face?" she tried to scrunch her brow into its usual scorn, knew her clean bare look with her hair pulled back was a naked shock. She hadn't replaced any of her jewelry or painted her nails or applied the masking makeup.

"It's . . . it's beautiful." Chuck's breathy admiration was flattering despite the repulsion Cori couldn't help but feel when she looked at his geeky face. She backed away from his open gaping and tried to think of some way to disparage him.

"I have something for you," Chuck said. His voice grew stronger with an apology and a promise of a gift that she would find later.

"What are you talking about?"

Chuck turned away, grabbed his large bag, and headed out without another word.

"Weirdo," she said to the closing door.

Emily lost her footing on the second to last step and stumbled just as Chuck's banging of the side door shook the house. She lurched into the hallway and hurried to the bathroom when she heard Cori's voice.

Weirdo was right, but weren't they all weird? The one closest to perfection was Ben and even he had his faults.

She finished in the bathroom and opened the door to find Cori looming over her. Her arms were crossed and she looked more like a housemother than a teen, as if she had aged ten years by washing her face. Her aspect had that accusatory look and she wasn't changing her stance. Emily couldn't duck around her. She lowered her eyes and waited.

"Well," Cori pointed her finger at Emily, "were you in there cutting yourself?"

She shook her head.

"It didn't seem like you had enough time. Let me see your arms."

Emily obliged her, mumbled that she had given her razor to Megan.

"And your legs?"

Emily backed up, glanced self-consciously toward the kitchen. If Ben was in there . . .

"Just pull your pajama legs up. The guys aren't here."

Emily conceded. The scars were red, but there were no new cuts.

"All right . . . good." Cori tried to sound compassionate, even gave Emily a pat on the shoulder as she let her pass by. Emily was surprised that she didn't hear the customary derogatory label; it had to be on the tip of Cori's tongue.

She went to the kitchen window and looked out. She had spied from her room and seen no new tracks. Ben hadn't come home. Now there was a snowless outline of where Chuck's car had been and two narrow lanes flattening out a trail to the road, going over a lump at the end of the driveway where the city plow had heaped a ridge.

She ate her breakfast in silence, noticing a newness about Cori. She scrutinized her as surreptitiously as she could. Megan came down dressed and ready. Emily could see Megan's surprise as she inspected Cori's style, but she, like Emily, held her tongue.

Emily had practiced what she wanted to say. She was sure she remembered word for word the note Mrs. Beridon had written. She had only ridden to school with Megan three times, but the oppressive feeling had become too weighty, the back seat too lonely, the jealousy too . . . too absolute. She had to tell her now before they got in the car. Before Megan became Ben's front seat girlfriend.

She opened her mouth to say that Mrs. Beridon was coming, something important was happening today, the judge was ruling.

But Megan spoke first, “So, uh, Ben said he’d be here the usual time to take us to school. He, uh, he had somewhere else to be last night.”

“Hockey?” She knew he stayed away lots of nights. It had to be because of hockey. Where else would he go? That other address? Emily felt a horrendous surge of hate. Apparently he didn’t keep secrets from Megan.

Megan wasn’t answering. A shrug of her lying shoulders was all she gave to Emily. Megan and Ben had a secret, didn’t they?

Emily rinsed her breakfast bowl and lumbered up the stairs to get dressed. The moment to tell Megan had passed. She’d try one more time. Maybe.

The window at the top of the stairs faced the back yard and something caught her eye. It was Ben. He jumped the neighbor’s fence and trudged through the deep snow, heading for the side door. She wasted no time in getting to her room and throwing on jeans and a sweater. She wanted to get back downstairs quickly in order to hear his explanation. Where was his car? Why had he come through the neighbor’s yard?

Ben parked on Birch Street and took a chance on cutting through the neighbor’s driveway and back yard. The chain link fence was an easy climb though he didn’t fly over it as easily as Cori had levitated the fat man. He reached the side door just as his step-father’s car turned the corner. He thanked his lucky stars that the door wasn’t locked and he could glide in before he was spotted.

“Hey! Get down. Everybody get down.” Megan obeyed immediately and left her plastic juice glass to clatter into the sink. Cori started to protest, but Ben grabbed her arm and pulled. “Listen. The car that’s pulling up out front is my step-father’s. He owns this place.” He watched Cori’s pretty blue eyes widen. “I don’t want him to see me. Or us, any of us. Where is Emily?”

“Upstairs,” Megan’s whisper was automatic.

“No, I’m here.” Emily crawled into the kitchen and crouched by the stove, her satchel mashed against her side. “What’s wrong?”

“I don’t have time to explain, but if he comes here we might be in a lot of trouble.” He took a closer look at Cori. “Hey . . . you look . . . you could be . . .” He chuckled, a plan formulating fast. “Cori, do you think you could pretend to be Mrs. Kremer if he comes to the door? The next door neighbors, the Petersons, complained that a bunch of teens are living here unsupervised. You could say they’re mistaken . . . that you’re just watching your niece and nephew or something, you know, and that they have a lot of friends over. Could you do that?”

“What, Ben, you want me to lie?” Cori’s sneer was so much less potent on a clean face. She smiled. “Sure, no problem.”

A brisk knock at the front door was followed with a stuttering of the doorbell.

“My big moment,” Cori said as she rose. If he didn’t believe her performance perhaps she could put him in a rolling coma, like she did to the fat dude.

She took her time and walked slowly to the door. Meanwhile Ben handed the girls their boots and coats. “We’re gonna cut through the back. My car’s on the next street.”

“But Megan can’t go,” Emily whispered.

“Shh,” Ben opened the side door carefully and directed them through as soon as he heard his step-father’s voice. He closed the door with ghostly softness when he heard Cori’s perfectly composed greeting.

Emily played with the strap of her bag all the way to school. She tried . . . she tried to tell Ben that Megan couldn’t go to school. She tried again as soon as they piled into the car. She tapped Megan’s shoulder and murmured the words she needed to hear. At least, she thought she did.

So Ben had a step-father. More lies?

When they got to the parking lot Ben pulled up close to the entryway to drop them off. Try again, one last time.

"Megan . . . you can't go to school today." There, that was part of Mrs. Beridon's message.

And Megan was nodding in agreement. "I know."

She knows. She knows she has to go to court. Of course she would know. That's why she doesn't have her school bag.

"She's right," Megan said as she and Ben watched Emily pull open one of the double doors at the entrance, "I can't go to school without my books. We left so fast . . ."

"Well, maybe it's safe to go back and get it now. We'll only be a few minutes late. I can afford a first hour tardy, can you?"

Megan laughed. "I've been so good this year that I can afford a first hour skip."

"Do you want to go to the Pancake House? I haven't had breakfast."

"Me either." She re-buckled her seatbelt. "Let's go."

It was a piece of cake walking into the school behind the Thursday morning chess club kids. Chuck had remembered weeks ago that those nerds met an hour before school. That knowledge became a small part of his plan, small but important. He wanted to be in place before the hall monitors started roaming, the teachers opened their rooms, and the students flooded the building. He had considered joining the chess club when he first started high school, but then he had . . . changed. The events that got him reassigned to the alternative school were best forgotten, but he would never forget the names and faces of the perpetrators. He was here to even the score.

First stop – an empty locker. He spotted one in the main hallway, but it was too close to the office. The side wings were better locations and he wanted a locker on the first floor. There. Number 413 was missing a padlock. He looked up and down the hallway as he lifted the latch and opened the door. The shelf was empty except for a broken pencil. The two coat hooks were twisted downward. Another glance, he was still alone. He used his body and the door to block the view as he stashed a gun there. Four thirteen. Four thirteen. He had to remember this locker. This spot.

Now, to the boys' bathroom. He found the only stall that locked and left the large bag there, arranged Adam's boots on the floor, removed one gun to hide under his jacket, and crawled out. He stood at the urinals and looked at the stalls. It certainly looked to him like some athlete was sitting there taking a dump. He cursed himself for not thinking of letting off a stink bomb or bringing some rotten eggs. The cackle that left his lips was otherworldly.

Cori closed the front door after her pleasant conversation with Mr. Ed Rose. Nice to meet you. Oh, yes, everything's working fine. There was a sticky doorknob, but my husband fixed it. I'd invite you in, but he just left for work, see the tracks? And I have to finish getting ready, too. Is there a problem? You're not raising the rent already, are you? Teenagers? Well, my sister's kids have been staying here. Did someone complain? The Petersons? Really? I'm so sorry. They must be playing that awful music too loud when they come home from school. I'll talk to them. Yes, you have a nice day, too.

She watched him drive away. That was fun. It was like she was in a play. She felt like doing a little dance now. Her heart rate had elevated, and the rush, the thrill, was just like shoplifting. She had fooled him so completely she should get an Oscar for that performance. It was so lucky that she hadn't put her makeup on yet or her chains and jewelry. Maybe she'd go to school like this and pretend she was a substitute teacher. Maybe something from Mrs. Kremer's closet . . . No. That was stupid.

The scowl returned.

She would just skip school. Strange that Chuck had left so early. Maybe he just went to get donuts or something. Boy, that sounded good.

She tried to concentrate on seeing the future. She definitely couldn't see herself in school today.

An image of that tortured nightmare stopped her cold. The blackened face multiplied into thousands of twisted skulls. Goose bumps pocked her skin, her hands began to shake, and her veins pumped fear along with the ice cold blood of dread.

She clamped her jaw shut, afraid that her screams would bring back Mr. Rose. Her mouth tingled. She *wanted* to scream, *had* to scream.

And then, as quickly and unexpectedly as it had enveloped her, the horrible impression of death left her.

Emily headed to her locker with a sense of relief. She wasn't a total loser. She had meant to tell Megan the message. She should get points for good intentions. But Megan already knew. That must have been the secret that Ben and Megan held between them. Of course. That was all it was. They had left so suddenly. Ben had a car; he would drive her home so Mrs. Beridon could pick her up.

That thing about his step-dad . . . that didn't mean what she thought. She could figure this out. What did it mean? Hmm, well, just like her, Ben had family problems, but instead of being abandoned he was running away from them. Yes, that was simple . . . and so like her own story. They abused him. It was probably mostly his mother's fault. She must have burned him with cigarettes.

Emily closed her locker, checked the time. She didn't want to get to class too soon. She had several minutes to hang out near the stairwell or sit behind the trash cans or . . . what else could Ben's mother have done to him? Maybe she didn't let him eat enough; maybe she gave his food to a younger brother. Or locked him in the closet when he had nightmares.

She passed the vending machines, the little door to the service room, the trash cans . . . something didn't feel right. No, something didn't *smell* right.

She remembered the nightmare she shared with Cori. An image of the stiff, burned body formed right before her eyes. She reached her hand out to the wall to steady herself. She could see the strange, sightless eyes. Two became four became thousands. It was too horrible. She couldn't look away; bony, scorched fingers plucked at her eyes. Look at us.

Look at us. It was nauseating; she hated the memory, hated herself.

And the smell.

It smelled like . . . it smelled like Chuck's bedroom.

The big man grumbled under his breath, cleared his throat, wiped his brow, and settled into the leather chair behind the mahogany desk. The bailiff, his good friend, had left him an iced tea. Even in the winter it was his beverage of choice. It seemed that he was always sweating. The extra hundred pounds of fat that he lugged around accounted for his loss of breath, high blood pressure, and poor health.

He gulped down half of the tea and then consulted his calendar. He read his notes and reviewed all that he had prepared for today's court appointments. He folded his hands and prayed for the wisdom of Solomon, the patience of Job, and the understanding and strength that he would need as he ruled on the child custody case that was first up on this morning's schedule.

He had gone round and round as he looked into all sides of this particular case. He had spent too much time on it. Still, he wasn't sure. He trusted that his instincts would lead him to the correct judicial response once he saw all parties in person. The young mother would most likely win.

Megan and Ben held hands under the table as they sat next to one another in a booth. While they waited for their pancakes they teased and laughed and goofed around. A few pointed stares from some senior citizens dampened their mood and quieted their spirits. It wasn't a good idea to draw attention to themselves since they were skipping school. They lowered their voices and turned serious.

"Can you believe what Cori did for me – pretending to be Mrs. Kremer? I wish I could have heard the whole conversation."

Megan agreed. "I told you she wasn't so bad."

"And she looked incredible. Pretty, actually."

"Hey, hey, don't make a girl jealous."

Ben kissed her cheek. "There's nobody you'd ever have to be jealous of. I just mean that Cori seemed to change pretty drastically. I don't get what happened to make her transform so completely in so short a time."

"Really? Where were you when she was playing puppet master with the bald guy? I think that would make anybody take on a new personality."

"Yeah, right."

"And look at us. This," she pointed her finger at him and then herself, "is pretty fast."

He gave her another chaste kiss. "I can't seem to get my head around all this . . . this paranormal stuff, though. There's got to be an explanation for everything."

Megan thought of all the changes she had gone through. Having a baby grow inside you was mind-boggling. Giving birth was unbelievable. But seeing that man float like magic had to be the most inexplicable thing ever. And the Ouija board was scary.

"What do think of Cori's claim that she can see the future?"

"I don't know. I wish I could see the future."

"Me, too."

"Is there something in particular you want to know?" He squeezed her hand.

"Well," she knew she wasn't going to say what he hoped to hear, "I'd like to know what the judge is going to rule . . . in my custody case. I'd like to know if I moved back with my parents if it would all work out. I'd like to see what my life is like in ten years."

"Ten years? Wow, that's a long time. I'd like to see two years ahead. What college will I be in? Will my mom be okay?" He leaned closer. "Will we be together?"

Ed Rose drove with one hand and pressed the phone to his ear. An automated message began. It was pre-recorded in the authoritative voice of the principal of Ben's school. "This is Mr. Mays. Your student has been reported as absent by the first hour teacher. Please call the attendance office before the end of the day to excuse your student. A total of six unexcused absences in a semester may result in reassignment." The message ended with a quick repetition of the attendance office's phone number and the ubiquitous 'have a nice day'. Ed began to fume. That little shit was skipping school.

He didn't really care. Except, if Ben was wasting gas, bombing around on slippery roads, flaunting the fact that he was not even in school when he should have been grounded from using the car . . .

His anger seethed. He scanned the other cars on the road, looking for Ben's car. At the intersection he swiveled his head in all directions. Where would Ben go? He decided to drive by the skating arena, the fast food joints, any other hang-outs he could think of. That little good-for-nothing was going to be sorry he even thought of skipping school.

Cori pulled out one of the boxes from under her bed. Attic dust left a trail, but she ignored it. She glanced upward to check that the paper she had taped over the hole in the ceiling was still doing its job. That creep, she thought. She had considered Megan's statement that Chuck was sick, but couldn't quite let go of the disgust, repulsion, and loathing she had cultivated.

And what was he mumbling about this morning? He had a gift for her? What the--.

Time to do her own spying. This box could wait. She had the house to herself and there was no time like the present.

She stood up and swayed. There it was again. That memory. That nightmare. Eyes floated toward her, dull, blank, like someone had sucked the life out of them. No gleam. No glint. Hollow, empty orbs.

She couldn't lift an arm for protection or a foot for escape.

Bodies swirled around and taunted her with their pointing fingers. Cackling laughs turned to silent screams then burst into deafening whistles of pain, teeth grinding, throats groaning, bones breaking.

And then it stopped.

She was afraid to think of Chuck again. She saw the connection now. Just a little while ago, in the living room, she had thought of Chuck and then experienced that nightmare again, a clear hallucination. It was the same now. Chuck crossed her mind and then spirits crossed her soul.

Like a warning.

The leg spasms had eased, the tighter muscles had loosened, and Chuck's hiding place remained undisturbed. He wasn't worried that he'd be seen, but someone might hear him; the jitters could give him away, his tapping feet were like tiny drums. He needn't have worried. The halls were hectic right up until the final tardy bell rang. The noises sheltered him. Protection. That's all he ever wanted.

Maybe he should stay right here in this very spot, so close to where . . . where it happened.

Where what happened? His brain was muddled, his mind disguised the faces, and his memory stole the names, cloaked and veiled them. What if he didn't recognize them?

Adam? Talk to me, please. What if they're wearing camouflage? What if I don't know them anymore?

Who will pay?

Does it matter?

Adam . . . I'll join you. I'll be with you. We'll be inseparable. Twins.

He fingered the trigger of the gun, ran his thumb along the barrel. Maybe, maybe there was an easier way.

How long before class change? How long before the halls crowded with chaos and confusion? How many bullets before he could command both pandemonium and order?

Ben paid the check and waited by the glass front door while Megan was in the restroom. They barely had enough time to swing by the house and pick up her books; they still might be late to second period even if they hurried. He stared at the blue salt that was scattered on the icy steps as he thought about the quickest route back.

An SUV exactly like his step-father's pulled into the parking lot. It *was* his step-father. The SUV slowed as it passed Ben's car. Ben had backed into a parking spot so his license wasn't visible, but the high school parking permit was clearly displayed on the dashboard. He watched Ed eye the car, hesitate, then look for an empty spot. He wasn't here for pancakes.

Cori felt a little hypocritical that she intended to go down the basement to trespass. She also felt afraid. She wished she had a weapon. But what for?

I'll tell you what for, she thought, remember last weekend when you came down here? You were alone in the house and that man broke in.

I proved I can take care of myself.

But this seems different.

She reached the bottom step. Chided herself for having an inane dialogue. Cursed Chuck. Walked into his neat and clean room.

"What the--" she broke off the curse to stare. "So where's my present?" she asked the empty room. She half-expected burnt and bony fingers to point the way, but she knew without a doubt where to look.

The tidied closet still smelled bad. Chuck's presence lingered, pungent. She tore the poster off the wall and revealed the hole. It was stuffed with clothing and other things. She didn't want to touch anything, but she held her breath and pulled each item out.

Ah, this must be it. A shoe box all wrapped up in notebook paper. Little hearts around the edges. Couldn't he have stolen some of Emily's Santa Claus wrapping paper? This looked like the work of a child. The tape was torn in places, as if he had unsealed and then resealed his handiwork. The paper, though decorated, was scrappy looking. Something had been erased. Four lines. A poem? How pathetic.

The box was heavy, too heavy for shoes.

She pulled the tape off the sides and lifted the lid.

Mrs. Beridon thought she saw some movement in the house, and a light flicking on, as she pulled into the driveway. Good. Megan got the message. It would be awful if she didn't know that she was picking her up.

She honked the horn lightly and waited.

Cori jumped as much from the nearby car horn as from the sight of an oily pistol resting on crinkly tissue paper. There was a note under the gun addressed to her. Two poems . . . about her. This was absolutely, positively creepy.

She didn't want a gun, knew she couldn't pawn it. Where did he get it? Was it from the attic? Were there more?

A sudden cold sweat chased away the tingling adrenaline rush. She put the lid back on and carried it out of the room.

She could have fainted when she reached the landing and someone knocked.

Mrs. Beridon knocked again. She could see a female shape within, but it was a girl larger and perhaps older than Megan.

"Hello? Is Megan ready?" she hollered, rapping again on the window pane.

The door opened and a fresh-faced teen screwed her face into a frown. "Megan's not here. Who are you?"

"Megan's not here?" She pulled back her coat sleeve and checked her watch. "Did she go to school? I thought she got the message."

"What message?" Cori contorted her face even more. "Is is about . . . her baby?"

"Yes. The judge is ruling on the issue of custody this morning. Megan has to be there."

"She went with Ben and Emily . . . to school. I don't think she got any message. Here, come on in. You can call the school."

Mrs. Beridon stepped inside. "Thank you. I don't think I've got the number on my phone."

Cori set the box on the counter and looked up the school's number in the phone book. She dialed it and handed Mrs. Beridon the house phone.

As it rang Mrs. Beridon introduced herself and Cori responded more politely than usual.

"Hello, I'd like to get a message to a student . . . No, I'm not. I'm her social worker. She's an emancipated teen . . . that's right. Her name is Megan Blakeney . . . Tell her Mrs. B will pick her up in ten minutes. She has to be in court . . . yes, that's right. Thank you." She handed the phone back to Cori with a whistle of relief. "Whew, that was close. She absolutely *has* to be there."

"You're a social worker?"

"Yes."

"What would you do if you thought someone, *maybe*, had taken guns to school?"

Mrs. Beridon searched Cori's face for the truth and slowly advised, "I'd call the school right away." She waited a beat to see if Cori had anything to add, then asked, "Do you think Megan has guns?"

"Hah! No, no way. I was just asking."

Mrs. Beridon put her hand on the doorknob and waited again. "Anything else you want to ask?"

Well, uh, do you believe in demons? Do you do exorcisms? She had lots of questions she wanted to ask, but she shook her head no instead.

Mrs. Beridon noticed then the empty piercings, didn't want to judge the girl, knew that some signs meant nothing. "I can stop back later and we can talk. All right?"

Cori twisted her face again. Was she a mind reader? "Okay, sure."

Chapter 21

Emily kept her head rigidly facing forward. Her teacher would pick on her the second she rested her head on her desk. Her stomach was unsettled and she ached all over. There was a weariness that made her feel fifty years older. She couldn't stop thinking about that smell. Right by the vending machines. Maybe something, a mouse, had died there.

Maybe Chuck was hiding there. That was funny. Chuck would never set foot in this school. Of course most people here wouldn't even remember Chuck anymore. Not even the kids who bullied him. Those jerks. The same things happened to her. Nobody could stop the bullying. It happened everywhere. Everywhere the teachers and administrators weren't, that is. They never saw anything. If they left the room, if their back was turned, if someone else had their attention then the bullies were free to deal out their favors.

She had learned the hard way that you had to be a bully or be invisible.

If only she could put her head down. Just fifteen more minutes until the bell rang. Could this class be any more boring?

Cori slapped her forehead over and over. Stupid, stupid, stupid. She amazed herself. How could she allow a total stranger, a social worker no less, to make an appointment with her? Okay, sure. Okay, sure. The words somersaulted out of her mouth, no jeweled stud to stop them.

And now she had another decision to make – call the school or not? What evidence did she have that Chuck might go berserk and start shooting up the place? Think. Decide.

She grabbed the shoe box again and examined the poems. Could these be clues? She didn't think so, but what did she know? What were the warning signs that someone was going to go on a shooting rampage?

She lifted out the gun, rubbed her fingerprints off with a paper towel, and set it back in. She didn't even know how to check if it was loaded.

What if she called the police? No, they'd come here and blow it for Ben. His step-father would get involved. No, not a good idea.

She could re-hide the gun. Maybe Chuck didn't have any other guns.

Maybe he was shooting it out at school right now.

She picked up the phone. Shit, she couldn't call from here. She needed to find a public phone. There were consequences for reporting a false alarm.

She groaned her annoyance. What happened to a nice quiet skip day? She slipped on the army boots, the coat, the gloves, and put the gun into her pocket. She would throw it in the dumpster at the gas station; she thought they had a pay phone there, too.

Ben caught Megan's arm as she came out of the restroom. He thrust the car keys into her hand and hurried through a set of instructions: "My step-dad is parking a silver SUV in the second row. Make sure he sees you get in the car. Then drive off. Circle around the block until he leaves and then pick me up across the street. Got it?"

"Got it." She rushed off and he watched from where he was, ready to duck into the ladies' room if Ed really was here for another breakfast.

Chuck felt the hum of voices throughout the building begin to intensify a full three minutes before the bell rang. Class doors opened, teachers allowed kids to move from their assigned seats. Gossip and whispers and stabs of laughter preceded the all out bedlam that followed the ringing of the bell.

Now was the moment. The air around him swished in waves as students passed. The vending machines rattled, candy and drinks clunked out, sophomores waited behind juniors who urged seniors to be faster. Freshmen rushed by in defensive clumps. Chuck focused on the tiny mirror he had taken from the drawer in the bathroom at home, his real home, where his parents were surprised to see him this morning. He changed the mirror's angle to reflect the ebb and flow of hungry teens. Their faces were intent upon the sugared drinks, the caffeinated colas, the candy, chips, mints, and gum. No one saw Chuck's blackened eye reflecting back from the finger of space between the two largest machines.

The plan was flawed.

Chuck's reasoning was built around a simple assumption: those whose debts were past due would visit this very spot sooner or later. Sooner or later.

Later.

Five minutes of frantic social interaction ended with the final tin can's clunk. The metal tab was popped and the fizz was muted by a pair of freshman lips. Who would have such a thirst this early in the day that he would risk a tardy to second period? Chuck knew. It was a freshman, someone bullied on the bus, someone whose head had been stuffed in the toilet bowl before first hour, someone small and scrawny who was pushed around, shoved into lockers, mocked, and cursed, and punched.

His anger filled his heart, his lungs, his mouth.

Don't scream.

Chill out. Take a pill.

He dug in his pocket for the matching pair of meds, popped them both in his mouth. He could wait another hour for the right moment. Or two hours. Or three.

Emily got up from her seat as soon as the teacher was finished with the project instructions. Most groups had three or four students boisterously arguing ideas. A few sat in quiet pairs, outlining their plans. Emily never considered joining the others and the veteran teacher was wise enough to allow exceptions. She had worked alone on the last project, earning a hundred percent. What was the big deal about group projects anyway? Everyone knew that one kid did most of the work.

"Library?" she whispered.

The teacher smiled and wrote out a hall pass. Name, date, time, destination, teacher's signature. Emily was out of the classroom in thirty seconds.

She walked through the quiet hallways as if she didn't know the way to the media center. Several classrooms had their doors open and she paused to listen to whatever teaching and learning was going on in the various subjects. She got to the end of the hall and doubled back, took the stairs, passed the main office, and headed for the vending machines. No one asked to see her pass; no one cared that she was out of class, wandering the halls. What was one insignificant girl in a school of almost two thousand?

She reached in the side pocket of her satchel. She had five one dollar bills and some change. She had not packed school lunches today; there was no time in the excitement of escaping through the back yards. Junk food from the machines would have to do; she could snack in the library, go back there during lunch. There was no way she wanted to see Ben in the cafeteria today.

She stood in front of the pop machine and decided on a calorie and caffeine free drink. The can plunked out and she collected the change.

She noticed the putrid scent again. Expected a flash of nightmare, but her memory stayed empty.

First the smell and now a sound. A tapping. Not the even clicking of a refrigerator motor. Not the four-beat finger drumming of a bored secretary. Not the steady rhythm of a dripping faucet.

Four slow clicks. One quick tap. Three measured taps. Four then one then three. Four. One. Three.

Almost a message. Or a warning.

She decided on the cheese and cracker snacks and a pack of two chocolate chip cookies. The machine rumbled and dropped the items. The tapping stopped. Had it been a foot? A shoe heel or toe that quivered against the tiles?

She bent and reached her hand for her treats and saw the eye. She froze. Her hand was part way in the dispenser; her satchel slipped down her arm. It wasn't the blind eye of that hellish vision. This eye could see. The skin around it was like black ash and the mesmerizing stare hypnotized her with a familiar ease.

She knew this eye.

Emily held Chuck's gaze. She gave him a nod of recognition, stuffed the food in her bag, and walked away.

Her mind rushed to make sense of it. Was this what Chuck would do when he thought he was Adam? Come to the normal school? Hide because he had no class schedule? Secretly watch the normal kids?

Goose bumps slithered down her body. Should she tell someone?

She passed the office, kept walking to the library.

Cori walked a couple of blocks, turned the corner and headed for the main street. She slowed to watch an ambulance back out of a driveway. A police car sat out front, its strobe light silently blinking round, making the snow seem red then blue.

If she hesitated or turned back, would they suspect her? That was stupid; they couldn't know she had a gun in her pocket.

She bent her head against a cold gust of wind, looked directly at the house, wondered if it was a heart attack victim they had carted away. A policeman was coming out the front door unto the shoveled porch where the second cop was waiting. They looked like they were locking up the place. They moved down the steps and Cori could see the house numbers that had been hidden by the one officer. And the metal mailbox, just like the one they had at their house. Only this one had large stick-on letters spelling out a last name: Burdick.

Funny. Wasn't that Chuck's last name? No, not funny. Disgusting. A disgusting name for a disgusting kid. Weirdo. Sicko. If she didn't have his gun on her, she'd walk up to these policemen right now and tell them he was out there somewhere planning a mass murder.

Oh, crap. The nausea hit her with the stunning force of a baseball bat to the gut. She doubled over, wretched on the snow. The yellow crime scene tape they were stretching across the porch provoked a conclusion too horrible to imagine, but as clear as yesterday's clairvoyant predictions.

Megan drove as carefully as she had the last time Ben entrusted her with his car. She watched for his step-dad's SUV in her mirrors, wondered if the angry man would spot the license plate, think she was stealing the car, and try to stop her. He might rear-end the car. The outlandish thought was motivation enough to make her turn down the next street, speed up, turn again and whip down an alley.

Ben's treasure was in this trunk. All kinds of crazy thoughts swirled around her head before she reached the end of the alley and had to stop. She inched out, caught a glimpse of the silver vehicle a block away going the opposite direction. She breathed, blinked, and circled back toward Ben.

Mrs. Beridon waited in the main office as the secretary first looked up Megan's schedule then sent an aide to the classroom. When the aide returned alone the secretary checked the hourly attendance reported on the computer and shook her head. Megan hadn't shown up to first or second hour. As an emancipated teen she could excuse herself for illness, doctor's appointments, or court, but she should have called in by now. The secretary had no suggestion for Mrs. Beridon other than to leave a message that could be relayed if Megan reported in later.

The social worker rubbed her forehead and glanced at her watch. She had no option but to race to the courthouse. Alone.

Ben leaped in the passenger side and grinned. "Wow, you were driving like a maniac."

"No, I wasn't. I was super careful. I kept worrying that someone was going to crash into me and wreck the trunk and send all your cards flying."

"Well, it looked like you gunned it out of the parking lot before Ed could see for sure that it was my car. Man, was I spooked. I was sure I was going to have to hide in the ladies' room."

Megan laughed. She signaled right and pulled out. "That would have been interesting because there was still a lady in there when I came out." She headed toward their house and asked, "Does he always chase you down when you skip? How did he know where you were?"

"I haven't a clue, but life sure has gotten exciting since you arrived."

"Tell me about it." She pulled onto their street and scanned for silver cars. "Should we park on the other street?"

"Nah, we won't be long. I'll quick make some sandwiches while you get your stuff. We'll be outta here fast."

Megan backed up the driveway to hide the license plate, just in case, and they hurried into the house. She bounded up the stairs while Ben slapped slices of lunch meat on some bread.

She stopped in her tracks when she saw Cori's door open. Maybe she was here; maybe she had skipped school, too. More crazy imaginings jigged around her head. They had left when Cori began talking to Ben's step-father. They didn't know how that conversation ended. What if he hadn't believed that she was Mrs. Kremer? What if she had told him about Ben? What if she was tied up in the back seat of an SUV?

Megan stepped into Cori's room and gently called her name. A box was on the floor next to the bed, the closet door was open, the ladder beckoned. She crossed the room and looked up.

"I'm done," Ben called from below. "Are you coming?"

"Be right there," she called back. She touched the ladder, felt a hand on hers. She closed her eyes and pictured Simon. So cute and warm and cuddly. So happy. He could crawl and pull himself up on furniture, tip and sway and bounce. His first steps would come any day now. He was early, the foster mother had said, doing things ahead of the curve, sooner than her own kids. But he was a worry when it came to eating. And the digestive problems meant repeated trips to the doctor. There would be operations, medications, check-ups. The weight of responsibility drained her of happy thoughts. She was ashamed that her precious son had become a duty to her, a once-a-week inconvenience scrawled on a calendar, but had she ever really bonded with him?

"What are you doing in here?" Ben took a step into Cori's room, saw Megan's hand come off the ladder and swipe away some tears. "What's the matter?"

Megan motioned him toward her own room.

"Mrs. Beridon," the judge sighed, "I appreciate your concern, but," he wiped his brow again, "this court will make its decision on the facts presented and," his voice grew louder and emphasized the grave pronouncement, "the obvious lack of interest by the young mother." He picked up his gavel, more for show than legality, and dropped it weakly on the wooden plate. "I hereby terminate all parental rights on the part of Megan Ann Blakeney. The foster parents may commence with adoption proceedings. The grandparents may make their petitions at this time."

Mrs. Beridon let the tightness in her chest and stomach relax away with a calm acceptance. What was done, was done. This wasn't how she wanted things to turn out, but sometimes you could look back years later and see the perfect construction of the world around you. Simon would have two mature and loving parents in a stable household. Megan would get to be a teenager. If the judge had ruled the other way both mother and son might be in for a very rough road ahead.

Who was she to question . . . question . . .

Her thoughts were interrupted by a vision, a fleeting scene. No faces. A panic. She hurried out of the courtroom and took a seat on a wooden bench. This had happened before. A thought, barely a thought, would come to her. Or a name would float before her mind's eye. And she would pray.

She took a minute, no more than that, and let herself be led in thought and prayer. It made no sense, but sometimes she never knew the outcome; sometimes she felt the peace before she said amen. She didn't understand it, but it was as real as any concrete evil she had faced. In this moment she felt the peace. Was it Megan she was praying for? Or Emily? Or the other girl at the house? Someone needed angelic support and Mrs. Beridon was an experienced intercessor. The demons would know her name, she hoped, as she knew some of theirs.

Cori made it to the gas station before she felt the need to vomit again. Thankfully the restroom on the side of the building was unlocked. She kept her gloves on, wrapped the gun in even more paper towels and stuffed it into the trash can.

Now she had to warn them at the alternative school.

Megan opened the yellow album. "This is Simon," she said touching the protective plastic. Ben looked at the baby scrap book. He put one arm around Megan and, with an awkward and self-conscious tenderness, listened to the unburdening of her soul. He asked soft questions, offered silent admiration, wrapped her in his arms and let things be.

When they had looked at every page of the album Megan closed it and tucked it back in the top drawer of the dresser.

"So, now you know everything," she sniffled. "I'm a horrible person."

"No, you're not. I think you're wonderful and brave." He cupped her chin in his hand and lifted her face. "You have a right to cry. You just told me you're torn between fighting for Simon and letting him grow up in a stable family. I can't imagine that there's a harder decision to make."

She rested her arms around his neck and buried her face in his shoulder. Her quiet sobs shook them both.

"Hey," Ben finally said, "I have a question for you." Megan looked up expectantly. Ben cleared his throat, held her close. "When my father died I couldn't stop crying. We stayed with my grandparents, my dad's folks, for a week. And all I did was cry or wreck things. My grandfather took me outside and said I had a choice. I could make a decision to accept things and trust that everything worked out for the best and grow up to be like my dad or I could keep being miserable and feeling helpless."

Megan nodded, understanding a little. "So, what's the question for me?"

Ben smirked one dimple. "Well, my grandpa also said he was willing to make the decision for me for that and for any other big decision I'd ever have to make in my life . . . so I'd never have to blame myself if things didn't work out. So . . . my question is – do you want me to make the decision for you whether or not you fight for custody?"

Megan bit at her bottom lip. "I'm not sure."

"Well, here's the thing. When I tell you the decision you have to tell me right away what you're feeling. But you're not bound by what I say. Okay?"

"Okay." Her eyes cleared, but her face was wet. Ben brushed his fingers across her freckles and dried the tears.

"Let Simon go." The silence stretched long enough for tears to form again. "Are you relieved? Is that what you wanted me to say?" Ben asked.

Megan nodded. "But . . ."

"No buts. You're not a bad person, Megan. Stuff happens. You can connect with Simon when you're older if you want, but you need to tell the judge what you feel."

Cori called 911. Her flustered attempts to give a reasonable excuse for calling the emergency number resulted in her hanging up before she named her school. She hoped she had said enough.

Her relief at having disposed of the gun and made the call cleared her thoughts. The nausea was gone; she was no longer edgy. Chuck was probably sound asleep in Murphy's class, meaning that Cori had just made a prank call. That would be funny. She started to laugh before she left the phone carrel. She glanced at the attendant whose attention was elsewhere. Good. It wouldn't be smart to draw attention to herself, not that she was memorable without her makeup and jewelry.

The emergency dispatcher called the police. The police reported the threat to the school district's administration. The administration called the high schools, the alternative school, the middle schools, and the elementary schools. Each one issued a lock down alert without delay. The practiced procedures included an announcement on the public address system. Teachers pulled any students wandering the hall into their classrooms and locked the doors. Shades were pulled, lights turned off, computers shut down. Students were directed to sit under their desks or grouped on the floor away from the doors and windows.

Emily knew the drill. She was at a back corner table in the library when the lockdown announcement was made. She nestled herself under the table with her satchel and books. She expected five minutes of bothered excitement as the librarian worried her way around the room. There were no blinds to pull in the large media center and turning the lights off wouldn't make much difference. Seven windows allowed an expansive view into and out of the room. If this wasn't a drill the librarian or her assistant would rush her into the back office. So far, though, no one had come out of the office. Maybe they were on break. Wouldn't it be funny if they had been swept into a classroom and made to sit under some kid's desk?

Five minutes became ten. Emily thought of Chuck in his hiding place. That might be hard to explain. He might be mistaken for a threat. She imagined the commotion. He would protest and his objections would get him into deeper trouble. He might attack someone like he attacked Megan.

Emily peeked out toward the hallway. She could hear the jangle of lockers being opened one by one. They were checking for bombs. Or weapons. She didn't see how she could get past them to warn Chuck, unless she waited until they went down the next hallway.

"Your grandfather is a pretty wise man," Megan said as she buckled her seatbelt. "But I still feel like a horrible person."

"Join the club."

"What? What have you ever done?"

Ben started the car, turned on the heater, and put his hand over Megan's. "It's more like what I didn't do."

Megan cocked her head, ready to hear whatever he wanted to share.

Ben pressed his other hand against the steering wheel until his knuckles popped. "I stood by and let a friend get bullied." He looked from Megan to the street. When all she did was grasp his hand tightly, he continued. "And it happened more than once. I'm pretty ashamed of myself. I've tried to make up for it, but . . ."

Ed Rose was starting to think that every other car on the road was a match for Ben's. He had been fooled by some little brunette at the Pancake House, then he had followed another car almost across the county line. He rounded his trip back by swinging by the hockey arena, but it was closed until noon.

He was irritated enough to go back to the house and take out his temper on his wife, but more appealing was the thought of discussing a harsher penalty for Ben with his principal or truant officer or whoever he had to see about such things. Grounding the boy was too light a punishment.

He exceeded the speed limit, spun his tires on a slippery turn, and cut someone off before he reached the roundabout. This particular traffic circle was bedlam before and after school when all the teenage drivers ruled the road, but Ed was the only one maneuvering through now. He pulled up to the school and looked for the visitors' parking lot.

"Shit! Shit, shit, shit." Cori's exasperation was matched by her anger. She was sure she had left the door unlocked. But it was locked now and she had no way to get in. She kicked her boot against the brick and stepped back.

Maybe, yeah maybe. She was as angry as before so . . . if she really concentrated she might be able to . . . uh, this wasn't going to work. Whatever demonic power she had before had disappeared. Option number two: kick in jerkoff's basement window. Ben might be mad at her for breaking in, but there wasn't an option three.

And then there was.

Mrs. Beridon's car pulled right up the driveway over Ben's recent tracks. Cori started kicking at the window anyway.

"I just want OUT!"

Cori kept up the chant even after Mrs. Beridon settled her in the front seat. "Out. Out. Out. I want OUT of my life."

"You know what, dear? Is there anything in that house that you absolutely have to have?"

Cori pictures all of her black clothes, the jewelry, the things from the attic. She didn't have much. She pulled off a glove and felt in her pocket. She pulled out two things: a wedding ring and a small pin still wrapped in its original package.

"What's that dear?" Mrs. Beridon held out her hand and Cori dropped both things in.

"They're not even mine. I found them." She jerked her head toward the attic.

"Oh, a wedding ring and a National Honor Society pin."

"An NHS pin? Is that what that is?"

"Yes," Mrs. Beridon smiled. "But you knew that. I think these two things represent two dreams of yours, don't they?"

Cori nodded. She knew she was grinning like a six-year-old, but she didn't care. "There's nothing in the house that I need."

"Good, then we can get started on your new life right now. If you'll trust me, I can make everything work out. I have really great connections."

Ben spotted the police car first. "Trouble at school. I wonder what's going on."

"Look. All the shades are drawn. Every classroom."

"Lockdown drill," they said together and laughed. Everyone liked the lockdown drill the best. It was like a time out from class without the hassle of a fire drill or the confusion of a tornado drill. A lockdown drill usually lasted only five minutes though a bomb scare last year kept everyone huddled for an entire class period. Kids texted each other and then their parents and soon half the town showed up and clogged the roads around the school.

Ben parked the car and sent a quick text to a friend in his second hour class to ask how long since the drill started.

"What did he say?" Megan leaned closer to look at the tiny screen.

"Twelve minutes so far. That's not good."

"You think it's not a drill?"

Ben shrugged, restarted the car, and explained, "We're going to loop around both parking lots and look for Chuck's car." He eased the car down the row.

Megan shivered. "What'll we do if we find it?"

Ben didn't answer at first. He stopped the car and pointed at a familiar vehicle. He exhaled with all the control he could garner. "I've gotta fix this. I know where he'll go, what he'll do."

Emily kept her eye on the parking lot. She had seen Ben's car come in and park and then pull out again. She crawled to the window and tried to solve the little mystery of Ben's parking game.

Oh, Megan was with him.

Now they were stalled in the lane. Now he was going in reverse all the way back to the first empty spot. He parked again. She watched them get out their doors then take their coats off and toss them back in. Smart, she thought, they were going to sneak back in and go straight to class, avoid the attendance office, and claim they were marked absent by mistake.

She raised her hand to wave. They wouldn't know there was a lockdown. They'd walk right into a locker search; they wouldn't be able to get into their locked classrooms.

She stood up and waved some more. If they saw her, maybe they would take the path to the library door. She could let Ben in . . . let them in.

She used both arms. She was almost doing jumping jacks. She hadn't moved this much in forever and it felt good.

They stomped their feet hard as they skated past Emily then dove for cover under the table with Emily's things.

"No one is here," Emily said as she joined them under the wooden table. "We don't have to hide."

"Have there been any PA announcements? What's going on?"

Emily kept her eyes down. "No, just the first one. They're searching the lockers now. I'm worried they'll find Chuck."

Ben grasped her arm, released her when she winced, "Sorry, but how do you know about Chuck?"

She risked a glance up. "I saw him . . . behind the vending machines."

Ben listened to the rest of what she had to say, nodded, and took off.

Ed Rose was not happy that he was being made to sit in the interior office. His anger had not abated, but now it was directed at the vice-principal and her rude brush off. This drill was ridiculously long. He wasn't going to wait any longer. He opened the door and glanced around the reception area. Empty.

He buttoned his coat and peered down the empty hallways. He could hear metallic clanging coming from the second floor, the sound echoing down the central staircase. And then a movement caught his eye.

"Well, I'll be . . ." he didn't finish the thought. He stepped into the hall, glad for the stealth of his rubber soles on the old vinyl floor. Of all the kids in this building, it was *his* step-kid who had the gall to sneak out during a lockdown. And for a soft drink no less.

"Chuck, I know you're there." Ben kept his voice as low as possible. He braced himself, one hand on each of the two largest machines. He could see the mirror where Emily had described it. Nothing was reflecting back except the gray cinder block wall behind the machines. He kept his head close to the crack, spoke into the tense air. There was a buzz growing throughout the whole school. Impatience was winning everywhere. "Chuck . . . it's me, Ben. I want to tell you that I'm still sorry. And I'll always . . . always be your friend. No matter what, buddy."

Ben saw a change in the reflection, a movement, some hair, then a brow, then a dark eyelid. Finally Chuck's eye filled the inch or so of reflecting glass. He had smudged some camouflage on his face; his eyes were masked with brown or dark gray shadow.

Ben sighed. "Chuck, there's a lockdown. They're gonna find you and you're gonna get in trouble. Come on, buddy. I can get you outta here."

Chuck felt his brother's absence, but there was another brother now. Someone or some *thing* was filling up that space. It came with more anger, fury, rage, and desperation than Chuck had ever experienced. It *was* his brother, but it wasn't Adam.

He listened to Ben's pleas with *other* ears. In his own heart he felt regret, he tried to hold onto Ben's words. Ben *was* his friend. He would *always* be his friend.

But a heavy crush of doubt left his heart and his hopes flat.

His ears stopped hearing. He moved the gun forward, shifted his weight. His head sought a better angle and he moved over the mirror until Ben's face was in his view. If there was remorse or pity or shame on that face, Chuck's eyes were blind to such emotion. The blackness within had sealed up all of Chuck's passions but one.

He angled the barrel of the gun to match the reflection.

Someone had to pay. It might as well be Ben. He was as guilty as any.

"Ben!" Ed's voice was a bombshell, a staggering surprise that caught Ben so off guard that between the sudden appearance of the gun's round end above the mirror, and his step-father's shout, he simply dropped to his knees.

The crack of the gun, the piercing of his flesh, the hardness of the floor as his head banged down – all were bolts of surprise.

Another loud and echoing shot blasted behind the vending machine. Ben rolled his head, looked back for Ed, saw him on the floor. Saw the blood. Rolled back. More blood oozed from under the dusty legs of the machine. He saw a ball of dust, a nickel, a friend's twitching finger. More blood.

Shouts. Trampling feet. Hands upon him. Voices. Shiny things.

Scraping.

Hushed and staggered questions.

Crackly intercoms.

But he was all right. His head was bumped. His arm was scorched. But he was all right.

How was Chuck? Was Chuck all right?

Yes, that's my step-father. Is he dead? You can tell me. I'm all right. Just grazed. I don't need an ambulance. No, just call my mom. Is Ed dead? Is Chuck all right? No, I don't know anything about any guns. Who? Yes, that's my girlfriend you can let her through. Yes, Emily, too, she's my friend, my very good friend. I'm all right. Please, just tell me about Chuck.

Emily rushed after Megan when they heard the shots. The closed classrooms they passed shook and shuddered; screams escaped. Ground floor windows were being flung open and kids were piling out into the snow, running for cover.

She slowed to a walk and let Megan go on. She'd have to cut herself as punishment if she didn't follow through and prove her hunch. She slipped down the side hallway that hadn't yet been searched. She checked the locker numbers, found number 413, four one three, like the taps she heard from Chuck, the message. The locker had no padlock. She hesitated, thought about the fingerprints she was about to leave, the incrimination, her bad luck, her nightmares, her guilt. And she opened the door and touched the gun.

When she came up behind Megan she touched her hand, gave a squeeze, and said that everything was going to work out. She even tried a smile, but Megan wasn't looking. Finally someone let them through to Ben. Emily watched Megan take his hand. Everything was going to work out fine, she thought. For Megan. For Ben. But not for her.

She listened to the policeman talk on his radio. They had confirmed the identity of Chuck Burdick, the son of this morning's homicide victims. They had a gun at the scene and had found another in a bag in one of the restrooms.

"Sir," she interrupted the police officer. He held the radio away from his lips. "There's another gun in locker 413."

She didn't hear his response or feel his touch as he moved her aside. She kept her eyes on Ben. She didn't expect to ever see him again. Megan blocked her view for an instant, but she saw him pass her the car keys. Wasn't that just like Ben? He wanted to be sure she had a way home.

It was the last thing she saw before her eyes went dark and her throat closed up. She let the demon take her, let herself be blind and mute. Out. She wanted out. Out of her life. Out. Out. Out. That wish was finally being granted. Infinite sorrow raped her soul.

Monday

Chapter 22

Mrs. Beridon parked in front of the school the same as any other Monday and watched for Megan to come out the door. With all that had happened she had hoped to wrangle one last visitation with Simon for Megan, but that was not to be. The poor girl didn't even know about the ruling yet and would get into the car with hopeful expectations.

And there she was, all smiles and anticipation, with a bounce in her walk.

"Hi, Mrs. Beridon, how are you?" Megan said as soon as she opened the car door.

"Fine, and you?"

"Great. Uh, listen, . . . I have something to talk to you about."

The social worker left the car in park after Megan buckled up. A calming presence guided her to listen to all that Megan had to say and only intersperse an encouragement, an "oh, Megan", or a "that's probably best, dear" to affirm the heavy conclusion that Megan had reached with Ben's help.

Then she broke the news that the judge had already made his decision: Megan's parental rights had been terminated. Mrs. B reached a hand out, smiled through the tears along with Megan, whose heart had miraculously been prepared. As hard as it was to hear the finality of the verdict, there was a burden lifted, a life returned, a bittersweet relief.

"And how is that boy you like?" Mrs. Beridon asked as she drove Megan home. "I heard he wasn't hurt badly."

"He drove me to school today, but he went back to the hospital," Megan said. "His step-dad is in a coma. They don't think he'll ever wake up. There's major brain damage, I guess. It's pretty sad. Ben hasn't left his mother's side."

"Oh, I'm so sorry, but, you know, things always work out. That bullet was meant for him and it only nicked him.

It's unfortunate that his step-father was in its path. Hmm. Mysterious. And how is Emily?"

"Well, they let Emily come back home. She really didn't have anything to do with it, you know, but . . . she's really messed up. She won't come out of her room."

"Is there anything I can do?" She softened her voice. "Technically, you know, I'm off your case, but I do a lot more than just the social work." She parked in the driveway for the third time that day. "Here, take this." She handed her a three by five card that was tucked in the visor. "I tried to help Emily before, but she resisted. Maybe now she's ready."

The card was the same one that Emily and Ben had. Megan stared at it for a moment, turned it over, and re-read the list of problems that Mrs. Beridon and her friends could help solve.

Megan dared to voice her fear. "The self-mutilation was scary, but . . . I think it's related to this." She pointed to the last thing on the list. "Can you help with that?"

"I can, and you'll never guess who my apprentice is."

Ben rang the front doorbell at 328 Elm and waited with a bouquet of flowers in one hand hidden behind his back. The door swung open and Megan practically pulled him into the foyer with an eagerness that matched his.

He kissed her and offered the flowers. "These are for you."

"Thank you."

"Hey, have you been crying?"

Megan turned to take the flowers to the kitchen. "A little."

"What's wrong? Didn't your visit with Simon go well?"

She filled a tall drinking glass with water and stuck the flowers in. "There was no visit. I'm not his . . . his mom anymore." She choked on the words, dropped her hands to her sides, but tried to smile.

"It'll be okay," Ben soothed. "It's all right." He sloughed off his coat and tossed it toward the side door. He put his arms around Megan and they stood by the sink in an embrace as she sobbed out the details. "See?" he said when she finished. "It all worked out for the best. It is kind of weird, though, that you came to the same conclusion on the same day that the judge ruled."

"There's a lot of weirdness around here."

Ben nodded. "Where's Em?"

"In her room, I guess. Why?"

"I thought she might want to go to the funeral home. Cori, too."

"Cori doesn't live here anymore. She's staying with my social worker. Can you believe it? Mrs. B is turning her life around."

"Good," was all he said before he kissed her again. "I've got something to tell you." He pulled back an inch and got serious again. "I don't live here anymore, either."

"What? Why not?"

"I told my mom everything and . . . well, she really needs me now. I can actually help her with Ed's business and stuff. But you and Emily can still live here and I'll come over and we'll . . . date . . . and stuff."

"So that's why you rang the doorbell and brought me flowers."

"Uh huh, it'll be like we're normal teenagers and all."

Megan smiled. Normal teenagers. Well, not quite. She lowered her eyes, stared at the floor.

"What?" Ben said.

Megan took a moment to raise her eyes.

Emily sat in her nest arranging Chuck's pills in a circle around Cori's pills. Cori was never coming back. Chuck was a different matter.

Emily had talked with him through the Ouija board. He was happy, he said. She wanted to believe it. He had gotten out. Out of all the hopelessness and pain. She didn't think she could do the same thing.

Megan had made a little noise when she came home, but hadn't bothered Emily, hadn't checked on her even once. Fine. Ben would be around sooner or later. He hadn't taken her around to the shelters last night. Surely he would make that up to her tonight. She had helped him, told him where Chuck was hiding. He owed her.

She took one of Cori's pills, waited, tried to chant, tried to levitate her bed. Took another pill.

The Ouija board stretched and widened before her eyes. Another message from Chuck spelled itself out without any help from her. D. I. E.

Then the pretty demons came; they swirled around her room like stars. They pulled her into a dark galaxy. Contentment, pleasure, ease. This was the out she wanted. Such ecstasy – to find a safe haven from every storm of life.

Then shame welled up in waves, like a foaming black sea of despair and misery. And more than she wanted out of her life she did not want to be damned.

What? The doorbell? Is it the police again? She pushed herself to stand up. Look out the window. Ben's car. In the street.

Why would *he* ring the bell? She looked down, could only see a grocery store bouquet of winter flowers, clear plastic protecting them from the cold. Flowers?

She dropped back to the nest, felt the air pressure change as the front door opened and closed, a solid thud. She grabbed a handful of pills and crunched them with her back teeth, swallowed.

There, that's done. She stepped on the planchette to the Ouija board, crushed it.

Ben. One last look at Ben.

Megan raised her eyes and said, "I want you to make a decision for me . . . so I can see how I feel about it."

"Okay, go ahead."

Megan measured her words out, "Should I go back and live with my parents?"

Ben looked for the right signs in her eyes. He took a breath and slowly, very slowly smiled his dimply grin. "Yes."

"Oh," Megan smiled back, "that's what I wanted you to say."

"I don't know, maybe I've got Cori's knack for premonitions, but I have a feeling that the only ones who will be living here are Emily, her mother, and her brother. We've never gone looking on a weeknight. Maybe we'll find them tonight."

"Can I come?"

"Of course." He bent for another kiss and was interrupted by a shriek as Emily fell down the stairs.

They found her on the bottom step, mouth foaming, eyes glazed, arms twisted at improbable angles.

"I'll call 911." Ben pulled his phone out as Megan knelt on the floor.

Suddenly Megan's body came slamming into his chest. The phone went flying and the two of them fell into the hallway. Emily's body rose and her limbs flailed in an outrageous show of demonic control.

"Oh, my god, oh my god, ohmygod!" Megan screamed as Emily loomed above them like a hungry carnivore. Soulless malevolence and a thin-lipped sneer preceded a response.

"YOU HAVE NO GOD." The voice reverberated with fiendish conviction. Then came the verbal attac. Filthy vile. Exploding from Emily's mouth in shards. Chirps of her own voice squeaking through. Scattering syllables of apology. Invectives pounding forth, pinning Megan to Ben's chest.

"Say it, just say it," Megan begged. "Say it, Ben. Make the demon come out."

Ben rolled Megan to the left and shielded her body. He punched his fist at Emily's face, heard her jaw crack. He punched again. "Come out of her, demon," he bellowed.

The demon laughed. A raucous bawl. It tore at Emily's clothes and ripped the sleeves away. It made her arms and legs move in a spider-like tour of the walls and ceiling of the narrow staircase. A roar of humorless screeching echoed back down to unbelieving ears. Emily's body reached the top and crawled away.

"Did it work?" Megan said, breathless. She jumped to her feet before Ben, spotted the blood on his sleeve and cried out, "Ben, your wound. You're bleeding."

"It's all right. Come on, let's get her." He leaped up the steps, gathered himself at the landing, and spoke in a whisper, "Stay behind me." They moved past the other doors and stood in Emily's doorway.

Her room smelled of sulphur and urine. The nest of blankets held an arrangement of paper scraps, each balled up into little pill-like rolls. The closet door was closed.

"In there?" Megan whispered.

Ben shook his head, listened. "The attic."

They reached Cori's room and entered.

"Help me," Emily's timid little voice persuaded them toward the ladder. Her body was in the attic, but her head was hanging down through the opening and her hands were on the top step.

"Em, I'm sorry I hit you." Ben reached for her hands, ignored the icy coldness of her skin. "I think you need to turn around and come down feet first."

The icy claws dug into Ben's hands, yanked him up with the strength of ten. The ladder toppled toward Megan and she screamed.

"Demon! Come out of Emily! Jesus says come out!"

Ben dropped to the floor. He stared wide-eyed at Megan. "That was it," he said. "Those were the magic words."

Emily's head reappeared through the hole, a lop-sided grin drooled saliva and blood. Her booming voice thundered, " Maaaagggiiiccc! Haaaaaa! Jesus I know, and his followers, too, but who are you to command me to leave? You have no authority!" Her whole body slid through, righted itself, and began to grab objects around the room. She threw the ladder at them and then the boxes and as they escaped out the door the dresser slammed against the frame.

Tuesday

"I still don't understand," Megan nestled into Ben's shoulder. They were sitting in the waiting room of the same hospital where Ed Rose lay two floors down. "The doctor said there was no evidence of drugs. They pumped her stomach and all they found were little pieces of paper. But you saw her, Ben, she must have been on something."

He looked at the large electronic clock on the wall, red numbers clicking off another second, another minute, fading the realities into foggy nightmares. It was barely dawn. Emily might not last the night. After she had cast herself through Cori's bedroom window and hit the white ground, they called the ambulance, rushed behind it in stunned silence the single mile to the hospital.

"I can't believe it," Ben let a tear escape. "She was my little buddy. I . . . I wasn't nice enough to her. I should have taken her to the shelters on Sunday, like we usually did."

Megan sighed, swallowed a sob, tried to bolster Ben, "If she doesn't make it, she'll be in a better place."

"You think so?" His left arm was around Megan, he crossed his right hand in front of her so he could crack each knuckle with stuttering finality. "I'm not so sure."

"Well, I'm sure of one thing," Megan turned her face into his neck and whispered, "I'm not going back there; I'm going home."

"Same here, and . . ." his voice dropped off as he thought about the 'authority' he desired, "and I'm gonna do some research. Next time . . . we'll have the power."

CPSIA information can be obtained at www.ICGtesting.com
Printed in the USA
LVOW091317161112

307657LV00001B/8/P

9 781475 249996